The Merlin Gambit

A Pequod Press Adventure Novel

An earlier and substantially different version of this novel was published as an e-book under the title *Tides of Chaos* by Dietmar Wehr.

Original Cover Art by Alan Gutierrez

First Edition

Printed in the United States of America
First Printing, 2014
V 10 9 8 7 6 5 4 3 2 1

ISBN: 978-0-937912-23-2

Cover art by Alan Gutierrez 2013 (*www.alangutierrez.com*)
Layout by Delaney-Designs.com

Pequod Press
P.O. Box 80
Boalsburg, PA 16827
www.PequodPress.com

THE MERLIN GAMBIT

JOHN F. CARR

&

DIETMAR WEHR

Pequod Press

Terran Federation Novels

Four-Day Planet

Little Fuzzy

Fuzzy Sapiens

Fuzzies and Other People

Fuzzy Ergo Sum

Caveat Fuzzy

The Cosmic Computer

The Merlin Gambit

Space Viking

The Last Space Viking

Space Viking's Throne

ACKNOWLEDGEMENTS

I would like to give special thanks to continuity editors John Anderson and Dan Radakovich for helping to keep this book true to Piper's vision. I'd also like to thank Victoria Alexander, Dwight Decker, Dennis Frank, David E. Williams and Wolfgang Diehr for their copyediting efforts and help in making this a better book.

Chronology

The Atomic Era is reckoned as beginning on the 2nd December 1942, Christian era, with the first self-sustaining nuclear reactor, put into operation by Enrico Fermi at the University of Chicago. Unlike earlier dating-systems, it begins with a Year Zero, 12/2/'42 to 12/1/'43 CE. With allowances for December overlaps, 1943 CE is thus equal to Year Zero AE, and 1944 CE to 1 AE, and each century accordingly begins with the "double-zero" year, and ends with the ninety-nine year—H. Beam Piper.

(*All dates in the Chronology are based on Atomic Era dating. jfc*)

28	First unmanned rocket, the *Kilroy*, lands on the moon.
30	The United Nations collapses.
31	Terran Federation formed.
31	The Thirty Days' War (World War III).
53	First human exploration of Mars; the *Cyrano* Expedition.
54 – 100	Further exploration of Mars, Venus, asteroids and moons of Jupiter.
92	Contragravity is developed.
95 – 105	First Federation begins to crack under strains of colonial claims and counter-claims of member states.
105	Venus secedes from the First Terran Federation.
106 – 109	World War IV (First Interplanetary War). Entire Northern Hemisphere devastated by nuclear bombardments.
110	First Terran Federation is re-centered in the Southern Hemisphere. Australia, New Zealand, South Africa, Brazil, Argentina, Uruguay agree to abolish nation states, creating a completely unified world.

This marks the beginning of a new civilization. Lingua Terra begins taking shape.

127 Reformed Second Terran Federation establishes a single-world sovereignty when Britain becomes the last nation to join.

172 Keene-Gonzales-Dillingham Theory of Non-Einsteinian Relativity developed.

174 Venus secedes from the First Terran Federation.

183 The First Terran Federation is dissolved and the Second Terran Federation is established. New Federation imposes system-wide pax.

183 Dillingham hyperdrive developed

192 First expedition to Alpha Centauri.

200 Atomic Era dating adopted.

200 – 800 Period of exploration, colonization and expansion.

350 Marduk colonized.

399 Fenris Company chartered and Fenris settled.

409 Chartered Fenris Company goes bankrupt.

526 Native revolt on Uller against Chartered Uller Company.

629 Zarathustra is discovered and settled.

650 Poictesme is discovered by Genji Gartner and settled.

654 Fuzzy sapience is recognized and Zarathustra reclassified from Class III to Class IV world.

716 Svantovit discovered and Svants encountered.

780 Foxx Travis born. Later he becomes the commander of the Third Fleet-Army Force headquartered on Poictesme.

812	Miles Gilbert and Foxx Travis thwart native revolt on Kwannon. Aditya is discovered.
839	System States Alliance secedes from the Terran Federation.
842 - 854	System States War.
851	Federation forces destroy city of Kindelburg on Ashmodai.
855	Ten thousand refugees from Abigor and the remnants of the System States Alliance Navy flee the Terran Federation and settle Excalibur, the first Sword-World.
871	Conn Maxwell is born.
888	The Fawzi Office Gang sends Conn to school on Terra; the prestigious University of Montevideo.
894	Conn returns from Terra to Poictesme.
895	Merlin is discovered and the Maxwell/Merlin plan to save the Federation is hatched.
896	Conn Maxwell and Sylvie Jacquemont are married.
897	Foxx Travis Maxwell is born.

PROLOGUE

891 A.E.

Captain Viktor Beauregard entered the bridge and dropped his Federation Space Navy uniform jacket over the arm of the command station chair.

He turned to his signals-and-detection officer and asked, "Anything coming our way, Chuck?"

The officer looked up at him and shook his head. Viktor's first impulse was to chew the man out for not showing the proper respect owed to a superior officer, then checked himself, remembering that he was no longer a Terran Federation Navy Officer and the *Valley Forge* wasn't really a Space Navy ship—not anymore.

Once she'd been a light cruiser carrying her proud name in defense of the Terran Federation. Now she was an old, decommissioned ship, given one last reprieve from being scrapped when the Navy agreed to lend her to the Technotron Corporation for use in testing new detection and evasion prototypes along with her equally old sister ship, TFSN *Kursk*.

Viktor looked around the bridge. Most of the equipment was clearly out-of-date but still functional. The most important units for the purposes of this mission had been upgraded by Technotron technicians who had been paid well to do their jobs and keep their mouths shut about it. The *Valley Forge* had been re-outfitted with offensive and defensive missiles and could confidently take on any spacefaring warship it might face other than a Federation Naval cruiser.

Viktor still didn't know the identity of the high-level executive who had provided the ship and retained his services, nor did he really care. What he did care about was the bank account back on Terra that was growing nicely, and would grow even fatter if he managed to bag an incoming Poictesmean freighter.

Supposedly one was due to arrive in-system shortly. And if a growing bank account gave him a nice warm feeling, the opportunity to command a former Navy cruiser made things even better. If he hadn't gotten kicked out of the Navy almost ten years ago, he might be in command of a real naval ship by now. Instead, he'd gotten caught accepting a bribe and been court-martialed for it. He had never forgiven the Space Navy for that humiliation, and being offered the chance to command one of the two pirate ships in this operation was just the ticket to soothe his still-bruised ego.

He was about to sit down at the command station when the signals-and-detection officer yelled out. "Bingo! A new transponder ID has just shown up. She's the *Pathfinder* out of Poictesme and she's one of the ships we've been alerted to look for."

Viktor cleared his throat and said in his best *officer* voice. "Excellent. Let's see her position on the main tactical screen."

The large viewscreen lit up with a Tri-D view of the vicinity of the planet Bifrost and the outer half of a sphere with a radius of a hundred and fifty million miles. Any incoming or outgoing ship traffic would be in the half sphere facing away from this system's star. The current amount of traffic was normal for this class of planet. Bifrost, for all of its grand name, was actually a third-rate economic destination and had the limited commercial traffic to prove it. The planet, two-thirds of which was coated with ice, was noted for its fine jewelry and gold mines, and even more for its chilly temperature.

That also meant that the increasingly underfunded Navy was less interested in patrolling it. The screen showed only two ships with active transponders. *Pathfinder* was a green triangle pointed and headed towards Bifrost at a distance of sixty million miles with a speed of just over twelve-thousand miles per second. The other ship, a tramp freighter headed outbound for Sarpanitum, was of no interest to Viktor or his backers.

But this *Pathfinder* was of great interest. Unfortunately, she was too far away from *Valley Forge* to try to intercept her on her way in. Viktor swallowed his disappointment. Actually, all other things being equal, he preferred to try for a ship when she was outbound rather than inbound since the freighter could increase acceleration if needed and be aided by the planetary well. The no-jump zone around Bifrost extended to just over fifty-five million miles. A ship that came any closer would be kicked back by its collapsing hyperspace field.

With the typical acceleration of 3.4 Gs that commercial freighters were designed for it would take that ship almost eighteen hours, after lifting from the Bifrost spaceport, to move beyond the no-jump zone. That would give *Valley Forge* plenty of time for intercept and capture.

As he sat down in the command station, he said out loud for the benefit of the bridge crew, "We can't catch her now but when she leaves this system...then we'll get her."

Captain Akira Yamato sat in the command station on *Pathfinder's* bridge. He wasn't happy about the fact that the cargo hold was only one quarter full but he understood that it took time for trade between any two planets to grow as businesses become aware of opportunities to either export or import goods. For the nth time he was glad that Tri-System Ltd. and Interstellar Spacelines had made it clear that they didn't expect miracles from him and that his position was secure. Especially since spaceship captains weren't exactly in demand outside the Tri-System.

He turned to the helm station and said, "Okay, Amanda, request clearance from traffic control for departure and take us up as soon as you get it."

She acknowledged the order and spoke softly into her headset mike.

Two minutes later *Pathfinder* broke through the cloud cover on its way into space. With artificial gravity keeping the inside of the ship at 1G no matter what the ship did, the only way the crew could tell the ship was moving was to check the radar altimeter or look at the external camera screen.

It wasn't long before the pilot reported. "We're clear of the atmosphere. No traffic in our flight path and ETA to the edge of the no-jump zone is seventeen hours, eleven minutes, thirty-four seconds."

"Understood. Thank you, Amanda. You have the conn. I'm going to my quarters. Tell your relief to wake me in eight hours if I'm not already awake."

"Aye, aye, Skipper."

Four hours later, Yamato woke to the sound of the buzzer.

"Yamato here. What is it?"

"Sorry to disturb you, Skipper, but radar is picking up an unidentified ship closing in on what appears to be an intercept vector. She's not squawking a transponder signal."

Yamato brushed away his fatigue. This was highly unusual and he didn't like the sound of it at all.

"I'll be right up."

With his cabin only one floor below the ship's bridge, Yamato was back in his command station in less than two minutes. He looked up at the main viewscreen. The bogey was ahead of them and off to one side and appeared to be maneuvering so that it would end up traveling parallel to *Pathfinder* at very close range.

"Any incoming transmissions from that ship?"

"No, Skipper. I've been scanning all ship-to-ship frequencies. Nothing yet."

"Well, then, let's ask them who they are."

Yamato heard the signals-and-detection officer ask the question, then a pause.

"Anything?"

"No response, Skipper."

"Okay, contact Traffic Control and advise them that we have unidentified traffic about to cross our flight path and ask them for permission to maneuver."

With permission granted, Yamato ordered his pilot to vector away from the approaching bogey.

As soon as *Pathfinder's* course change became apparent on the viewscreen, the Signals-and-Detection First Officer snapped his fingers.

"That ship's calling us. Audio only."

With the flick of a finger, the message was heard over the loudspeaker. "*Pathfinder, Pathfinder.* You are ordered to resume your original vector and prepare to be boarded for anti-smuggling cargo inspection."

Yamato walked over to the comm station and said, "Advise Traffic Control that an unidentified ship has ordered us to let ourselves be boarded. Transmit that system-wide. I want everyone to know what's going on. When you've done that, tell that ship that your Captain wants to speak with their captain with a screen connection."

"Okay, Skipper."

When direct contact was established, Yamato was surprised to find himself speaking with Captain Thoroldson of the Terran Federation Navy ship TNS *Valley Forge*. Thoroldson wore the uniform of the Federation Space Navy and Yamato recognized the background as a navy cruiser bridge. After introductions were made, Thoroldson took control of the conversation.

"You will comply with my instructions, Captain Yamato. Revert to your original vector and make no further transmissions of any kind. We will rendezvous with you and then provide more instructions. I'm sure your ship isn't carrying any contraband but I've been ordered to make sure of that.

"Once we've checked your cargo hold and assuming no contraband is found, your ship will be on its way again. Are you prepared to comply with my instructions, Captain?"

Yamato thought about it for a few seconds, then nodded and said, "Yes, Captain. We'll cooperate."

A strange smile appeared on Thoroldson's face before the connection was cut. Yamato felt a chill go up his spine. He had a bad feeling he had just said the wrong thing.

I

Conn Maxwell's three-year-old son, Foxx Travis Maxwell, pulled at his pants leg as he made his way toward the door. "Sylvie, could you help out here?"

His lovely wife shrugged. "I keep telling you, Conn, the boy misses his father. You're spending way more time with Merlin than you are with your own family."

There was a note of sadness in her voice, as well as disapproval. He had to admit her complaint was valid. However, Merlin was in the middle of the year-end economic projection and State of the Federation analysis. Conn needed to be there to make sure the super-computer had all the necessary information. If an important economic index or data field were missing, the results could be catastrophic to Poictesme's emergent economic engine. Plus, there were new elements, like the growing space piracy, that hadn't yet been entered into this year's data base.

Six years ago there had been banditry and pirates on Poictesme, like the Blackie Perales Gang. The new prosperity and resurgent government forces had eliminated those problems, but now these divisive elements were cropping up elsewhere in the Federation. Maybe things were coming apart faster than Merlin had predicted. He needed to get back to Force Command Headquarters and find out.

"I'm sorry, Foxx, but daddy's got work to do."

The little boy's face crumpled, his eyes starting to flood.

"I need you here to take care of Mommy. Understand?"

Little Foxx brushed the tears out of his eyes before answering. "Yes, Daddy."

He looked down at the boy, bent over and mussed his curly brown hair.

Sylvie looked at him and shook her head. "Okay. But one of these days...."

Their apartment was on the twenty-first floor of the remodeled Gartner Building in mid-town Litchfield just north of the mall. Tri-System Investments had picked up the building for a song just before the Merlin Boom revived the local—and planetary—economy. Conn took a lift up to the building-top landing stage where there was a battery of anti-vehicle weapons and several Barton-Massarra private police, now known as the Company Police. The Barton-Massarra Agency had been purchased by Litchfield Exploration and Salvage and was one more company-owned affiliate. Litchfield, one could say, was a company town—a Maxwell Company town that is.

Patrolman Bruce Mayher tipped his hat as Conn started to get into his recon-car. "How are you doing, Bruce?"

"Pretty well, Mr. Maxwell. It was a quiet night all around. Not much excitement these days."

Conn grinned. "We had enough excitement last month to last me for the rest of my life." It hadn't seemed so amusing at the time. Somehow, probably when his former aircar was at the garage for service, a Merlinolator had found a way inside the car and hid in the back. Conn hadn't noticed him until he landed at Force Command and the man tried to subdue him. Thankfully, the nutcase hadn't been much of a fighter; all he really wanted to do was worship at the feet—or in this case—the base of his deity, Merlin. Conn had been able to wrestle him to the floor after landing, and the Company police had quickly subdued him.

After that incident, the Company—in the person of his father—had insisted he drive to work in a combat car. He argued against it and they'd finally compromised on a collapsium-armored recon-car.

Even in a recon-car it was a six-hour flight, over some of the harshest land on Poictesme, to where Merlin was housed. The super-computer was hidden inside the walls of the Duplicate Force Command in the Badlands, over between the Blaubergs and the east coast. Fifty-seven years before, the Third Force Corps of Engineers had come to this isolated mesa in the Badlands and dug a huge pit into the butte where they had emplaced the super-computer. Inside it they had built a duplicate of the headquarters for Third Fleet-Army Force Command, a thousand feet in diameter and more than five hundred deep. They ran a shaft a hundred feet in diameter like a chimney at one side, and ran a tunnel out through solid rock to the head of a canyon half a mile away. Afterwards, they buried the whole thing. When the System States War had ended, they sealed both entrances and went away, leaving it intact with clothes and personal possessions still strewn about.

After landing, Conn nodded to the waiting guards with rifles brought up to port. Two of the guards accompanied him down the vertical shaft that led to the cave-like entrance to Duplicate Force Command Headquarters. He used his keycard ID, then entered his personal code into the keydock that opened the collapsium doors. If the code was off by even one symbol, sirens would ring out and guards from all over the installation would come on the run. This was the home of Merlin, the super-computer that had helped the Federation win the System States War. At that time, its very existence was the most guarded secret in the Federation. Its memory banks contained all available human knowledge and its positronic brain was capable of superhuman feats of combining and forming associations, as well as reasoning with uncanny accuracy and extrapolating to produce new facts. Merlin was even able to predict future events.

Unfortunately, its decisions were only as good as the knowledge and data it contained in its memory bank.

Recently there had been an unsettling worldwide trend: more and more of Poictesme's ignorant and uneducated citizens were beginning to attribute Merlin with superhuman abilities, even godlike qualities. This had been a problem, even before Merlin's rediscovery, when the first worshippers or Merlinolators began to make themselves known. The oldest and most vociferous being Dmitri Costanzia's First Church of Merlin.

Old Professor Dolf Kellton compared them to the followers of the Cargo cults on Terra in the South Sea Islands during the Second World War. The natives living there had grown accustomed to parachute drops of supplies from Allied planes, many of which were off-target. The islanders took those that missed the mark, believing they were manna of divine origin. When the cargo shipments stopped, the natives had felt abandoned by the gods.

It was a close parallel to the situation on Poictesme forty-five years ago when the war abruptly ended. Millions of troops had been stationed on or routed through Poictesme during the twelve years of the System States War, when the System States Alliance had seceded from the Federation, and war had been declared. The mines and factories had worked around-the-clock producing armaments and other vital items. The Federation had spent trillions upon trillions of sols, piled up mountains of supplies and equipment, leaving the face of the world cluttered and pockmarked with installations. Then, almost without warning, the System States Alliance had collapsed, the rebellion ended and the scourge of peace fell on Poictesme.

The Third Fleet-Army Force had abandoned the planet, leaving behind mountains of supplies, ordnance, bases, half-built starships, even the troopers' uniforms. Everything had been jettisoned: even the most expensive military equipment had been worth less than the cost of its removal. An avaricious few had made fortunes selling off the mountains of remaining supplies and equipment. Those who grew wealthiest left Poictesme, taking their riches with them as they departed for more civilized worlds, like Terra, Odin, Aton, Isis and Baldur. For the succeeding four decades, those who had stayed behind had made a bare living scrounging off the remaining salvage.

Then six years ago Merlin had been rediscovered. Among other questions, the Fawzi Gang had asked Merlin about the future of the Terran Federation. When Merlin predicted the fall of the Federation—which would be hastened if news of its prophecy were leaked—the Merlin-12 group had been formed to keep her location secret.

The original prediction had given General Foxx Travis and his staff the impetus to cover up not only its prognostication, but the very presence of the super-computer: "In two hundred years there won't be any Terran Federation. The Government will collapse, slowly. The Space Navy will disintegrate. Planets and systems will lose touch with Terra and with one another. The economic depression will spread from one planet to another, even to Terra. Just a slow crumbling, till everything is gone; then every planet will start sliding back, in isolation, into barbarism."

In trepidation, the Merlin-12 had asked: "What is the best course to be followed under these conditions by the people of Poictesme?" The answer had been: "Export trade, specializing in luxury goods. Brandies and wines, tobacco; a long list of other exportable commodities, and optimum markets. Reopening of industrial plants; establishment of new industries. Attainment of economic self-sufficiency. Cultural self-sufficiency; establishment of universities, institutes of technology, research laboratories."

Then the Maxwell Plan became the Merlin Plan; the breakup of the Federation was a fact that entered into the computation. Merlin suggested: "Build-up military strength to resist aggression by other planetary governments. Defense of the Gartner Tri-System. Lists of possible aggressor planets. Revival of interstellar communications and trade; expeditions, conquest and re-education of natives...."

The majority of the Merlin-12 Group was comprised of the core of the old Fawzi Office Gang, a group of Litchfield Town Merlin believers who had helped finance Conn Maxwell's education at the University of Montevideo on Terra. They were Planetary President Kurt Fawzi; Professor Kellton; Franz Veltrin, the group historian; Colonel Zareff; Head of Security; Tom Brangwyn, the Minister of the Interior; Lorenzo Menardes, the distiller; Lester Dawes, the banker; Morgan Gatworth, the lawyer, and Judge Ledue.

The rest of the group was comprised of the Maxwells—father and son—and Dr. Wade Lucas, Conn's brother-in-law. The Merlin-12, or M-12 as they called themselves, was the unofficial designation of the twelve key insiders who knew about Merlin's gloomy projections and who collectively held a majority of the shares in Tri-System Investments, Ltd, which owned among its other interests all the shares of Litchfield Exploration & Salvage. Among Litchfield Exploration & Salvage's many assets was the Force Command Duplicate Headquarters site where the super-computer Merlin was located.

Within M-12, Conn and his father led a core group that could outvote the rest. M-12 was able to exercise control of the holding company, Tri-System Investments. Both Conn and his father understood how fragile the whole structure was and how easily the Maxwell/Merlin Plan could be derailed by losing control of Tri-System Investments. The M-12 Group wasn't just protecting the most advanced computer the Terran Federation had ever known; it was protecting the Federation from Merlin's prediction of the coming apocalypse.

Now, even some of those who should have known better, like melon grower Boris Menendez, were encouraging the deification of Merlin. If they didn't watch out, in another few centuries the masses of Poictesme would be on their knees worshipping Merlin and taking its predictions as Word From On High. In his mind's eye, Conn could see robbed and hooded acolytes tending the Oracle of Merlin and giving the roughly garbed hoi polloi its revelations while the priesthood lived off the bounty.

Conn shook his head to dispel the vision; it was all too real. It was up to him and the Merlin-12 Group to make sure this never came to pass. Unfortunately, too many members of M-12 still saw Merlin as an infallible and omniscient deity that had all the answers to mankind's questions.

In truth, it was just a machine with a big brain, and if that brain didn't have damn good data, its predictions were worthless. Like the old maxim everyone learned in elementary computing classes: "Garbage in, gospel out."

In Conn's mind, education and prosperity were the real answers to Poictesme's problems. Poictesme was still too dependent upon trade with the Federation to stand on her own. The planet was ripe with agriculture, but poor in heavy metals and energy sources with little oil and few deposits of radioactive ores. Fortunately, the dead planets of the Gartner Tri-System were rich with minerals and rare earths, but still everything had to be shipped in.

In the six years since Merlin's rediscovery, after decades of decline, the economy had begun to grow again. The unemployed were getting jobs and interstellar trade was on the upswing. Bands of tramps and hobos no longer wandered the countryside aimlessly searching for work. Port Carpenter on Koshchei now had over fifty thousand permanent colonists living under the dome city. And, while it was too early to say prosperity had arrived in the Gartner Tri-System, it appeared to be right around the corner.

However, the Terran Federation as a whole was still caught up in the post-War depression. Over a hundred planets of the former System States Alliance had been impoverished, while others had been bombed into the stone age. Many Federation worlds hadn't escaped the war unscathed and had suffered damage to their economic base as well as to their bombed cites. After the war, high taxes and military casualties had devastated their economies and left many worlds with depressed and failing economies.

As more and more worlds like Tanith, Malebolge, Seth, Gilgamesh and Aditya became decivilized; it was growing harder for Merlin to access the data it needed to make accurate predictions. Conn had spent the last standard month reviewing the data fed to Merlin and awaiting the computer's latest projections with increasing anxiety. As part of the team that had rediscovered the Big Brain, he had once taken it on faith that the super-computer and its predictions were omnipotent. Now he knew better, but Merlin was Poictesme's—and maybe even the Federation's—last hope.

Six years ago, after reading Merlin's prediction about the dissolution of the Federation in the Tenth Century as interstellar revolts and wars consumed planet after planet, it had been decided by M-12 to keep this information top secret. Especially since Merlin predicted its dissemination would only hasten the Federation's end as people lost faith in the future and in the Terran Federation.

Unfortunately, due to the media blitz that had followed Merlin's discovery, everyone on Poictesme and throughout the Federation knew that Merlin was located inside the former Federation Third-Force Command Headquarters in the Badlands. This explained why Force Command was so well protected by Company Police and the Planetary Government; besides dozens of small patrol craft, there were three interplanetary destroyers and one battlecruiser in the vicinity.

In Conn's mind, the biggest threat to Merlin wasn't off-worlder saboteurs or modern day Luddites; no, it was the Merlinolators themselves, the multitudes of worshippers who saw the super-computer as some sort of deity or magical father figure, like the God Ghu to the Thorans.

Recently, the Poictesme Air Patrol had caught several aircars entering the Badlands. Two of them had contained true-believers who wanted to visit the site of their "god" to worship in his presence. One of them, a modified gunboat, had fought back. The Company destroyer had made short work of the gunboat, which was destroyed with all hands aboard. Unfortunately, they still didn't know who had sent it or why.

II

Ward Shawley took a stool next to the smooth-looking Asiatic gentleman who looked like a card sharp except for the blue-triangle scars on both cheeks. He was reputed to be a member of one of the Dizang triads, but no one knew for sure; it wasn't healthy to ask personal questions at the End-of-the-Line bar in Tramptown. They were seated at the end of the bar, several barstools away from the nearest drunk.

"Have you been able to obtain a handle on this M-12 Group?" Shawley asked, looking both ways to make sure no one might overhear.

The man known as Xu shook his head. "I've tried to bribe some of the clerks but they won't play." His voice was gruff and lower than one would expect, as if he'd taken one too many hits to the throat.

"How persuasive were you?" Shawley asked.

Xu sneered. "I worked one over pretty well with my blade; he never made it back to work. Still, he didn't know nothing."

Shawley had played with the idea of putting his own man up as a programmer, but apparently all new applicants were recommends from former hires and thoroughly vetted with a veridicator. Not even cold cash could suborn a truth machine.

"Any ideas where we can get what we need?" he asked.

"I gave you Gatworth, didn't I?"

He nodded. "And he's been useful. But I need more leverage."

Xu said, "You might try Dmitri Costanzia; he's a crackpot, but he claims to know all of Merlin's secrets."

"I'll talk to him. Here's a thousand sols for your trouble." He passed off the cash under the bar so no wandering eyes might see the payoff.

Xu frowned as if he didn't think it was enough, but slowly got off his stool after taking measure of Shawley's two guards. Both were former Federation Marines with dishonorable discharges and experts at hand-to-hand combat. They'd been assigned to him by the principal and were well worth the sols they cost. While Poictesme was not a frontier world, it still had its rough-and-tumble edges.

Now, he needed to find the man who called himself the Patriarch of the First Church of Merlin.

I

Conn was winded by the time he reached the bottom of the vertical shaft. *We need to install lifts*, he told himself for about the hundredth time. *True, but this is just about the only exercise I get.* Being Chief Programmer meant that he spent most of his time sitting in a chair or pacing the floor. *I need to spend more time at home chasing little Foxx*, he decided. *Sylvie is right; I am spending too much time with Merlin, who is quickly becoming the "other woman" in my life.*

As Conn entered the commander-and-chief's office where Merlin's interface had been reinstalled, he saw his programming assistants, Myra Atherton and Jessie Alfonso. Myra started waving the moment he entered the office.

"Communication drones just arrived from several of the outer worlds, Hoth, Beowulf and Jagannath. Your idea of setting up trading posts throughout the Federation rim has really started to pay dividends."

Due to the difficulty of obtaining accurate and timely data from the rim worlds, Conn had come up with the idea of setting up trading outposts on selected worlds that would act as a central collection base for the more isolated groups of planets. Rather than having to visit each world, or depend upon Federation reports and statistics, they would have real-time data from the planets themselves. The plan was that the outposts would send bi-annual data bursts via hyperspace drones regarding their sectors. The comm drones were put into orbit in the outer heliosphere of the target planetary system. Every standard six months the outposts would send their reports via tight-beam transmission to the system communication drone. Once the data had been received, the drone would then enter hyperspace and emerge into real space only when it entered Alpha System.

The program was only two years old, but they were already getting reliable transmissions from forty worlds that had been previously hit or miss when it came to Merlin's biannual State of the Federation Surveys.

"Yes, this Year-End Survey is going to be the most detailed ever," Alfonso added.

Conn nodded. "But it hasn't been cheap." President Fawzi had been screaming about runaway costs and, to an extent, he was right. However, the trading outposts they were building throughout the Federation rim would one day soon serve as depots for arriving Tri-System Interstellar freighters, and even passenger ships. He liked to view them as investments in the future.

He sat down at his desk and looked at the wealth of data that had not yet been converted to machine readable code. *It's time to teach Merlin Lingua Terra,* he decided. *Sure, but when—in all my spare time?* Unfortunately, the best programmers in the Gartner Tri-System were already working at Force Command. What they should be doing was teaching at the new Litchfield University, but until they imported more teachers that was just a pipe dream. Emigration from Terra was out since all the risk-takers, explorers and wanderers had left Terra centuries ago. All that were left behind were the yes-men, corporate drones, glad-handers and mamma's boys.

Maybe it was time to shift their target to Odin or Baldur where there were still ambitious young men anxious to get ahead or bored with the same old same old.

Conn paused to take a deep breath and push everything out of his mind but the documents he was putting into code, and went to work. His assistants and a dozen other programmers were just as busy. There was a nightshift, too. Each year there was more data to enter and not enough time to train more help. He was going to have to spend the night here again. And Sylvie wondered why he wasn't home more often....

II

The next day at noon, Conn quickly walked over to the salvaged Third Fleet-Army Force reconnaissance vehicle and climbed in. After announcing his destination to the Litchfield airport, Conn settled back to wait until the sleek little vehicle had gone supersonic before putting it on autopilot and calling his father. It took a few seconds for his father's image to appear on the console viewscreen on the secure feed.

"Ah, Conn. You're on your way?" he nodded. "Good. If you push it to the max, you should get here just in time for the M-12 meeting at 1800 hours."

"I know I'm cutting it close, Dad, but I wanted to finish reviewing the latest projections." He paused for a few seconds. "The news isn't good."

Rodney Maxwell raised his eyebrow. "How so?"

Conn sighed. "Well...apparently the loss of our second hypership to piracy is a major new development. Merlin's baseline projection of a slow, gradual collapse of the Federation didn't project any space piracy for another forty to fifty years. The fact that it's happened this quickly is interpreted by Merlin to indicate that we're veering towards the worst-case scenario, a much quicker and violent collapse. The Civilization Index has dropped another two percent from our last projection!"

His father was shocked. "Great Ghu! That much in just six months? That *is* terrible news. Our Planetary President isn't going to like that."

In spite of the serious nature of the conversation, Conn couldn't help but chuckle. President Kurt Fawzi was Merlin's biggest fan. His belief in the super-computer was unshakable. Like many of the other members of M-12 Group, he believed that the super-computer, used by the great general Foxx Travis to win the war against the System States Alliance half a century ago, would reveal the path to glorious prosperity for all the citizens of Poictesme. Therefore bad news from Merlin caused the President no end of conflicting emotions. It was like the Christian god telling its most faithful followers that He wasn't going to answer their prayers.

"Our Beloved Leader will just have to deal with it," Conn said. "The trouble is that I'm having trouble dealing with it, too. I'm starting to have serious doubts that the Maxwell/Merlin Plan is the right thing to do."

Now Conn's father looked really shocked. "I can't believe what I'm hearing, son. You're the one who proposed the Maxwell Plan in the first place. True, the rest of the Federation seems to be going to Nifflheim in a handbasket faster than we expected, but things on Poictesme are improving. That can't be a bad thing, right?"

"Yes, things are improving planetside, but maybe that is the problem. Are we making things worse for everyone else in the Federation in order to make things better for a few Poictesme citizens? Remember what the cause of the worst case scenario was?"

Rodney nodded. "'If news of Merlin's projection of a long-term decline and collapse of the Federation became common knowledge, then people and planets all over the Federation will scramble to protect themselves economically and militarily as much as possible at the expense of other planets, resulting in trade dislocations and eventually wars.'"

"That's right. And do you remember what question we asked Merlin six years ago about Poictesme?"

"We asked Merlin what the best course of action was for the planet of Poictesme. What was wrong with that?"

"Don't you see, Father? That approach is exactly what Merlin predicted other planets would do. We've been assuming that what's good for Poictesme is also good, or at least neutral, for the Terran Federation; but what if it isn't? What if we ourselves are becoming the very catalyst that's causing the worst-case scenario to happen?"

His father looked puzzled. He paused to take his pipe out of his suit pocket and pack it with tobacco grown locally on Poictesme. "I don't see how. The only properties we've taken over are the Federation facilities here in the Gartner Tri-System that the Federation abandoned over fifty years ago. We're paying fair prices for goods that our ships import from other systems. No other planetary government is angry with us, as far as I know."

"Terra-Baldur-Marduk Spacelines isn't happy with us," he replied.

"Okay, so they're not making as much money from having their large hyperspace freighters stop here on their way to Marduk as they used to. They're a privately owned company, not a planetary government. What could they possibly do that would speed up the collapse of the Federation?"

"I don't know," Conn said, "I just have this nagging suspicion that we've put things in motion that we aren't even aware of, some of which will have unintended consequences."

His father looked thoughtful for a minute or so, then said, "Let's hope that's not the case. Is that something that we could ask Merlin?"

Now it was Conn's turn to be surprised. "You mean ask Merlin if the Maxwell Plan is causing the Federation Civ-Index to plunge faster than expected?"

His father nodded.

Conn had to think about that before answering. "That's something that I've never considered before," he said. "We would have to ask the question in a way that Merlin can understand, and even then it may not be able to make the necessary computations. It's too bad General Shanlee passed away. He might have been able to shed some light on this question."

Conn remembered how General Shanlee had almost succeeded in destroying Merlin before Conn and the other members of the "Fawzi Gang" had realized that the super-computer was within their grasp. It had been General Shanlee who first revealed the awful news that Merlin had predicted the Federation was doomed but—when Merlin had justified its own continued existence—the General had become a willing supporter of the Maxwell/Merlin Plan. Shanlee was also one of the founding members of the Merlin-12 Group, the cabal of Litchfield civic and political leaders who had kept the existence of the super-computer a closely guarded secret for the past six years.

"Certainly his input would have been useful," Conn said. "We'll have to wait until tomorrow before I can formulate the question for Merlin, so don't say anything to the others at this meeting. Let's wait until we have an answer to that question—if it's even possible to get an answer—before we raise the issue at the M-12 meeting, okay?"

"Okay," his father replied.

"Has *Trailblazer* arrived yet?" he asked.

Trailblazer was another medium-sized hypership freighter like *Pathfinder* that was used exclusively on runs to nearby inhabited planets, those too insignificant for Terra-Baldur-Marduk Spacelines, Odin Trailways and Pan-Federation Spacelines, to bother visiting more than once a decade or two.

Conn's father's expression became somber. "No, and they're now six days overdue. Are you thinking that they've run afoul of pirates, too?"

"Aren't you?"

"It's starting to look that way." His father paused again.

Conn waited certain that his father had something else on his mind. He was right.

"Tri-Systems Investments' stock traded again yesterday at one hundred and forty-four sols per share, up twenty-one sols from the previous trade a week ago. The bid price has gone up, too, to one hundred and seventy-five sols per share. Considering that company profits have been trending lower for the last two years, this persistent rise in price to another new all-time high can mean only one thing."

"Someone is trying to buy control of the company?"

"Yes," his father replied.

"Any idea who's buying?"

His father shook his head emphatically, almost spilling his pipe. "That's the scary part to this. All of the share purchases over the last six months have been by different buyers. Individuals for the most part, but also companies that suddenly popped into existence with cash in their pockets. I haven't been able to find out who's bankrolling any of them. None of the individuals are known within the Storisende or Litchfield business community and no one seems to know where they got the money to buy the shares. We're talking over ten million sols worth of shares over a six month period.

"It's obvious to me that someone with very deep pockets, maybe even someone off-planet, has gone to a lot of trouble to buy a major stake in Tri-Systems Investments without revealing themselves. If this were just an ordinary investment, why all the secrecy, son?"

Conn gave it some consideration. "Could it be the same people who wanted to buy Merlin from us a few years ago?" A large corporation from Terra had set up a local company to hold their commercial interests on Poictesme and had been buying up shares in local companies, including the M-12 firms.

"They were pretty upfront about who they were and what they wanted, weren't they?" his father asked.

"True, but if it's the same bunch, why be secretive about it now?"

"Doesn't makes sense to me, son. There's no law or company prohibition against selling shares of Tri-System Investments, Ltd. to off-planet investors. We decided not to try that because having company bylaws restricting who can own shares would have opened the door to lawsuits that might have resulted in Merlin's gloomy predictions becoming public knowledge in courtroom testimony."

"Good point," Conn said.

His father leaned back in his chair, pointing at his son. "No. This secret takeover smells like someone is doing something they know we wouldn't like, or is downright illegal and they don't want to get caught at it. As long as the M-12 Group keeps their combined controlling interest in Tri-Systems Investments intact, we're okay, but I'm worried that these sky-high prices will entice someone to cash in their shares in spite of our oaths to each other not to do that."

Conn pondered that comment for a while. "You know…back in the beginning, when there were five operating companies, it made sense to put them all under one corporate holding company for administrative purposes so that cash resources could be moved around to where they were needed the most. But things have changed. Both Mainland Medical Materials and Litchfield Exploration and Salvage have squeezed as much revenue from the sale of salvaged materials as possible. There's not all that much left to salvage anymore. Litchfield Exploration & Salvage is now really just a holding company for the Merlin site and the spaceport over on the Barathrum continent. Koshchei Exploration & Development is still making money and will continue as long as we need more ships, but there's a limit to how many interplanetary and interstellar ships we'll be able to use. And off-world sales are next to nothing."

"Since the war, there's been a fire sale on interstellar ships."

"That just leaves the two main sources of income right now, which are Alpha-Interplanetary and Tri-System & Interstellar Spacelines. Maybe the time has come when the whole is worth less than the sum of its parts. What if Tri-Systems Investments just spun-off all of its holdings in the other companies? That would make it harder for some outsider to buy control of everything and if that someone then concentrates on one particular company, we'll know exactly what they're after. Maybe whoever is buying Tri-System Investments stock isn't interested in Merlin but rather Koshchei Exploration & Development or Tri-System Interstellar, instead."

"I've been wondering the same thing," his father said. "I was planning on sounding out the other members of M-12 about it privately. Let's you and I talk about it some more after I've done that." Another pause. "Was there anything else you're going to report to the M-12 Group?"

"There's another thing or two. Well…we can discuss this some more after the meeting. I'll see you in about…six hours."

Conn knew that some of the members of M-12 were only interested in the future of Poictesme and couldn't give a fig what happened to the Terran Federation, except as it impacted Poictesme and their personal lives. And its fall would affect them, more than they could imagine: revolutions, internecine warfare, piracy, planetary warlords, interstellar conquerors of every stripe. In the end, the deaths of billions.

"Yes, that ETA is about right," his father replied. "See you then."

They both signed off and Conn switched the viewscreen to the external view in order to contemplate the scenery while he organized his thoughts for the upcoming meeting of the Merlin-12 Group.

I

Morgan Gatworth slunk through the alleyway behind Acaire Street. He couldn't afford to have anyone he knew see him in this part of town. The stench of garbage, stale beer and human effluvium filled the air. This was not a reputable part of Litchfield, only two blocks away from Tramptown. The few derelicts he walked by, lying passed out on the ground, had missed the prosperity boat and had dropped down into the sea of misery for the third and possibly last time. *If I'm not careful, I'll be joining them,* he worried.

And I was doing so well. Last night at the Risky Business Club he'd been fifty thousand sols to the good, then Lady Luck deserted him. Shat on him, you could say. A couple of spins of the ball and not only had he lost everything in his hand, but he'd lost another twenty thousand on account. *Shawley's going to own me right down to my last pair of skivvies.*

The family house, no mansion, was mortgaged to the gables. He should never have sunk so much of his liquid capital into it. And, his wife, totally unaware of his financial status, spent money as though it came out of a faucet. Not only that, but he was selling out his friends. He'd turned spy and—*be honest for once in your life, you miserable cur*—traitor!

His law practice brought in a good five-figure income and the dividends from Tri-System Investments were substantial—but never enough. *Not when your luck at the roulette wheel is as bad as mine....*

His biggest fear—other than the fact that Shawley might hurt him physically—was that he'd cut him off. Make his debts public. Then he'd be lost for sure; his friends would turn on him and he'd end up as just another Tramptown bum. Maybe today's news, just off the Koshchei packet ship, would buy him some breathing time, maybe even settle his debts. A man could hope.

II

Ward Shawley felt sweat bead on this forehead. His principal didn't take well to failure, and he'd been on Poictesme for ten Galactic Standard months and was no closer to taking control of Tri-System Interstellar than he'd been after landing at Storisende Spaceport.

Shawley was a big, rough-looking man who few would take for a lawyer, but he'd gone to Law School at Melbourne University and had graduated at the top of his class. However, his penchant for high-risk games of chance had caused him to borrow sols from loan sharks. To pay them back he'd siphoned cash out of some of his escrow accounts, gotten caught when he couldn't return the funds, then he'd been disbarred. Now, he took any jobs that were offered, whether they skirted the law or not.

Back on Terra, he'd been approached by an intermediary from some large company or corporation. He'd been offered half a million sols and reinstatement to the bar if he could engineer a takeover of Tri-System Investments. As an inducement, they'd given him a quarter of a million sols cash for expenses and to pay off the locals for information—and unlimited funds to purchase a majority interest in the Maxwell's holding company. One of the problems was that it all had to be done through intermediaries. No one—not even himself—was to know the identity of the principal. *It makes sense*, he thought wryly, *I'm not the soul of discretion, nor above selling out my bosses whoever they are.*

Shawley heard a tenuous knock at the door and looked down at his wristwatch—right on time. He'd been careful to rent an office space in a marginal area of town. When people asked what he did, he answered speculator—a respectable position on a world that had made a living off selling army surplus for the last fifty-five years.

He didn't press the door release right away; he wanted Gatworth to sweat a little more, the degenerate gambler. However much he despised the man—maybe because they shared the same weakness—he was Shawley's only link to the Merlin-12 Group. Now, he had to squeeze Gatworth for everything he was worth; otherwise his replacement would be arriving in the near future on the next inbound spaceliner.

He hit the door release and Gatworth stumbled inside; he looked bad, his skin was fish-belly white and he was perspiring heavily. Gatworth was a tall, thin man who might be considered handsome were he not so much on edge. His hat was tilted to one side and his left eye was twitching.

Shawley knew about last night's fiasco and he was sure the lawyer wanted to hit him up for another advance. *He can't be that stupid, can he? Of course, he can.*

Gatworth actually took off his hat and approached his desk hat-in-hand. "Sir, I—"

"I know all about your losses last night at Risky Business," he interjected. "Did it ever occur to you that the name might actually have a secondary meaning? Casinos are there to make money, not give it away to bums like yourself."

Gatworth flinched.

This is too easy. It's not even fun anymore… "It's time you started paying up—"

"That's why I'm here, Mr. Shawley."

The wheedling tone hurt his ears. "I know the M-12 meeting isn't until tonight, unless you made an error."

"No, sir. It's still on." Gatworth's face suddenly took on a duplicitous cast. "But I did get some new information—important news. Really, a new development. An old friend was on the Koshchei packet today for a ten-day leave and he told a *very* interesting story. And he wanted my help, due to this information, on how to capitalize on it."

Poor bastard. He must be desperate if he's counting on Gatworth's help. "What is it?" he asked, interested despite himself.

"I think it's worth a lot. Even more than the three hundred and forty thousand sols I owe you, Mr. Shawley."

"Well," he replied. "You've got my attention. What is it?" If the fool didn't spit it out soon, he was going to pull it out with tongs, if need be.

Gatworth lowered his voice to a throaty whisper, as if there might be listening devices abroad. *Not in this room, my fine feathered friend. I check it for eavesdroppers and micro-dot listeners every morning.*

"My friend is part of an engineering group on Koshchei working on improvements to the Dillingham hyperspace engines."

Now, he had his attention. "So?"

"It's an ad hoc project by young Maxwell's father-in-law, Yves Jacquemont, the First Engineer. They've made a big breakthrough. If it pans out, and it looks like it will, their new drives will cut hyperspace travel times in half." Gatworth leaned back with a big grin pasted on his face, as if he were saying "now, top that."

"Hmm." This was a startling, but welcome development. It wasn't what his principals were looking for, but on the other hand this development could turn the Terran stock market upside down—especially, if an insider knew about this before even the Maxwells….

"That is helpful, Morgan. It's not what we were looking for, but I believe this will be useful to interested parties."

"I've got some of the details locked in my office safe. How much are they worth to your principals?"

Shawley's first impulse was to slap the smile right off Gatworth's face. But, he needed him too much to actually injure him, visibly anyway.

"Okay, deliver those papers to me right now and I will write-off your entire debt. Plus, pay you another fifty thousand sols cash."

"Come on, Shaw. This is worth *real* money, not chump change. I wanna see some sols and lots of them."

He was practically salivating.

"Never call me Shaw, you degenerate freak! As far as chump change, how about I sell your markers to Vinnie Two-Fingers? Yeah, how about I do that?" Vinnie hadn't earned that sobriquet by any shortage of his own fingers, but by cutting off the index fingers of known welchers with a dull blade.

Gatworth's face turned white, and he looked as if he were about to faint.

"Now, I'm going to give you one chance. Bring me those papers now! If you're quick enough, I might still see it in my heart to give you the fifty thousand sols I mentioned."

"Yes, Mr. Shawley. I'll be back shortly."

"No, no. This time I'm going with you. I don't want you to have any second thoughts or maybe develop a conscience between here and your office. Stranger things have been known to happen. We'll walk together."

"But what will people think?"

"Nothing. I'm not well-known in your circles. I'm just another client in need of a good lawyer. Right?"

"Right, Mr. Shawley. Yes, you're right."

I

Conn Maxwell met his father at the Litchfield airport. His father picked him up in a ground car and they drove to the Airlines Building, which was Tri-System Investments' company headquarters. As they drove through downtown Litchfield, he couldn't help but compare the town to how it had been when he'd returned from Terra six years ago. The roads had been repaved and most of the buildings rehabbed, even those that didn't have occupants. The Mall was teeming with customers and there were people walking on the sidewalks. The town population figure was up to thirty thousand from twelve thousand six years ago. For a Federation town, Litchfield was still a backwater, no contragravity towers and spires like in Storisende, and people still rode around in ground cars. And, true, they still had their disreputable parts of town, like Tramptown. But, overall, Litchfield was alive again and the townspeople's confidence in the future had returned.

Maybe a visitor from Terra would see it as a provincial backwater, but to Conn it looked pretty damn good and a far cry from yesteryear.

On the way he and his father discussed the upcoming meeting. Conn said, "Besides, the Year End Report, I've been working with Merlin, trying to figure out what strategies could be implemented that would accelerate the recovery of civilization after the coming collapse has hit rock bottom." That was an issue that M-12 decided should be looked into two meetings ago.

Rodney Maxwell nodded. "Yes, I remember. What's the latest on that?"

"We ran into a brick wall. According to Merlin, the basic problem is that further computations are impossible, since there's no way to estimate how bad things would get or how people on different planets might cope with the breakdown of the Federation. So I had to approach the question from a completely different angle. Rather than try to figure out what will happen, I set up a hypothetical simulation of the Federation after a general collapse and made some rough assumptions.

"Based on those assumptions—which is a *big* caveat I might add—Merlin was able to identify three strategies, which if implemented before the collapse, would contribute to a faster recovery after the collapse. Here's what Merlin came up with: The first strategy is to establish a brain trust on certain key planets. This brain trust would be a collaboration between universities and industrial companies that would set up a remote site—away from major cities which are prime targets for any attack—that would store technical data, books, records and key technological components in a way that would stand the test of time. Therefore, if civilization crashes, as Merlin predicts one or two hundred years from now, the survivors would be able to access the site and bootstrap their way back up to an interstellar civilization in a few hundred years.

"The next strategy would be to establish a secret society, with a religious front, that would engage in interstellar trade and therefore not be tied down to any one particular planet. This society would have as its goal the preservation of interstellar communication and trade, and to enable technology transfers even during the lowest point of the collapse's aftermath.

"The last strategy is the most difficult to execute but has the best chance of success. It would involve exploration beyond current Federation borders for habitable worlds to be colonized in secret and kept isolated from the rest of the Federation during the collapse. By being self-reliant, these colonies would not be subject to the forces that are causing the collapse and—at the right time—would send ships back into the Federation to begin reconstruction."

Conn waited for his father's reply.

"Hmm. It seems to me that setting up brain trusts and exploring for new colony worlds would be pretty expensive. And an iffy situation since the colonists may have their own problems and will not be concerned with their charters or ancestral issues. And I certainly don't have a clue how we'd go about creating a religious front."

His father paused long enough to unwrap a cigar and light it. He took a few puffs, and then said, "I wonder if it would really be necessary to find a new habitable planet beyond Federation territory. You know there are literally thousands of planets in star systems scattered between Federation planet systems that have never been colonized or exploited."

"You mean planets that would require domed cities?"

His father nodded.

"We'd want to avoid those," Conn said. "If I remember correctly—Merlin would have this in its databanks—there are also some planets that have breathable atmospheres but have other variables that makes them less than ideal, such as high or low temperatures, little water, hostile wildlife, climate extremes, etc. If we could identify a marginal world that wasn't too hostile to life, but hadn't yet been colonized, it would be a lot less costly to set up a colony there. With some terraforming, such a world could be made more hospitable to Terran life forms. Since we wouldn't have to send ships out for months or years on exploration trips that would prevent those ships from carrying cargo and earning revenues. Did Merlin estimate the cost of these strategies?"

"Yes," Conn said. "The cheapest is finding underused known worlds and rehabbing them, but even that one would cost almost three or four billion sols to do properly."

Rodney Maxwell snorted. "If all of Tri-System Investments' subsidiary companies sold every asset they have, we *might* be able to raise that kind of capital...maybe! And that's a big maybe."

"I know, it's frustrating, Dad. The replacement cost of those industrial facilities on Koshchei alone are in the hundreds of billions of sols, but no one would pay even a fraction of that for them because of the depressed local markets and the cost of shipping goods by hypership."

His father shook his head sadly. "I know, and there's no way we could convince M-12 to go along with that kind of expenditure without the promise of a real return, which just isn't feasible. They remember the hard times too well. We're just going to have to come up with something else, or let Merlin do it."

Conn felt his heart drop to his stomach. "Let Merlin do it," that was everyone's response to any seemingly insurmountable issue. But, as he knew, Merlin was far from infallible, and only as good as the information it was programmed with. He was beginning to think that Merlin was coming to the end of its usefulness, and starting to become part of the problem.

II

They parked in the Airlines Building's parking lot. At the building entrance Conn's wife, Sylvie, and his son, Foxx, were waiting for him. Foxx was playing with a small animal that he recognized as Klem Zareff's Fuzzy, Stonewall Jackson. Even from a distance he could hear its "Yeek! Yeek!"

The fact that old man Zareff would entrust Stonewall to Foxx demonstrated just how much the curmudgeon dotted on Conn's three-year-old son. Fuzzies were a rare sight off their homeworld. Everybody loved Fuzzies, but not everywhere loved Fuzzies. It turned out that the first Fuzzies taken off Zarathustra did not reproduce on other worlds. As a result, the Federation had banned their export from Zarathustra and made it a federal crime to take one off-world.

This prohibition had broken down during the System States War when Zarathustra had joined the System States Alliance. Klem had never visited Zarathustra, but had been given Stonewall Jackson by Morgan Holloway III, a major in Klem's regiment, who'd been the head of the 32nd's scouts. Holloway had received a fatal wound during a Federation bombardment and had entrusted Stonewall to Klem's care for life.

"Hi, Daddy!" Foxx cried out. He ran up to Conn, hugging him just above the knees. Conn leaned over to pick him up and swing him around.

Sylvie sighed. "I know you don't like him out this late, but you've been so busy lately he hasn't spent any time with you."

He leaned over to kiss his wife. "I know, but with a ship missing…well, it's been hectic."

Sylvie nodded. She was still as beautiful as the day they'd meet, when she'd been a prisoner of Blackie Perales' gang. Meeting her was the best thing that came out of that rescue, he thought.

Stonewall came over to Conn, and he scratched the Fuzzy behind its ears. "Hi, Unka Conn. Pappy Klem's inside with lots of Unkas." The Fuzzy's fur was still mostly golden, but recently silver streaks had started to appear. He knew Stonewall had to be at least seventy years of age, if not older. *How long do Fuzzies live, anyway?*

"Thank you, Stonewall."

He picked Foxx up again and gave him a big hug. "I'm sorry, big guy, but Daddy's got to go back to work."

"Can I take Stonewall home with me and Mommy?" Foxx asked.

He shook his head. "Stonewall has to come with me. You know Unka Klem, he doesn't let Stonewall go on visits without him."

Foxx nodded, since previous requests to take the Fuzzy home had been denied.

"I'll be home, late, I suspect."

Sylvie gave him a wry smile. "I'll keep the home fires burning," she said, taking Foxx by the hand, heading back to their ground car.

All the other members of the Merlin-12 Group—melon farmer

Klem Zareff, Chief Tom Brangwyn, Judge George Ledue, banker Jethro Sastraman, Franz Veltrin, Professor Dolf Kellton, melon-brandy distiller Lorenzo Menardes, lawyer Morgan Gatworth, banker Lester Dawes—were there except for Planetary President Kurt Fawzi, who had business in Storisende to take care of. They were seated in the company boardroom waiting for Conn's arrival. Filling in for Fawzi, Judge Ledue chaired the meeting.

As soon as they entered the room, Stonewall ran over to Klem and jumped up on his shoulder. There he'd remain for the rest of the meeting, not making a single yeek. Conn wasn't sure if he was well-behaved for a Fuzzy, but he was certainly the best behaved person at the meeting.

Judge Ledue banged his gavel to let them know the meeting was about to begin.

Conn wondered how much longer the Judge would be around. His remaining hair was now completely white and surrounded his bald head like a tonsure. He'd already been past retirement age back when Conn had left for his computer education at the University of Montevideo thirteen years ago.

Naturally there was an agenda and that meant reviewing the minutes of the last meeting. Once the formalities were out-of-the-way, they got down to business. Rodney Maxwell, as Company Treasurer, advised the M-12 Group on the latest month's operating results of the various companies in the holding company portfolio. Business was down again, but no surprise there. They'd sold off most of the desirable army surplus; interstellar freight hauling and trading were a slow-growing proposition for a new outfit. Planets had their own freighters or were used to dealing with bigger commercial outfits, like Odin Trailways.

When his father brought up the disappearance of the *Pathfinder* and mentioned that the *Trailblazer* was also now overdue, that got everyone's attention.

Chief Tom Brangwyn, head of company security, asked, "How certain are we that the *Pathfinder* was indeed the victim of pirates."

Rodney Maxwell looked grim as he answered, "A tramp freighter came in from Bifrost, where *Pathfinder* had picked up a cargo before returning here. The tramp brought an audio recording of the last transmission that Bifrost traffic control received from *Pathfinder*, which shows that our ship was intercepted by an unknown vessel that did not have an operating transponder. This unknown ship ordered the *Pathfinder* to cut their acceleration and prepare to be boarded. That sounds like piracy to me."

"Well, damn," Judge Ledue interjected. "This will make two ships now, the *Pathfinder* and now the *Trailblazer*, taken by pirates. Any more losses like that and we're out of the interstellar freight business."

Conn nodded. The Judge was just about right. They only had five remaining ships, the *Ouroboros II*, the *Genji*, the *Vanguard*, the *General Travis* and the *Wayfarer*. The new spaceliner, *The City of Litchfield*, was still under construction on Koshchei.

"What I don't get is: why haven't we heard from these pirates?" Lester Dawes asked.

"That's a damn good point!" Klem Zareff interjected. "Historically, pirates ransom prisoners. Or the ship's cargo. Did the insurance company ever hear from them?"

"Yes, I want to know what happened to my son," Raymond Fitch demanded angrily. His son, Jock, had been the astrogator aboard the *Pathfinder*—the first hijacked ship.

There was rumbling up and down the table. Almost everyone here had lost a relative, friend or neighbor to the pirates.

The Judge banged his gavel when Conn's father raised his hand. "Let the man speak. Yes, Rodney?"

"I haven't heard from Lloyd's of Melbourne since the last ship from Terra landed. We should be getting an update when the *City of Nefertiti* arrives any day now. According to Lloyd's, who paid off on the cargo for the *Pathfinder*, they haven't heard a word from the pirates—no ransom demands or cargo sales. Space piracy is as new to Lloyd's as it is to us. However, they did tell me that if another ship is overtaken, they will not issue any insurance to merchant ships from the Gartner Tri-System."

There was a chorus of boos along the table.

"You can't blame them," Judge Ledue said. "They're not in the business of insurance to give out money, but to take it in."

"What about the Federation Space Navy?" Tom Brangwyn asked.

The Judge shrugged. "Their official position is 'we'll look into it.' Which pretty much means—maybe and maybe not. Piracy is bad for interstellar trade, no one can argue that point. But, because it's all against just one system, nobody on Terra appears all that concerned."

"How do you know that, Judge?" Zareff asked.

"President Fawzi's had several talks with the Federation Minister-General. Sam Murchison doesn't seem to be that concerned. Remember we ruffled the feathers of a lot of Federation bigwigs with the Merlin fracas. They don't like upstart planets showing them up. Plus, there are commercial interests on Terra that aren't happy about our successes."

"So, we're on our own, Judge?" Conn asked.

"Yes. Lloyd's is about to drop us and no other interstellar insurance group will even talk with us."

"So then it's up to us to deal with this piracy," his father said. "Maybe we need to send out a few ships of our own."

Klem Zareff nodded, saying, "I agree. When the System States Alliance sent some commerce raiders into the Federation during the War, they were told to operate exactly like that."

"Like what?" Tom Begawan asked

"We'd send out warships disguised as freighters, board enemy ships—if possible. If we captured a ship, the first rule of order was to maroon the crews in lifeboats or on out-of-the-way planets or moons. The cargo we'd keep, of course. Of course, with scalawags like these pirates, they'd find it easier to space all the prisoners."

"Space?" Raymond Fitch asked. "What do you mean by that?"

"Just what it sounds like," Zareff snorted. "Push 'em out the air locks."

Fitch, a heavy-set man with a big gut, rose to his feet swaying.

Tom Begawan went over and helped him over to the restroom.

Everyone at the table appeared shaken.

Finally, Conn's brother-in-law Wade Lucas asked. "So how did the

Federation stop the commerce raiders?"

Klem Zareff replied. "They used warships disguised as freighters and when the raiders attacked them, they attacked back."

Lester Dawes said. "Well…we don't have any warships. Can we build some?"

"We could," Conn said, "there are lots of almost finished warships on Koshchei, but I'm not sure that's a good idea. The Federation has pretty strict rules about hyperspace-capable armed warships. Not prohibiting them before the War allowed the System States to cause serious mayhem to shipping during the System States War. According to Federation space law, ships can be armed if they're not hyperspace capable and they can be only hyperspace capable if they're not armed.

"Only the Federation Navy has ships that are both. But I believe there's a way around this problem. We have one of our freighters carry smaller armed but not hyperspace-capable vessels, like the gunboats that we found inside Force Command Duplicate—"

Old Klem Zareff tapped his silver cane-head on the table to get Conn's attention. As the only member of M-12 who had military experience, he didn't hesitate to interrupt. He had been born on Ashmodai, one of the System States planets, where he'd been a military commander during the war against the Federation. He still wore a little rosette of System States black and green on his coat. "Unfortunately, those gunboats were built for use on planets and weren't designed to operate in deep space."

"True," Conn said. "However, it shouldn't be too difficult to design and build a gunboat variant that can operate independently away from the motherships."

His father turned to Conn. "Can Merlin design something like that for us quickly?"

Conn nodded. "In a heartbeat."

"Good," his father replied. "Then I propose that Merlin do exactly that and we'll build some of these gunboats and deploy them on our trade ships."

Klem frowned. "But won't putting gunboats on our freighters displace a good deal of their cargo space?"

Conn shrugged, saying, "Sure, but we're not filling the cargo holds anyway. Trade is still building. If we don't have enough room in the holds, we can always lamprey them onto the hull. Besides, if we lose many more ships it won't matter; we'll be out of business."

"Okay," Klem said reluctantly, "but I still don't like it."

"None of us do, Klem," his father said. "Building these gunboats will take time, too. In the meantime, if anyone has any ideas that can be implemented sooner, let me know."

Everyone sitting around the boardroom table appeared stumped.

Rodney took notice, saying, "If no one has any ideas, then Conn is going to brief us on the subject we discussed at our last meeting."

Conn got up and gave the group the three possible ways to speed up recovery after the worst of the collapse predicted by Merlin. When he described the alternative of exploring for new habitable worlds outside the Federation, he noticed Klem Zareff sitting up straighter.

Judge Ledue appeared to notice it as well. When Conn finished talking, the Judge said, "Klem…is there something about this alternative that you want to comment on?"

Klem didn't answer right away, then shrugged and said, "Well…I don't suppose it will make any difference if I tell you all this now. I'm sure the Federation military already knows about it, anyway. Right after the War, there was a mass exodus from Abigor of around ten thousand people. They took what was left of the System States Alliance Navy and went off in search of a new world to colonize that was as far away from the Federation as they could travel without running out of fuel and foodstuffs."

Tom Brangwyn said, "Great Ghu! You mean that someday they might come back and try to rebuild the System States Alliance all over again?"

Klem shrugged and said, "Who knows? It could take centuries to build-up a planetary civilization to the point where they would have the means to return. I can't imagine their descendants having any loyalty to the System States at that point. Still, there's a chance they'll come back with a spacefaring technology base when the planets of the collapsed Federation will need someone to show them how to rebuild civilization.

"As for the other two options, considering Merlin's cost estimates, I don't see how we could seriously consider starting anything like that now."

Rodney nodded. "Does anyone disagree?" No one did. After discussing some routine business issues, the meeting ended.

I

Morgan Gatworth sat slumped in his chair, inside his beautifully appointed law office, with his head cradled in his hands. He took the pistol out of the lower side drawer, checked to see the clip was full, then pointed it at his temple. *I can't go on betraying my friends like this…*

His right hand was shaking so bad he had to brace it with his left. He started to pull the trigger, then his finger froze—*I can't do this.*

I've got to find a way out. Maybe Judge Ledue can help. He's my mentor and old friend….

He buzzed his receptionist. "Marci, please get the Judge on the line."

"Yes, Mr. Gatworth," she replied.

Am I nuts? I can't explain this to the Judge. I know that look he has for those who've gone beyond the pale. "Wait a minute, Marci," he interjected. "I've changed my mind. Why don't you leave early; I'm going to be going over some old files."

"Yes, Mr. Gatworth."

There was no way he could avoid disgrace, no story he could spin that would save his friendships, his name, his wife's trust.... No, he'd given all that up at the gaming table last night—and the scores of nights before. Instead of going home after the M-12 meeting, he'd gone back to the casino and lost everything, the fifty thousand sol advance, markers for another thirty thousand and most importantly—the last of his self-respect. His life insurance was about all he had left; it was a big policy. *She'll be okay, better than living in disgrace—an object of pity. This way they'll only feel sorry for her.*

He knew that Shawley was expecting him this evening for his M-12 report, all saved—every word—on his micro-recorder. He took the micro-recorder out of his jacket pocket. *This little item is more dangerous than an A-bomb.* He took the memory stick out of the recorder, put it on the ground and stomped until it was crushed and fragmented. Then he bent down and used a paper and the edge of his hand to gather the fragments and put them into the trash. If Shawley got hold of this information, M-12 and his friends, they were all through—finished.

Morgan was sick to death of his weakness, his compulsion. *I even make myself ill...*

He put the gun back into his hand. This time it didn't shake—

Marci Velasquez heard a sharp crack coming from her boss's office. Through the thick walls it sounded like a heavy book hitting the parquet floor. *He must really be busy today,* she thought. *Maybe I should check on him and see if everything is all right.*

Then she reconsidered. *No, he's been in a bad mood the last couple of weeks. I should be leaving. That's what Mr. Gatworth told me to do. Maybe I can get home in time to watch the* New Marrieds *on Tri-D.*

II

Conn was just returning to his office after lunch in the Force Command cafeteria when he heard his phone chirping. He was startled when his father's face appeared in the viewscreen; his hair was mussed and his face drawn.

"What is it, Dad? Is Mom okay?"

"It's Morgan. He shot himself last night. According to his receptionist, it was an hour after the M-12 meeting. She heard a sharp crack, but thought it was a falling book or knickknack. Not that finding him then would have done him any good—his brains were splattered all over the wall."

"That poor bastard. But why, Dad?"

"I've had J. Fitzwilliam Sterber and his firm going over the books all morning doing a quick forensic autopsy. Sterber just got off the line. It looks bad. Morgan is as good as broke. Thank Ghu, he kept up his insurance payments to Storisende Mutual; otherwise Valerie would be out on the street."

"Has anyone notified his son?"

His father shook his head. "Remember, he took the berth as First Mate on the *Trailblazer*. With his son unaccounted for, Gatworth sure picked a bad time to check out."

"Poor Charley."

"Poor Valerie; if the *Trailblazer* was taken by pirates, she'll have lost her entire family."

He nodded. "Was there anything suspicious about his death?"

"No. As I mentioned, Marci was in the office when it happened. Morgan was supposed to be going over accounts, or at least that's what he told her. She's always been half in love with him, probably why she never married. Now, she's blaming herself." His father shook his head in wonderment, as if at the foibles of the human mind. "She did say he's had a few strange characters visit his office recently, probably strange to Marci because most of his clients are long-time residents. But we're going to check it out. I've got the Chief on it now, and Barton-Massarra Investigations, too."

"That's smart. From the outside, Morgan had everything to live for. A thriving practice, good investments, a loving family—it just doesn't make sense. I would have never thought he'd take the suicide way out. Maybe somebody had something on him."

"My thoughts exactly, son. We should know by morning. Maybe you should take the day off tomorrow and meet me in my office. Say 1400 hours."

"Sure, Dad. It'll give me some time with Foxx and Sylvie. I've been spending way too much time out here at Force Command. I believe Merlin can survive a day or two without my ministrations."

"I should hope so."

III

The next afternoon Conn Maxwell stopped by his father's office. His father looked more put together than he had yesterday, but there were new furrows in his forehead. Or maybe he was just paying more attention. People get older and mostly you never notice it until one day you look up and it hits you in the face. Suddenly it seemed as though his father's brown hair had turned mostly gray, and there were more lines and furrows on his face.

"Have a seat," his father told him. "We've got a number of things to go over."

"That bad?"

"How about a drink first." His father took a bottle of Baldur rum from his office bar and poured four fingers worth in both glasses. After a deep drink, he said, "Yup. I've known Morgan Gatworth for over forty years—we went to first school together. But it looks like I hardly knew him at all."

Conn said, "You can say that about most people. We all have our 'secret lives' or hidden selves."

"Well, Morgan had a good one! Did you know he was an inveterate gambler?"

"No, but then I wasn't part of his crowd. Still I wouldn't have guessed it. If anything, I thought he was a skirt chaser. He was always a little too well-dressed and groomed, and that cologne—phew."

"Well, he was a bit of that, too. But he was smart enough to keep it away from his office—although poor Marci might disagree. Early this morning, the syndicate that owns Risky Business casino and nightclub put in a claim for three hundred thousand sols against the estate."

"Already! They've got their nerve. Can't you do anything about it?"

His father grinned. "Already have. I sent Sherm Worley from City Services over to do a quick inspection. He found a hundred thousand sols worth of necessary improvements in just one visit, and promised them more if he had to come back. I think we've heard the last of them."

"Good. Any other hidden problems?"

His father's face turned serious. "Joe Massarra went over the office with a fine tooth comb. He found an empty micro-recorder in the office desk and the fragments of a crushed memory stick in the trash can."

"Damn! You're thinking he recorded the last M-12 Group meeting?"

"Yup, I do, son."

"Did he have time to send it out?"

"Sure, but we don't think he did; otherwise, he'd still be alive. And why else would he have ground that memory stick into the floor? I think his conscience finally got to him. About time."

"I hope so, if any of what we discussed ever got out...."

"Yeah, it'd be the end of M-12," his father finished. "Unfortunately, it probably wasn't his first recording, which means the enemy—whom we don't know—knows a lot about us. We knew there was a leak, but I thought it was out of one of the Interstellar offices."

"Still may be," Conn added. "I think we need to veridicate everyone in Tri-Interstellar, Ltd. and the rest of our companies from the office boys to the president."

"I'm with you, son. I've already talked it over with Joe Massarra and Rolf Barton. They're going to have Barton-Massarra veridicate all of the Merlin-12 Group, including ourselves."

"An even better idea. Klem Zareff will blow a fuse, but it needs to be done."

His father grinned. "Old Klem may surprise you. He's ex-military and knows more about security than you and I ever will."

Conn sighed. "Then we'll just have to assume that our unknown opponent knows about all our plans and inner workings up until last night."

"Agreed. But from now on they're going to have to work in the dark—like we are. Now, back to business: Have you made any progress determining whether or not the Maxwell Plan is the cause of the coming decline?"

Conn nodded his head. "According to Merlin, it's the piracy that's the trigger. Due to interstellar distances and long travel times, piracy is like a disease. If it's successful anywhere in the Federation, and the Space Navy doesn't stamp it out, it will spread like wildfire as planets and shipping companies see it as a way to prevent economic ruin.

"Merlin was way off on its original calculations regarding how quickly piracy would rear its ugly head, just like it was also wrong about where it would show up first. The original prediction was that the outer planets would suffer piracy first, because that's where there would be minimal Federation Naval protection due to budget cutbacks."

Conn paused, then added, "I'm beginning to wonder if we should be rethinking our whole strategy. I'm beginning not to trust Merlin's predictions..."

His father shook his head. "If you can pin down the actual trigger that points to something we've done, then I'll agree that our strategy will have to change." He stopped for a couple of seconds and then said, "Speaking of rethinking strategy, you know our plans to build missile gunboats that our medium-sized freighters could carry for defensive purposes?"

"Yes."

"Well...the bean counters at the Company Head Office have been doing the number crunching and they tell me that unless we're going to build hundreds of those gunboats, the cost to set up the tooling for a limited production run of a couple of dozen would be prohibitive. It looks like we're going to have to figure out something else for a long-term anti-pirate solution."

Conn sighed and said, "It's too bad we can't make use of those hundreds of interplanetary ships that were abandoned on Koshchei. I'll bet we could modify some of them pretty quickly with ship-to-ship weapons, but they're too big for our local freighters to carry."

"True. A half dozen of our biggest hyperships could carry some of the smaller interplanetary crafts, the two-hundred to three-hundred foot diameter ones, but that wouldn't leave much room for cargo space. The ships we're using for local hub and spoke shipping weren't built to carry anything larger than a hundred feet high."

Conn's eyes widened and he snapped his fingers. "That's it, Dad! Our thinking is too conventional. Our freighters don't have to carry their defense with them all the time. The window of attack is limited to when they're leaving the star system to return here or go to another system. That's the only time they're vulnerable because of the no-jump hyperspace zone. The pirates won't be able to intercept them when they arrive because they won't know in advance when they're arriving and what part of the system they're jumping into. So they have to wait until our ships leave the visiting planet and then catch them on their way out, right?"

His father nodded, as he pulled out one of his cigars.

"Okay. So…if we had armed interplanetary craft of our own, stationed at each of the planets we trade with, they could escort our ships to beyond the no-jump zone and then our ships would be safe from interception."

His father looked puzzled. "But we don't have any armed interplanetary craft of our own and it's too expensive to build any from scratch."

"Ah, but we can get some," Conn said, "Remember those old ammunition resupply ships that Third Fleet-Army Force abandoned here after the war? We used one of them to help us pacify the area around Merlin's Force Command Duplicate. There're still more than a dozen of those ships sitting on Mothball Row at Storisende, and they still have their weapons and armament. We can claim them and upgrade them with more missile launchers and missile storage. Then we can use our soon-to-be-idle hyperships to carry a couple of these upgraded ammunition ships to each of the planets we do a lot of trading with. We drop them off and they remain there in orbit until our freighters show up, then they escort our ships planetside and back—which will keep the pirates at bay."

Rodney Maxwell paused to think that over carefully. "Well, that does follow the letter of Federation law. I suppose it's no different in principle than paying crews to man gunboats that would have to be transported back and forth all the time. But do you think our trading partners will be happy about us stationing a couple of heavily armed ships in their systems?"

"Why not? If left unchecked, piracy will damage their economies, too. Any system that refuses; well, we stop trading with them. We could even make a profit by offering our escort service to other outgoing ships when they're not busy escorting our ships."

"Great Ghu, son! I think you've come up with another great idea. We'll have to charter a new company for that of course. What do you think of the name Tri-System Interstellar Security?"

Conn chuckled as his father talked excitedly about creating *another* company. He was happiest when he was wheeling and dealing.

IV

The next day, Rodney Maxwell canvassed the rest of the M-12 Group, which endorsed the idea wholeheartedly and began the process of creating a new company.

Interstellar Security was granted a charter and immediately applied to the Planetary Government for all of the still unclaimed Army combat freighters under the Commercial Enterprise Encouragement Act of 858 A.E. With the Planetary President sending the word down that this request was to be expedited forthwith, it was approved in record time. Interstellar Security began hiring staff and crew to move the ammunition resupply ships one at a time over to the Barathrum Spaceport, inside the extinct volcano, where they could be refurbished and their weapons upgraded out of sight of any gossips, spies or pirate agents.

Meanwhile, Barton-Massarra started the first shifts to veridicate everyone in the Aircraft Building. They would start there first, then work out to the smaller satellite offices here in Litchfield, and later in Storisende City. Already three employees had gone AWOL and Security Chief Tom Brangwyn had men out searching for them. Now, bank accounts were being accessed.

"They won't get too far," Brangwyn told Rodney Maxwell in his office.

"Good. We need to put them under the veridicator."

Brangwyn nodded. "Rod, it's a big planet, but there really aren't that many places to hide. None of them are going to survive out in the Badlands, or even here in farmlands in the Gordon Valley. Plus, I have people posted at the spaceport here and in Storisende. No one leaves the planet without a visual and proof of identification. We'll get them, dead or alive."

"Why do you say that?" Rodney asked.

The Security Chief's gray eyes narrowed. "I suspect we're not the only ones looking for them. If they're lucky, we'll find them first."

I

As soon as he heard the news of Gatworth's death, Wade Shawley was tempted to pack up his things and move out of Litchfield lock, stock and duffle bag. He knew that the Maxwell's private and company dicks would be all over the dead man's office building. And, first thing, they'd be checking all the building recordings to see who had come and gone from Gatworth's office. And, front and center, would be his mug. It would be even worse if Gatworth had left behind a suicide note or recording....

Next, they'd have men stationed at all the spaceports, airports and the rail and bus depots. Probably with his picture in hand. For just this kind of contingency, he kept a beautician robot in his back office. He'd have it cut off all his hair, fabricate a false mustache, darken his skin and give him blue-colored contacts. By the time it was finished, even his own mother wouldn't recognize him.

Fortunately, he hadn't used his real name on the office lease and had been living in various low-rent hotels and boarding houses, paying cash. Still, it would behoove him to find new digs, and soon. Now that he'd lost his only contact within the Merlin-12 Group he was going to have to find a new way to provide the information his principal demanded.

In fact, he'd better update him right away. Shawley took a chance using his office phone, without the viewscreen, but he doubted the public ones would be any safer—and a lot harder to blank. If they were already on to him, they might be able to break his scrambler code. On the other hand, if they'd identified him, he'd already be in jail or on his way to an interrogation cell.

He used the mission-in-jeopardy prompt, and his call was answered by the third ring.

"What's up?" asked the distorted voice.

"Prime Number One was found dead this morning from a self-inflicted gunshot."

"Hot damn! But why?"

"Beats me? He lost again at the wheel last night; maybe that's why. Or maybe his conscience got the better of him—I don't know."

"Is he replaceable?"

"Not now. Maybe never—the others don't have any verifiable vices I could learn. I did get him to sign over his shares in the holding company, but I doubt they'll be worth anything now."

"Yeah, a straight line to us. Burn them all."

Ouch! That's about a hundred million sols worth of paper. Screw the boss, I'll keep them—maybe they'll come in useful.

"Sure, boss. I might have to go on the run for a while—"

"Why?"

"They've got my picture. I had to visit his office more than once."

"Stupid."

"The man had a bad case of nerves. I had to babysit him a few times, and give him some inducements. He had a conscience, you know."

"Got it. The mission hasn't changed. Find a way to break into the Group, destroy the machine if you get a chance."

"Yes, sir."

"Where are you going to hide?"

"Around."

"Keep us posted."

"Will do," he ended, hanging up the phone. He was already wiping off his fingerprints. Not that it would make any difference. In a case with this heat, they'd probably bring in chromosomal sniffers. *I'm going to have to burn the place down before I leave. The last thing I need is a sniffer on my trail....*

II

Conn was coding the latest manufacturing statistics from Marduk when there was a ringing from the off-world comm-line, direct from Koshchei. It was coded red and he excused himself and went into his private office. *What fresh hell is this?* he asked himself. *Did one of the air domes implode, or was there another robot insurrection?*

One thing he knew for sure, that code was rarely used—never for chit-chat; and when it was used—it was usually trouble.

Conn activated the viewscreen and Yves Jacquemont's lean face appeared. His father-in-law's face was flushed and he appeared agitated. "Conn, are you alone?"

"Yes, sir," he replied, knowing full well that it would take six minutes for his voice to make journey from Poictesme to Koshchei. He ran a mental list of all the possible problems he could come up with and before he was done his father-in-law's voice returned.

"I can see the worry written on your face. This is not trouble, for a change. No, I've got some very good news. News that could change everything, for us, for Poictesme—for the Federation."

"We can use some good news down here. Morgan Gatworth committed suicide and it looks as though pirates have seized another ship. M-12's in a tizzy."

Before his father-in-law spoke again, his face dropped. "I'm sorry to hear that. I counted Morgan among my few close friends. Was his death related to work?"

"Yes," Conn replied. "It looks like he sold us out." He gave Jacquemont all the details of Gatworth's death and the mess he'd left behind.

"I'm sorry to hear that. I would never have pegged him as a gambler, or a sell-out."

"Only his wife knew about his gambling, and she was so ashamed that she never told anybody."

"Well, then the group does need some good news," his father-in-law said. "Let me tell you about our latest success."

"*Success.*" Conn liked the sound of that.

"Now that most of the industrial and plant work here is automated and working fine, I put my engineering team to work on some ideas I developed during my career as a hyperdrive engineer. It had always seemed to me that there was no real limit to a craft's velocity in hyperspace, other than those limits imposed by the Dillingham drives themselves. Over the years, I came up with a few interesting hypotheses on how to rectify that, but never had a lab at my disposal to check them out."

Uh-oh! he thought. He didn't know much about hyperspace drive engines other than the fact the Dillingham Hyperdrive was developed in 183 A.E. and had been in continuous use since the Third Century. Currently commercial ships traveled at roughly one light year in roughly 4.4 hours, with military vehicles approaching a light-year every 4 hours.

"We haven't come up with anything new, in case you're wondering. Just an improvement of the current hyperspace drive." His father-in-law smiled like the cat that'd just eaten the canary. "Hell's bells, son, let me just cut to the chase. The team has used my ideas to cut hyperdrive travel time in half!"

Conn had six minutes to mull over that bombshell. At first, he was excited; Poictesme freighters and passenger ships would be able to put every spaceline in the Federation out of business within a year! It would revolutionize space travel. On second consideration, that would cause no end of economic disruptions, bankruptcies, consolidations—maybe even war. He couldn't see Odin Trailways stepping back passively and letting Tri-System Interstellar steal all of its business. Terra-Baldur-Marduk Spacelines and Pan-Federation Spacelines would be in an uproar—and they were based on Terra with their lips pressed against the ears at the top levels of government. He could easily see the Federation President confiscating their discovery, using the Federation Navy to carry it out, then parceling their discovery out to selected interest groups.

Not if I have anything to say about it, he decided. *We have to move slowly on this. I need to discuss this with my father.*

Before the time his father-in-law's face started to speak again, he'd already made up his mind. He said, "We need to put a lid on this—Top Secret. I don't mean stop work, but just keep it secret. There are a lot of ramifications to your discovery, some of which could have a negative effect upon both Poictesme and the Federation in general. Also, I need to run this by M-12 and see what they have to say. Can you do that for me?"

When his father-in-law began to speak again, he could read the disappointment on his face. "I don't get what you mean. Why this discovery will give us an unparalleled opportunity to… Oh, I get it! I hadn't thought it through."

Conn hated the six-minute delay; he was antsy. When his father-in-law stopped speaking, he said, "If we're not careful, we're going to have another invasion by Federation forces, only this one will be aimed at us."

He needed to discuss this in detail with his father, but not over a commline, no matter how supposedly secure. Not until they had a better handle on the *enemy*. He saw them as such after Morgan's death. They weren't above using any means to get what they wanted, industrial espionage, sabotage, misdirection—even murder.

III

Later that evening, over dinner at Senta's, Conn told Sylvie about her father's bombshell. His wife not only had a good head on her shoulders, but she wasn't emotionally invested in Merlin like almost everyone else in Litchfield City. Senta had put them in a secluded corner of the restaurant for her own romantic reasons, but it suited Conn's purpose. In addition, he'd activated a white-noise field with his pocket projector in case they were being monitored.

"So what did your Dad have to say?" Sylvie asked.

Conn refilled both glasses with melon-brandy. "He wants me to run it past Merlin, but we're not done with the Year-End Projections and this could really throw things off. Once the data is entered, it's not like the computer will disregard it when it's making other predictions."

"I see your problem, Conn. Too many of your cronies take Merlin's projections over their own common sense."

Conn had to grin at that. "Isn't that the truth. Still, your father's bombshell could cause no end of mischief. With all the ship-building facilities we have on Koshchei, we can build our own interstellar craft for half the price that Pan-Federation or Terra-Baldur-Marduk Spacelines can on Luna. Not that anyone's building new ships these days, due to the economic downturn. It does mean that when the economy turns, we'll be in a great place to take advantage of any Federation-wide trade increase."

"I agree. However, once word gets out that my father's improvements have cut hyperspace travel times in half, the other interstellar firms will have to take action—no matter what our stated aims appear to be. The economic advantage that will give Poictesme would be impossible for them to surmount. Is that not correct?"

Conn nodded, then took another drink. He was a lucky man; his wife was not only beautiful, but smart. "Yes, which means either a covert war or they'll use their political muscle to get the Federation involved. And, if that happens, we know who the loser will be."

"Yes, it'll be Poictesme. Here's what I think you should do," Sylvie said. "Take Dad's findings and give them to the Federation Space Navy, maybe in exchange for contracts to build new vessels. Let them deal with this bombshell. They can parcel it out as they please, which they'll do anyway. Once our ships' drives are retrofitted and word about the speed increase gets out, the Space Navy will grab the first one they run across and declare eminent domain, then let their own engineering staff reverse engineer the Dillinghams. And there won't be a damn thing we can do about it. It's not like we can declare war against the Terran Federation."

He had to laugh at that. "No, no. Not in a million years. In fact, that's the last thing we want to see happen. However, I can't see telling the Old Fawzi Gang that we're going to hand this over to the Federation. Klem will burst a gasket and Fawzi will foam at the mouth. These guys are still bitter as Niflheim that the Federation pulled out almost fifty years ago and left this planet in the lurch."

Sylvie shook her head. "It's time they grew up, Conn. The Federation's not their mommy, and it was never responsible for Poictesme's economic health. The Federation used the Gartner Tri-System as a military base, not for our own good, but because we were the best forward system in their grand plan to end the System States War. We were fortunate that they did so because it gave us two decades of unparalleled prosperity. Sadly it had to end, but nobody promised us that it was going to last forever. We've been living off the table scraps ever since. With the Maxwell plan, we've finally taken the first steps toward real independence."

"You're right, but can you imagine me trying to sell that to Zareff, Fawzi and Judge Ledue? I can't."

"But you're going to have to, darling. There's no one else for the job. You're their protégé. Plus, you still wear the mantle of the Man Who Saved Poictesme and Found Merlin. They'll begrudgingly listen to you, and will even do as you demand if you yell loud enough and stomp your feet. They look up to you, Conn. After all, you're Merlin's acolyte. I know it's hard for you, but you need to use everything in your arsenal to bend them to your will or this all will end badly."

"You're right. I know, I know."

"I'm still having difficulty accepting the idea that Mr. Gatworth was spying on M-12," Sylvie said.

"Me, too. But we've got all the evidence we need to convict him, if he were still alive. His wife's devastated."

"Of course. That poor woman.... Now, that we know for sure the *Trailblazer* has been taken, why she's lost her entire family."

"We don't know that for sure, Sylvie. It's possible the pirates might ransom the crews at some point."

"That's not what you told your Dad."

"No, I was sugar-coating my worst fears. A lot of those crewmen were friends; I've known Charley since we played ball together. I think Old Klem was right when he said the pirates probably spaced them all. For most of them, their families couldn't raise enough sols to pay for their transport back to Poictesme, much less a ransom."

"But wouldn't Tri-System Interstellar pay the ransom?"

"Probably, but how would the pirates know that? All they know is that what they have are common spacemen. It's not like they captured a big spaceliner with lots of wealthy first class passengers."

Sylvie nodded in agreement. "We can only hope for the best."

SEVEN

I

A word placed in the right ear had drawn in Dmitri Costanzia like a moth to a bright light. Shawley was seated in a half-derelict hotel room in Tramptown that rented by the hour—no questions asked. Even so he was taking a big risk. As he'd expected, all the depots leading out of Litchfield were armed and guarded. Low resolution pictures of his face had been posted on the news services, but they no longer resembled his new disguise.

He watched as the fat man moved sideways through the door.

Costanzia was an overweight man with a stomach that overflowed his belt like a sagging beach ball.

"Have a seat, Dmitri," Ward Shawley said. His plan was to start out soft, then work his way to tempered-steel hard.

The fat man didn't just sit down, he enveloped his chair. "Phew, I'm kinda excited to hear what you've found out about Merlin."

It was hot in the room since it had no temperature control, but not as hot as the sweat pouring off Costanzia's mop of curly hair would indicate. Dmitri Costanzia was the Patriarch of the First Church of Merlin and, according to his sources, the biggest Merlinolator on the planet.

"I think you got your information backwards," Shawley said, his voice hard. "I came to you for information."

Costanzia flinched. "What do you want to know? I can tell you the entire history of Merlin's development and how He ended the War."

The man's nuts, Shawley realized. He would have to play him carefully, act as if he too were a true believer. "Oh, yes. Without Merlin the Federation may well have lost the Big War. We all owe Him a great debt."

Costanzia gave him a patronizing smile. "Yes, but He is more than a machine. Merlin has been given a divine gift, one that needs to be shared with the universe. Merlin is the only One who can create order out of the chaos we humans have created in our wake."

The way the fat man's eyes glazed over every time he mentioned the computer convinced Shawley that he was a complete nut case. "Yes, but as I understand it, the Merlin-12 Group have imprisoned Merlin and refuse to allow his worshippers access to Him."

Costanzia's eyes almost bulged out of his skull. "You do understand. We must free Merlin from these unworthy infidels. Twice I have led bands of true believers into the Badlands to visit Merlin. Both times we were repulsed by the Maxwells and their armed minions. How dare they keep us from our God!"

Shawley needed to shush the fat man up. He was drawing attention to the two of them in a bar where any normal skullduggery would go unnoticed. "Let's go to my room since you have so much to teach me."

No true believer could resist such an invitation. Shawley led him back to the small room, off the stockroom, where he had a simple cot and chair, which the fat Merlinator's fleshy thighs completely encased as he sat down.

"Tell me about the Merlin-12 and maybe that will give us an idea of how to save Merlin from their clutches."

Costanzia nodded eagerly. "Yes, yes. The Maxwells are very well protected. Rodney Maxwell lives in a penthouse atop the Airlines Building, which is protected both by the company police and the Barton-Massarra Agency. So are Judge Ledue and Chief Tom Brangwyn, who's the head of security for M-12. Then there's the Planetary President, Kurt Fawzi. Morgan Gatworth, the lawyer, is dead. The doctor, Wade Lucas, may or may not be part of their cabal, but I do know that Klem Zareff is one of the founding members. He's so smug about it!"

"Who is this Zareff? I've never heard of him."

"He's an old man, has his own melon plantation—a big farm outside city limits."

Now, this sounds like easy pickings, Shawley thought. "Does the old man have any guards?"

"Humph, not that old man. He's too ornery. Klem does have an old mastiff; almost got as many years on its hide as the old man."

It wouldn't be hard getting directions to the old man's farm; now, it was time to silence this ball of blubber for good—who knew what he might reveal under a veridicator—and find a new place to hunker down.

"Come here, I want to give you a donation for your Shrine."

Costanzia's eyes lit up with greed.

Shawley pulled a roll of sols out of his pocket with his left hand. When Costanzia leaned forward to grab it, he slashed his throat with a knife. He choked, then a ribbon of red blood spewed out of his mouth. Shawley caught the fat man before he hit the floor, and eased him down. He didn't need any accidental witnesses.

II

Conn joined his father in his office for a drink before dinner; at least, that was his excuse for getting him alone. After cigars were lit, he said, "Dad, I had a good talk with Sylvie the other night about this hyperspace development. She thinks we should keep it to ourselves for now."

"Smart woman, you married. I'll go along with that. The boys are upset enough about this piracy issue and Morgan's suicide. This would just compound their confusion."

"Right. And the first thing they'll want me to do is run it past Merlin. Great Ghu, that machine's busy enough with the Year End Projections. Add this development, and it's likely to blow a circuit."

"I'm beginning to develop a case of Merlin fatigue, son."

Conn smiled. "Yeah, me too. I'm beginning to suspect the super-computer isn't all-knowing like the rest of M-12—or should we start calling it M-11—believe."

"Hell, we always knew it was just a machine, not the godhead of wisdom. I'm surprised it hasn't crapped out before now."

"True. But we now know for sure that there's another group, or groups, out there who are determined to take control of Tri-System Investments and were using Morgan as a crowbar to break in. I wish I knew how far he'd sold us down the river?"

Rodney Maxwell shook his head. "Do you think they might be connected to the ship hijackings?"

"I do," Conn replied. "I wish Morgan hadn't taken the easy way out; he could have answered a lot of these questions. His wife is sure in a tizzy."

"I'm not surprised. She's one of the nervous ones, like your mother. She's lost a husband and her son is in the hands of pirates. Fortunately, Morgan didn't have whole life insurance or she'd be facing destitution."

Conn snorted. "Yeah, the tightwad would have cashed it in and blown it at the tables a long time ago. His gambling problem sure explains a lot of questions I always had about Old Man Gatworth. Charley was the best baseball player this planet has ever seen; he could hit, he could field—even pitch. He almost single-handedly took the Litchfield Dodgers to the Planetary Championship game—"

"Come on now, Conn. You were a damn good first baseman. And how about Anse Dawes; he could hit the stitches off a ball. You kids were lucky to have that."

"What do you mean, Dad?"

"There were no baseball teams on Poictesme before the Big War. It was all those soldiers from Terra, Isis, Baldur, Odin, Ishtar and Aton who brought it with them. They fielded the first teams and got a lot of us locals involved. For a while, it was baseball mania. Even after the War, when all the soldiers left." There was a note of wistfulness in his voice.

"Well, Charley could, not should, have been a ballplayer. He was even scouted by the Baldur Boulders. But Morgan wouldn't give him the price of a ticket to Baldur. We always thought it was because he was just cheap, although he never spared a sol on his suits or that mansion they lived in."

"I always wondered where all his money went," his father replied. "Although that wife of his could spend sols faster than a robo-mason can lay bricks."

"Charley, if he's still alive, is going to be devastated. He always believed his father wouldn't let him go off-world because he wanted him to follow in his footsteps, be another lawyer. Although that might be partially true, since Morgan was shooting smoke out of his ears when Charley signed up as a spacehand."

"I remember that day!" Conn's father hooted. "Phew. I'm glad we don't have those problems."

Conn felt good about that. Very few of his friends had the close bond that he shared with his father. "But, getting back to this hyperspace development, why don't we table it until we can run it by Merlin after the end of the year? If we don't like what it has to say, we'll follow Sylvie's idea and make it the Federation Space Navy's problem."

"Good idea, son. I'm glad you're spending a few days at home with Sylvie and my favorite grandson."

"You mean your only grandson," Conn replied, laughing.

I

Ward Shawley could hear the boards creak as someone snuck past his door on the way to the boarding house phone. He'd been stuck in this crummy joint for a couple of standard weeks and his nerves were fraying. Ever since Costanzia's death, when one of the bar's cameras had picked up a fuzzy image of him leaving by the back door, carrying the fat preacher over his shoulder, he'd been constantly on the watch. Fortunately, the picture had been out of focus—it was a dive after all—and even the police reconstructions were vague. Still, he didn't like the idea that every nosy parker in Litchfield was on the lookout for yours truly. So he'd removed his mustache and was wearing a blond wig.

He had contacted his principal in an effort to get help, but the line was dead—disconnected. He was on his own.

Shawley had been fortunate to find this boarding house on the fringes of

Tramptown; the landlady was deaf and half-blind so he hadn't had to worry about being identified. He made a point of leaving late at night on his foraging trips for food and information, but occasionally he ran into one of the other boarders. One of them, a derelict with rusty red hair and a broken nose had given him the once-over when he'd gone to the john about an hour before. He'd briefly considered taking him out right then, but so far the rough stuff hadn't been paying off.

He had a telltale on the phone so he could listen in. It was an old unit with a blackened screen. He heard the sound of numbers being punched in, then a voice said, "Litchfield hot line."

"I think I know—"

Shawley was out the door, knife already in his hand, before broken nose could even turn around. He went in low, going for the kidney. The redhead made a half-hearted moan, then collapsed into his arms like a folding chair. After dragging the body back into his small room, he returned to quickly wipe up the blood and pull the phone off the wall.

Too late for that now. This whole operation is dead.

He knew they could trace the call and Litchfield's finest would be at the boarding house in just a few minutes. It was 0200 hours and impossible to find a place to stay inside. He'd have to find a back alley or abandoned building to hide in.

Maybe tomorrow night he would pay Mr. Zareff a visit. Yeah, a vacation out in the beautiful Gordon Valley away from all his problems. *That's just what I need.*

II

Tor Handler had been planetbound for the past two months, ever since the shutdown of the interstellar transport business due to pirate activity. As ship captain, he'd been one of the first to be laid off when the *General Travis* was put in drydock. Tri-System & Interstellar Spacelines said it was temporary, but that didn't pay the bills or cure a bad case of cabin fever. He loved

Melissa and the children, but he found their small house in Litchfield even more confining than a cabin in one of the Company's freighters. So when he'd read the ads in the *Litchfield Record* about a job for trained skippers, he'd jumped at the opportunity.

The new company, Interstellar Security, had been very secretive about what his new job would entail. Only that he'd be spacebound before the end of the month. That was good enough for him. Now he was aboard a company shuttle headed for their secret hideaway.

When he stepped off the company shuttle, Tor got his first look at the inside of the Barathrum Spaceport, which was located on the floor of an extinct volcano. He'd read about the old abandoned spaceport, but this was his first visit. It certainly didn't look abandoned any longer.

Unlike spaceports out in the open, buildings and ships were much closer together; yet it still managed to look huge when compared to the dozens of people who were moving around them. He heard someone shout his name and looked around. It was Chief Tom Brangwyn waving him over. They were old friends and had taken classes together at the University of Storisende.

Tom shook his hand, saying. "Glad you were able to get here so quickly."

"I thought this outfit might have something to do with Tri-System Investments."

"Right on the money," Tom said.

"Good to see you, Tom," Tor said. "What's this all about? And why all the hush-hush?"

"Come with me and I'll show you what you left your nice, cushy, boring job as interplanetary freighter skipper for. Don't worry about your gear, it's being looked after."

The two of them walked over to a mid-sized globular craft that was split open. He could see that workers were welding something in its cargo hold. "Well…there she is. One of Third Army's old combat ammunition supply freighters. She's in pretty good shape considering that she's been sitting at the Storisende spaceport for half a century."

"She's so small compared to the *General Travis*."

"I know. Your freighter measures a thousand feet in diameter. This one's about a third of that, but unlike the *General Travis* this ship was built for combat. Higher acceleration even with the collapsium armor, short-range cannon, two long range missile launchers with lots of room for troops and ammunition. She's a powerful little fighting craft, meant to supply ships under battle conditions, but we're going to make some improvements. Look over there."

His eyes followed where Tom was pointing, at a large piece of equipment being moved by crane. "That's a ground-based, anti-ship missile launcher designed to defend important ground facilities like this spaceport and Command Force Duplicate from space attack. We've removed it from the contragravity vehicle that carried it and we're installing it in the cargo hold of that ammo freighter along with three more just like it.

"Each missile launcher will have two different missile pods. One pod contains nine anti-ship missiles and the other sixteen anti-missile missiles for a total of thirty-six offensive and sixty-four defensive missiles. When you add in the twenty-four internal anti-ship missiles that feed the two built-in missile launchers, I pity the pirate ship that tries to take on two of these ships at one time."

"Two ships?" Handler asked.

Tom looked surprised at Handler's question. "Sure. I guess no one's told you yet. We're currently trading with eighteen inhabited planets all within a fifty light-year radius. We've taken possession of a total of twenty combat freighters like this one. The plan is to keep four here on Poictesme, for our own security, and assign two each to eight of our major trading planets, disregarding Terra, Baldur and Odin for the time being, as well as some of the poorer worlds. You'll be happy to know that Interstellar Security, the new company that's been set up for this operation, has created a rank structure such that each one of these ships will be skippered by a commander. Both in-system ships will be under the authority of a senior officer. You will be in charge of the first two corvettes—that's what we're calling these ships—that we deploy near Asgard when *Ouroboros II* makes her next trip there.

"So congratulations, Senior Commander!" Tom offered his hand.

They shook on it.

"Thank you, Chief. I'll do my best to justify your confidence in me. When will my two corvettes be ready and what kinds of crews will you let me have?"

Tom laughed. "You don't waste time, Tor. I like that. This one here is the *Lester Dawes*. She's the craft we picked up years ago when everyone was still looking for Merlin. Klem Zareff convinced the powers that be that this corvette should be kept for local anti-pirate defense for sentimental reasons. But that's not a bad thing. She'll be the prototype for all the rest; there are bound to be bugs that have to be worked out with all the modification that we're doing to these ships.

"So by the time the next two are ready, which we estimate will be in two weeks, we should have all the kinks figured out. As for your crews, well, you're going to be lucky there, too. Our recruiting call, which you answered, has gotten a lot of responses and you get first pick of the applicants. The Tri-System Security boys will be running all the applicants through a veridicator—you too, my boy. Even the M-12 Group members, after Gatworth's suicide, are going through it. The last thing we need is to have one of the pirates' agents infiltrate Interstellar Security."

"What makes you think they have any agents on Poictesme?" Handler asked.

"Because, as Conn Maxwell's pointed out, the only ships they're hijacking belong to Tri-System & Interstellar Spacelines. As far as we've been able to determine, no other spaceline or interstellar shipping outfit has had any trouble with these so-called pirates."

"Why in the Gehenna are they targeting us?"

"The Board's been tight-lipped about that, but I suspect somebody on Terra doesn't like our little outfit."

"Meaning, Terra-Baldur-Marduk Spacelines or Pan-Federation Spacelines is unhappy with the competition."

"Something like that. Old Klem's convinced it's a Federation plot to see that Poictesme is kept in a backwards state, although he doesn't have a clue as to why. 'They just do,' he says."

III

Gerhadus Venter, the Chief Security Officer of Panstellar, positioned himself at the rear of the bar so that his seat faced the entrance of the La Casa del Becho, one of the old tango bars in downtown Montevideo. The del Becho dated back to before the First Federation and was located in a house that once belonged to Mattos Rodríguez, a famous tango composer. Venter took another deep drink of his apricot *clericó*, one of the bar's signature drinks. He didn't think anyone was following his boss, but one couldn't be too careful.

Venter had some new information for him that had just arrived from a hyperspace message drone direct from the Gartner Tri-System. Tarkington's latest move was a bold one, but not one shared by the Board or by most of Panstellar's top executives. He'd only gone along with Tarkington because he had promised him a big bonus and the presidency of a new security firm that would have all of Panstellar's business. He had three ex-wives and a mistress to support, and wasn't making ends meet on his present five-figure salary.

However, that didn't mean he trusted President Howard Tarkington; although, he knew where most of Tarkington's skeletons (and there were a lot of them!) were buried. Tarkington's latest gambit was a move to buy enough stock to take control of the Maxwell firms; thereby gaining control of their super-computer. It could prove to be his boldest move yet. However, they needed more information on what Rodney Maxwell and the Merlin-12 Group were up to. So far, they only had one inside man, and he was shaky.

He watched as Tarkington made his way through the crowded bar like a tugboat pushing aside lesser craft. The President, with his affected eyeglasses and diffident manner, didn't appear at first glance to be anything more than an accountant or light scribe pusher. But upon closer look one could see the steely gray eyes and their disconcerting stare that left one feeling like a rabbit looking into the eyes of a rattlesnake.

President Tarkington gave Venter a quick glance-over that said in no uncertain terms, "This better be important," before taking a seat at the cocktail table.

Venter lit another cigarette while he waited for Tarkington to order a drink from the robot-tender. When he was finished giving his order, Venter said, "I just got a message from our principal in Storisende via a comm-drone."

The President shook his head. "It's about time, Gerard. First, is the area clean?"

He nodded. "First thing I did was use my detection wand. No devices other than the usual security scanners and detectors. I've also set up a white-noise field around the table.

"Good. What's up?"

"Murchison just got an important packet from our mole. He sent it out-system straight away." The hyperspace comm-drones were an expensive way to send messages, but they were far better than waiting for the next freighter or packet ship.

"Tarkington shook his head in disgust. "So far I've spent over three million sols and all I have to show for it is a bought-and-paid-for Federation rep and one mole who's afraid to stick his nose out of his hole. So what's the latest? Have we made any progress on gaining control of Tri-System Investments?"

Venter shrugged. "Nothing new, there. This Merlin-12 Group is tight-knit. Most of them have known each other since childhood, and they all have a foolishly naïve belief in their super-computer's predictions. Just the name Merlin is a tip-off to what kind of nutcases we're dealing with. And, by Satan, these M-12 boys are at the top of the food chain. From some of the reports I've read, some of the hayseeds on Poictesme actually think this Merlin is a god. No wonder the Federation is going to hell in a handbasket."

"Yes, yes," Tarkington replied. "We've talked this to death. I've spent more than enough time at the Planetary Assembly to know how out-of-touch and backwards most of our off-world citizens are."

"There is one other development I think you should know about. One of the engineers on Koshchei has come up with a way to cut hyperdrive speeds in half."

Tarkington reared back. "Now, this is news! Very bad news.... Tri-System Interstellar could put us all out of the freight business if they quickly replaced their old hyperspace drives with the new ones, and then built up their commercial fleet. We know they've got the facilities on Koshchei to do it, too. Unless we get our hands one of those drives, Panstellar stock will be selling for centisols this time next year."

Venter nodded. "Our mole got the heads-up before M-12, although they probably know all about it by now."

Tarkington swore a blue streak. "It takes the drone four months to travel sixty-five light-years. They may have already retrofitted all their ships by now."

"I don't think so, sir. From all evidence, it appears that the Merlinites are more worried about the economic effects on the rest of the Federation than they are on a quick profit. At least, that's what our mole believes, and he's their chief counsel."

Tarkington leaned back with a thoughtful expression on his face. "This just ups the ante in our little takeover game. Just the thought of halving travel time of our ships will have most of the Board salivating. Still, I'm not sure I want to let them in on this news yet. It does mean that we have to do something serious to stop M-12."

"How about having our man in the Office of Colonial Ministry hit them with an unfair trade practices suit?"

Tarkington smiled in a way that sent a chill up Venter's spine. "Yes, I like that idea. Their use of Federation-built plants and equipment on Koshchei and Poictesme has given them an unfair trade advantage. I'm sure we can get Pan-Federation Spacelines and Trailways to sign on with us. Are you sure you don't have a law degree?"

They both laughed.

NINE

I

Klem Zareff was watching a documentary about the fall of the System States—it was mostly poppycock, but then the Federation was never going to broadcast the truth about their greatest rival—on his Tri-D screen—when one of his outside motion detectors began to beep. At first he thought it might be Stonewall Jackson; the Fuzzy had a habit of roaming the plantation late at night. *Nah, he'd never set off an alarm. Probably a lost dog, shovel-snout or some tramp looking for work,* he decided as he used his controller to switch to the outside screens. With military surplus being so cheap, Klem had long ago installed a first-rate surveillance net over his property.

Occasionally, his network caught the out-of-work hobo or kid stealing melons, or some jasper trying to stir up trouble. With his outspoken anti-Federation views, Klem was the target of a lot of hate. Then, of course, it wasn't impossible that Terran Military Intelligence might want his voice stilled. *If so, I'm ready for the bastards!*

Klem watched the infra-red gray-green images as the hunched-over intruder, which was what he thought of him now, made his way down the long flagstone pathway leading to his front door. He had planted a thick brush cover to hide the detectors and recorders that lined both sides of the pathway.

He watched as the intruder softly stepped up the stairs leading to the porch. He could have ended it right there, since there was a deadfall rigged into the porch right before his door. *It'll be more fun to see how it plays out,* he thought grimly.

II

Stonewall Jackson saw the bad man even before he stepped foot on the plantation. He could tell he was a "no-good-sum-bitch!" by the way he slunk down the path leading to the farmhouse door. *Maybe him be the "Sumbitch-Fed agent that's going to stab-me-in-the-back" that Pappy Klem always talked about.*

He knew that Pappy Klem had cameras all along the pathway and was probably watching the sumbitch make his way to the door.

Stonewall decided it was his job to go around the back and warn Pappy Klem in case he'd fallen asleep.

III

Old Klem Zareff lived farther outside of Litchfield than Wade Shawley had expected. The melon plantation was huge, some ten thousand acres, or at least that's what people said. No one seemed to like the old coot, but then the lowlifes he'd talked to in Tramptown weren't exactly Litchfield's leading citizens. For a moment, he'd considered bringing help along but had nixed it when he found out Zareff was over eighty years old.

When the day comes where I need help sandbagging an old man, it'll be time for me to retire.

Shawley had a long evening planned. First he was going to question the old buzzard—easy or hard, it would be up to him. Then once he squeezed everything of value out of him, he was going to have him sign over all his ownership in the Maxwell Companies to him. That would give him real bargaining power with the people he worked for. They wouldn't like it, but so what. They'd dropped him like he was radioactive slag the minute things went south.

What happened after that depended upon how helpful the old man had been; either way, he was headed for an unmarked grave.

There was no sign of the old man's house along Potter Road, but someone had told him to watch for a big oak tree. When he spotted it, he parked his ground car and crossed over the gravel road. Most travel here these days was by aircar or contragravity lifters and the roads were poorly maintained. He went over a rise, past a small copse of feather trees then down a small hill where he spotted a stone pathway bordered on both sides by rows of large bushes, some of them flowering, others heavy with thorns.

No wonder people don't like him. Antisocial old coot. I bet he's got a lot of hidden loot on the property. Maybe real gold. People like him don't trust banks.

Shawley made his way carefully down the pathway, which in the darkness seemed to go on forever. It was several hours past midnight but he knew a lot of old-timers didn't get to sleep until the wee hours and he didn't want to warn Zareff that he was coming. The old porch was made of wood and creaked with every step. He tried to keep the noise down, but he was beginning to get angry. *Why was the old geezer making things so tough?*

The door was key-locked, which surprised him. No one on Terra used anything but lock cards or thumblocks. *Remember, you're on the frontier. These hicks wouldn't know civilization if it smacked them in the face.*

He used his knife to work the lock, but it wasn't getting anywhere. Instead, he drew back and slammed his foot into the door. There was a loud crash but the door held. He didn't care anymore if he woke the old buzzard or not, slamming into the door with his shoulder. Some of the boards cracked and now the door was leaning crookedly. Another hard hit with his foot and the door blew open.

Shawley barreled his way through the entry hall into the parlor, where an old man sat on his chair with a silver cane in his lap. His white hair was tousled, like cotton candy, showing the pink scalp underneath.

"Are you Klem Zareff?" he asked.

The old man looked him right in the eyes, saying, "That's what my parents named me. And who are you and why have you broken into my house?"

His voice was surprisingly steady and held steel.

Shawley pulled his knife out of its sheath. "I'm the Revelator."

"What in Ghu's Name is a Revelator?"

Shawley smiled as he tested the blade with his thumb. "The man who's going to reveal whether you live or die."

The old man smiled. "And what's going to determine that?"

"The answer to my question," Shawley stated.

"I have no doubt about that. Well, get asking, then."

"I want to know where your Company stock is located," he demanded.

"So that's what this is all about. You're not from Terran Naval Intelligence?"

Shawley shook his head, wondering what kind of kook he was facing. "I represent a party that's going to pay me a lot of money for those certificates. That's all I'm going to say on the subject."

Klem Zareff shook his head. "I don't think so."

Shawley slowly raised his knife blade so that the dim light of the Tri-D reflected off of it. "You'll talk."

Before he could advance more than two steps, the old coot had drawn a sword out of his cane and was up and out of his chair, aiming the sword right at his gut. He couldn't believe his eyes—the old man was as fast as a rattlesnake!

He moved forward with his knife extended, but the old man pushed it aside with his sword, then drew his sword back and—

Shawley felt as though a burning hot poker had sliced into his abdomen and his knife dropping out of his suddenly numb and trembling fingers.

He must have passed out for a few moments. The next thing he saw was the old man standing over him with a cold smile on his face. A Fuzzy was perched on his shoulder like a parrot. His hand was still gripping the hilt.

"Who really sent you?"

"Ahh. Go to hell—"

The old man pressed the sword deeper. "You might still live, if you talk, sonny. I wouldn't advise raising your voice again."

"Un-who," he managed. "I don't know who sent me. My, my orders were sent to a postal drop on Terra...." He paused to cry out in pain. "I, I was given instructions and a quarter of a million sols to buy the information."

"Tell me where the money is," the old man said, as he bent over.

Shawley told him everything, including where he hid the key to the safe deposit box.

"How many more of you are there?"

"Ahh! I don't know—"

Klem put some pressure on the sword.

There was a short scream, then Shawley stammered, "Okay, okay. I know there's a couple, but the only ones I worked with are two ex-Marines and a killer name of Xu. That's it...I swear!"

"You done good, boy. But, in clear-cut cases like this, I don't believe in trials."

The last thing Shawley remembered was the white-hot heat of the blade as it sliced through his intestines and straight out his back, and then everything fell into a black swirl—

IV

"Damnit, Klem!" Rodney shouted. "You should have called the Company police. Or got a hold of Tom."

They were holed up in Jude Ledue's chambers. The Judge nodded in agreement. He wasn't happy about the way things had turned out. But, if there was one thing he'd learned in his long life, it was deal with the hand you're dealt, not the one you wished you had.

Leaning on his silver headed sword cane, Klem Zareff said, "I got everything that scallywag had to give, Rod. He was just a gun for hire."

"Yes, but under a veridicator we might have gotten something substantial out of the son of a diseased Khooghra."

Klem shook his head, then made a V out of his fingers and pointed into two ice-blue eyes. "These babies are the best veridicators around. That jasper told me everything he knew. No sense wasting taxpayer money on some trial, and take a chance of him getting off because some high-priced lawyer from Storisende bests the local yokels."

Judge Ledue nodded. "Rod, Klem's right. The last thing M-12 needs is more publicity. A trial would have brought news service reporters into Litchfield from all over Poictesme, maybe even off-world. A spotlight like that is the last thing we need while we're trying to deal with this piracy angle."

"Dad, I agree," Conn Maxwell said. "We already have too many outsiders trying to get to Merlin. We don't need to have news reporters digging into M-12 and our other companies. The people we're dealing with are too smart to leave any dangling loose strings. I say, let's do what Klem suggested, drop the body into Klem's melon-farm recycling tank just like he'd do with any other dead animal. Let the dead man's handlers back on Terra wonder what happened. It's time they started worrying a little."

"What about the other hard cases he mentioned?" Klem asked.

Judge Ledue tugged at his Van Dyke. "Let's pick them up in the morning." He paused to rub his eyes. "Then we can veridicate them, see if they know anything."

Klem shook his head in disgust. "Waste of time. They're just cannon fodder for the suits back on Terra."

"You're probably right," the Judge said. "Still, we can keep them on ice until we wrap up this piracy business. Hold them as 'persons of interest' in our case of interstellar piracy."

"That works for me," Rodney Maxwell said.

"I think we need to start doing serious security checks on every off-world passenger, especially those arriving on Terra-Baldur-Marduk Spacelines ships," Conn added.

"Good point," the Judge said. "As Klem would say, it's time to weed our own melon patch!"

"I agree," Conn said. "I think we're speaking for all of M-12. Only let's not just start with new arrivals, let's go over the T-B-MS passenger manifests for the past five or six years. Tom's got a lot of locals on the payroll. I say it's time to give them something to do."

Klem's usually stern face crinkled, as he broke into a big smile. "Now you're thinking, sonny." He rubbed his hands together briskly. "I haven't had so much fun since the time my outfit got pinned down on Ashmodai…."

"I've gotta run, Klem," Judge Ledue said, before Klem launched into another one of his interminable yarns. "I haven't had a wink of sleep tonight."

"Me, either," Rodney Maxwell added.

TEN

I

After showing Tor Handler around the Barathrum Spaceport, the next morning, Tom Brangwyn said, “You’ll be able to train them here in a section that we’ve never needed to use before, the tactical simulation center two levels down. Wait until you see it!”

They walked over to take a closer look at the work being done on the *Lester Dawes*. While Tom kept on talking, Handler wondered if he was going to regret leaving that undemanding but mind-numbing job as captain of an interplanetary freighter.

As the days passed, Handler gradually picked out his crew and the crew of the other corvette from the dozens of candidates. They were all experienced spacers. With the ships all down, they had a lot of prospective crewmembers to choose from. If they couldn’t come to the spaceport in person, he interviewed them by viewscreen. Each corvette would have a crew of twelve.

When both crews were chosen and had arrived at Barathrum Spaceport, Handler had them start training in the simulation center, throwing every scenario that he could possibly think of at them. The upgraded corvettes fared favorably against any kind of armed freighter, but not very well against hypothetical warships, such as those of the Federation Space Navy. *Praise Merlin, the pirates don't have any of those*, he thought to himself.

When he ran out of realistic scenarios, he programmed some way-out scenarios just for the heck of it. The most far out was a fleet-to-fleet action where both sides had dozens of corvette-type craft deployed from multiple large hypership transports. It lasted almost twenty hours and by the time he and his team were finished, their two corvettes were ready for their shakedown cruise.

II

The Terra-Baldur-Marduk Spacelines freighter *City of Asgard* came out of hyperspace and arrived with more bad news. Terra-Baldur-Marduk Spacelines had lodged a complaint with the Federation Office of Interstellar Trade, regarding unfair trade practices by Tri-System & Interstellar Spacelines. The basis for their complaint was that Tri-System & Interstellar's ships—which were carrying cargo between Terra and Poictesme—had been built using facilities and equipment on the planet Koshchei that the Federation had abandoned. Therefore, those facilities, most of the materials and equipment had been for all intents and purposes free and the only real cost to build those ships had been the labor cost of the personnel required to construct them.

As a result, Tri-System & Interstellar Spacelines had been able to purchase those ships from Koshchei Exploration & Development at much lower prices than Terra-Baldur-Marduk Spacelines had paid and continued to pay for its ships and therefore could offer lower shipping rates that T-B-MS couldn't match. They had asked—and the Federation Office of Interstellar Trade had agreed—that a three hundred percent tariff be imposed on *all* goods carried by ships belonging to Tri-System &

Interstellar Spacelines. The Terra-Baldur-Marduk freighter carried the official notification.

Not only would Poictesme's ships not be able to sell their cargo on Terra at anything other than a huge loss, the same tariff applied to anything that those ships would normally bring back to Poictesme. The tariff effectively put the shipping company out of business. And because they still had to pay the salaries of the crews who were in transit, there was a good chance that Tri-System & Interstellar Spacelines would go bankrupt within six to nine months.

The news sent shock waves throughout the Poictesme business community. The ripple effects of diminished exports would end up affecting the entire planetary economy. Planetary President Kurt Fawzi called an emergency meeting of M-12 in Litchfield. He called upon Conn Maxwell to ask Merlin what the long-term impact of the tariff would be.

III

President Fawzi chaired the meeting. Conn couldn't help but notice his new shimmer-sheen suit, cut in the latest style from Terra—or latest style, some six years ago when Conn had last been on the homeworld. Fawzi looked freshly barbered and manicured; what happened to the old Fawzi? Klem Zareff would have called it "falling in with the First-Families-of-Storisende," the original settlers who still felt entitled and pretty much ran things in the capital.

Kurt Fawzi was the first president from "outside Storisende" in several generations. Litchfield City had always been viewed by the Storisende crowd as Hicksville. Conn wondered if Fawzi was beginning to feel that way now that he'd moved, lock, stock and gun barrels, to the Presidential Tower. Conn did know that four years ago Fawzi had fought the new Litchfield spaceport bonds, tooth and nail, when they were first introduced under his new administration. Fortunately, the Merlin Could Do No Wrong crowd was strong enough to push the bonds through the lower house anyway.

Now Litchfield had its own spaceport, which made sense since most of their planetary exports, melon-brandy and tobacco, were grown and refined in the Gordon Valley and outlying areas.

After the minutes were read, Conn Maxwell stood up before the group. "I'm sorry, but according to Merlin, if this new tariff isn't rescinded within one year, the Poictesme economy will be in worse shape than it was before Merlin was discovered."

Everyone tried to talk at once.

Klem Zareff was yelling that Poictesme should secede from the Federation and build its own navy. He was so excited that Stonewall Jackson was bouncing up and down on his shoulder.

Chairman Kurt Fawzi finally managed to regain order and recognized Rodney Maxwell.

Conn's father stood up and looked around the conference table. "Let's not lose our heads! The worst thing we can do is go off half-cocked. This news is six months old and any of our ships in transit to Terra will be affected by it no matter what we decide so if we take a few days, heck, even a couple of weeks to decide how to respond, it won't really matter. However there is one action that must be taken immediately."

He looked at President Kurt Fawzi. "It's just our good luck that the *City of Asgard* arrived on a weekend. When stock trading resumes on Monday morning, the shares of Tri-System Investments will likely bottom out and take the rest of the market with it. Kurt, you need to order the Storisende Stock Exchange to remain closed for at least a couple of days, maybe longer."

Fawzi jaw dropped, but kept his outrage to himself.

Conn knew this gang would laugh him off the podium, if Fawzi said anything about his dad using his first name. *When did he get so pompous, and how did I miss it?*

Everyone agreed to Rodney's proposal.

"Okay, if everyone's agreed," Fawzi announced with poorly concealed ill-humor. "It'll give us all some breathing room."

Lester Dawes the banker said, "I'll bet whoever was buying our shares at those inflated prices will be sorry they did now."

Conn was about to agree, then thought it through. Finally, he shook his head. "I disagree, Lester. I'm beginning to suspect that pushing our share price to new, all-time highs is part of the same effort as this trade complaint."

"I don't understand your reasoning," Dawes said, shaking his head. "Please explain."

He looked at his father and nodded.

Rodney said, "Suppose that Terra-Baldur-Marduk Spacelines, or perhaps its parent company, Panstellar Industries, wanted to not only put us out of commission permanently as a competitor, but wanted control of the Koshchei facilities, all the interplanetary ships operated by Alpha Interplanetary as well as Litchfield Exploration & Development assets, such as Barathrum Spaceport and Merlin. How would they go about doing that? My gut feeling is that they would use the carrot and stick approach."

"What do you mean?" Klem Zareff asked. "Make it simple so even a melon farmer like me can understand."

"First, buy as many shares in Tri-System Investments as they can at almost literally any price, and then engineer a financial panic. One that they hope will stampede enough shareholders to sell at a centisol to the sol; thereby enabling them to exercise control of the holding company, and through that all of the assets. In this case, the other companies."

Rodney Maxwell paused to give everyone time to digest the information, then continued, "I said a minute ago that Tri-System Investments shares would probably crash. Now I think it's more likely that there will be a standing buy order at or near the recent high prices for all shares being offered for sale. The rest of the market could still crash but Tri-System Investments' shares will remain enticingly high; it will be very difficult for those of us in this room to resist that temptation and stick with our agreements not to sell any Tri-System Investments' shares to outsiders."

"Great Ghu, that's diabolical!" Lester Dawes the banker piped up "Surely they know that none of us in this room would betray the group's trust. Not to mention the larger stakes involved with the collapse of the Federation...."

His father looked grim as all get-out. "Well, let's hope they don't know about Merlin's long-term predictions, or they're more evil than even I'd paint them. But as far as this group sticking together to maintain control—they might just pull it off. Morgan was set to sell us out, we know that now."

There was a flurry of throat clearings and other noises. While several of the people seated around the table started to express their indignation at the implied suggestion that their word was no good, but Rodney cut them off.

"Think about it! Every one of us here either has a business or a job that would be negatively impacted by the tariff and a stock market crash. Klem, if your melon-growing business went under and the only asset you owned that was still worth anything was your Tri-System Investments' stock, are you positive that you wouldn't sell, especially if you knew that the stock wasn't worth the price they were willing to pay for it?"

Klem Zarcff looked angry. He stood up and pointed a finger at Rodney. "You picked the wrong person to use as an example, Rod. I'd rather live on the street and eat garbage than sell out to a bunch of Terran corporate carpetbaggers! But, that's just me and my System States Alliance prejudices. I don't have a family to worry about, but most seated around this table do. And you have a valid point about what some of us might feel forced to do, if push came to shove. A man's gotta do whatever he has to, to provide for his family. The question is: What can we do to stop it?"

Everyone looked to Conn's father as the acknowledged expert in corporate wheeling and dealing. He looked around the table and said in a hesitant voice.

"Well…if we try to resist the takeover, we'll probably lose. So…maybe what we should do is…let them think they've won."

He held his hands up to forestall any protest. "I'm still pondering this, mind you…but here's what I'm toying with. What if those of us in this room, as well as a couple of other Tri-System Investments' stockholders that are sympathetic to our cause, were to swap our shares of Tri-System Investments for controlling interests in Litchfield Exploration & Salvage and Koshchei Exploration and Development? That would effectively keep control of the key assets of Koshchei and Merlin in our hands, and Tri-System Investments would still have control of the interplanetary and interstellar shipping companies which will very rapidly be turning into financial black holes.

"By handing our Tri-System Investments shares back to the company, Terra-Baldur-Marduk Spacelines or whoever is buying those shares, they will suddenly find they already own enough to control Tri-System Investments and there's no point in buying any more."

Lester Dawes spoke up. "But Rod, you've been telling us for years that we need those interplanetary ships owned by Alpha Interplanetary and the hyperspace ships owned by Tri-System & Interstellar Spacelines. If we let those ships slip under Terra-Baldur-Marduk Spacelines' control, then we're back to square one, aren't we?"

"No. Not at all. First of all, we found hundreds of abandoned but still usable interplanetary ships on Koshchei, remember? Some of those ships were sold to Alpha Interplanetary but most weren't. If Terra-Baldur-Marduk Spacelines decides to shut down Alpha Interplanetary operations, we'll just set up a new company and use ships that are still sitting on Koshchei. Second of all, T-B-MS isn't after our ships. They already have enough of their own! They just don't want *us* to have any ships. But if we have Koshchei intact, we can build more ships for our own use."

"But won't the Federation just slap another tariff on those ships as well?" Professor Kellton asked.

"I grant you that, Professor. We'll have to be damn smart as to how we use them to prevent that from happening again, but that's a relatively minor detail. What I don't know right now is whether we can make this proposed transaction a done deal before the markets open again in a few days. John, you're our expert on corporate law, what do you think? Can it be done that quickly?"

J. Fitzwilliam Sterber, the companies' lawyer, looked thoughtful, then said, "We'll have to call an emergency shareholders' meeting to ratify the transaction. Company bylaws require at least a seventy-two hour notice before a shareholder's meeting. That means that the soonest we could have one is four days from now. Because it involves a significant change to the company's structure, we would be justified in asking the Stock Exchange to halt trading in Tri-System Investments' shares until after the shareholders meeting regardless of whether the rest of the market is open or not. So, the answer is: yes, it can be done."

Rodney Maxwell smiled for the first time since the meeting began. "Good. Here's what we'll do, then. We announce a shareholders' meeting for four days from now. Tomorrow, we'll have a meeting of the Board of Directors and vote on the proposed purchase of Litchfield Exploration & Salvage and Koshchei Exploration & Development from Tri-System Investments in exchange for shares of Tri-System Investments which, thanks to our mysterious buyer, are worth far more than the individual values of the two companies involved. Then the shareholders' meeting will ratify the deal since we in this room control a majority of the shares.

"With the sale of Tri-System Investments' shares halted, no one will be able to sell on the exchange. I'm asking all of you here and now, to pledge that you will not sell any of your Tri-System Investments' shares to anyone that approaches you with a direct, private offer, prior to the exchange of shares being made."

Everyone around the table made the pledge.

Next, Rodney turned to Kurt Fawzi. "Kurt, order the Exchange closed for as long as you can."

Planetary President Kurt Fawzi nodded.

Conn knew it was only because Fawzi held a good chunk of shares that he was so amenable to his father's advice.

Turning to Lester Dawes, Rodney said, "Lester, our shipping companies will be running out of cash within a few months. As soon as they're in violation of their bank loan covenants, you should have the bank seize whatever ships you can lay your hands on and then the new shipping company that we'll set up will buy them from the bank for the amount of the unpaid loans plus one sol. That will legitimize the purchase price and not even the Federation Office of Interstellar Trade will be able to declare that unfair." He paused.

"Another thing, I'm beginning to think that we should stop trading with Terra anyway. We should concentrate on Baldur, Isis, Odin, Aton, Ra,

Marduk—they all have the population and wealth to provide markets for our brandy, tobacco and a lot of our manufactured goods. They're a lot closer, too. Hell, by the time we get the new company up and running smoothly, we'll be making more money that we were before.

"However, that won't happen overnight. Things will be difficult for about a standard year so be prepared."

With the main issue settled, everyone relaxed and the serving robot brought out drinks for everyone.

I

The next four days were hectic and tense. Planetary President Kurt Fawzi managed to keep the Stock Exchange closed for four days. After Tri-System Investments' Board of Directors met and voted to approve the share swap deal, a public announcement was made along with notice of the shareholders' meeting. That meeting was televised live with company police guarding the building and only allowing news people and registered shareholders inside. Only one shareholder—who had proxies from dozens of shareholders, and apparently represented several of the mysterious new investment companies that had bought Tri-System Investments' shares at record prices—was against the deal. He was outvoted.

Immediately after the meeting, Rodney Maxwell was interviewed by reporters and announced that a new shipping company would soon be chartered. The new company would acquire both interplanetary and interstellar ships which would resume exporting Poictesme goods in a way that would not incur the punitive tariff imposed by the Federation Office of Interstellar Trade. The day after the shareholders' meeting, both the stock market and Tri-System Investments' shares were open for trading.

There was some selling early in the morning but by then the market as a whole recovered to close higher on the day. Tri-System Investments did not trade at all and the record high bid had been withdrawn.

Conn Maxwell was worried that the change in control of Tri-System Investments would allow the new majority owner (Terra-Baldur-Marduk Spacelines?) to interfere with the anti-piracy operations involving Tor Handler's team and the *Vanguard.*

His father reassured him. "Conn, don't worry about it. *Vanguard* is owned by Tri-System & Interstellar Spacelines. A majority of its shares are held by the two companies that the M-12 Group now has solid control of. It will eventually run out of cash when the ships that are in transit on their way back from Terra arrive with their last tariff-free cargoes and sell them here. That will take about six months, by which time, I hope the pirate situation will have been solved.

"Don't forget that I'm the senior executive of all of the companies we set up. That means that I'll still be able to manage the day-to-day operational affairs of the shipping companies until such time as the new owner of the holding company can vote in a new slate of Directors, which they won't have the opportunity to do for some time.

"But when they do, they'll be able to kick me out of the top spot for both the holding company and the interplanetary shipping company that we don't care about anymore. If things go according to plan, the banks will have repossessed most of the ships due to loan covenant defaults, and that's when the new company will buy them from the banks and start exporting again."

Conn still looked worried. "Will the new company have enough cash to buy those ships by then?"

His father thought about that for a few seconds. "Now that the Maxwell/Merlin Plan has established its credibility, I think we could probably raise some seed capital by selling shares to the public, then leverage that with new bank loans, so I don't see a problem."

II

A week after the corporate reshuffle the *Ouroboros II*, the first hypership built in the Gartner Tri-System since the System States War, arrived back from its trading trip to Terra. As soon as it landed at Storisende Spaceport, Rodney Maxwell went on board and asked the captain to call the crew to a special meeting in the mess hall.

"First of all, welcome back. I know that it's been almost half a year since you were here last and that you're anxious to go home and see your families. But, before you do, I have some important news. I think you deserve to hear this from me rather than from inflated rumors told by outsiders. I'll try to be as brief as I can. I come bearing both the proverbial good news and bad news.

"First the bad news: Our competition, Terra-Baldur-Marduk Spacelines, has managed to convince the Federation Office of Interstellar Trade to impose a three hundred percent tariff on all goods carried by our ships. Never mind how they managed that, it's not important. What is important is that the tariff now makes exporting our usual cargoes to Terra completely uneconomical, which is exactly what Terra-Baldur-Marduk Spacelines intended."

There were mutterings throughout the mess.

"So for the foreseeable future, we will not be sending any more cargo to Terra. The good news is that we have other things to transport aboard *Ouroboros II* and her sister ships over the next few months. It will be company policy to continue to pay your salaries, regardless of whether these hyperships are actually doing anything or not, for as long as the company has the cash to keep doing so. Now there's obviously a limit as to how long the company can keep doing that, but plans are being implemented that we hope will allow us to rehire all of you at some point in the not too distant future. So don't pay any attention to any rumors that claim otherwise."

"You heard the man," the Captain said. "Anything else, Mr. Maxwell?"

"Yes, the next year, maybe two, may get a little rough. But, believe me, when I tell you that beyond that—the future looks bright. I'll stop here and let you get back to your unloading so that you can finish and get back to your homes."

One of the mates asked, "Is this another one of Merlin's plans?"

Maxwell just grinned, but didn't say yea or nay. *Let them think it's Merlin's idea and they'll jump through hoops just to prove it right.*

III

The shakedown cruise went well, and they even engaged in mock combat with the *Lester Dawes* playing the role of the pirate. By the time both corvettes settled back down at the Barathrum Spaceport, Handler was pleased with his crews, especially his second-in-command, Commander Rachel Montoya. One last problem remained to be solved before they could become operational. The two corvettes had to be named.

Tom Brangwyn had left that up to each corvette's CO. Tor finally decided to call his ship *Dragon Hunter*. Commander Montoya named her ship *Amazon Warrior*. After one more briefing by Tom Brangwyn, both crews manned their vessels and carefully docked them in the large cargo hold of the *Ouroboros II*, which hovered over the spaceport. It then joined up with the smaller hypership, *Vanguard*, and the two of them set course for Asgard.

During the hyperspace journey to the Gaulthwait System, Commander Tor Handler and his crew kept to themselves and rested up for the ordeal ahead. When both ships made their final microjump to within sixty million miles of Asgard, *Ouroboros II* launched the two corvettes, which then accompanied *Vanguard* down to Valhalla City. The freighter landed at the main spaceport while the two corvettes found a suitable hiding place about five hundred kilometers away in a canyon. As they found out later, no one at the spaceport queried *Vanguard's* captain about the corvettes so they had apparently avoided detection by the spaceport radar.

Ouroboros II stayed a considerable distance beyond the no-jump zone to see what, if anything, happened.

Asgard was one of the first-wave colonies and least developed. It was a much larger world than most with a diameter of some twelve thousand miles. However, it was a less dense world than Terra, and the gravity was 1.1 galactic standard gravities. It was known for its large seas and temperate climate; however, it had very few heavy metals and almost no radioactives, which meant the planet was highly dependent upon imports. Rodney Maxwell had noted this and believed it would prove to be a great market for Tri-System Interstellar war surplus. It also had turned out to be a great dumping ground for surplus metal vehicles, robots, machinery and metal junk that no one else wanted—and they paid top sol.

This was Tor Handler's first visit to Asgard and he would have liked more time to explore Valhalla, but this time the trading was only a cover for the real mission and he had very little time for sightseeing. After the usual turnaround time to unload incoming cargo and load outgoing cargo, *Vanguard* requested and received permission to lift-off for the voyage home. As it gained altitude, it sent a pre-arranged signal in the general direction of the canyon, which *Dragon Hunter's* communications technician detected and then informed his CO. Both corvettes left the canyon minutes later and quickly took up position behind *Vanguard.*

The freighter, as per standard commercial procedure, had an active transponder but the corvettes kept theirs turned off. Before the *Vanguard* had reached a distance of fifty-five thousand miles from Valhalla, all three ships received a signal from a ship that declared itself to be the Federation Space Navy Cruiser *Valley Forge* with instructions to cut acceleration and wait to be boarded for inspection.

Vanguard's Captain and Commander Handler discussed the demand over a laser line-of-sight link.

"Should I follow instructions and stop accelerating?" Captain Anson asked.

"No!" Handler ordered. "If that was really a TFSN vessel, why weren't you informed that she was in-system inspecting cargoes when you were on Valhalla? Why doesn't the *Valley Forge* have an active transponder? Why all the secrecy? A pirate ship pretending to be a Federation Naval ship would explain how *Pathfinder* and *Trailblazer* were both captured before they could run away. They fell for the deception, and didn't realize their mistake until after they'd been boarded.

"Stick to the plan and you continue to accelerate until you're far enough away to make your first microjump. Commander Montoya and I will take care of this intruder. I'll take full responsibility."

"Aye, aye."

When it became obvious that *Vanguard* wasn't going to obey orders to stop accelerating, another message arrived from the suspected pirate ship. This one much more belligerent.

"Stop accelerating and prepare to be boarded or the *Valley Forge* will fire!"

Commander Handler snorted. Now he knew he was right. No Navy ship would fire on an unarmed freighter unless it was in clear violation of Federation law, and refusing to be boarded didn't count as such. Besides, the most efficient and foolproof way to prevent the transportation of contraband and prohibited material was at the receiving end. That's why all spaceports had Federation inspectors checking all incoming cargo.

The Commander ordered both corvettes to drop back in the general direction of the incoming messages so that they would be between *Vanguard* and the *Valley Forge*. More minutes passed. *Vanguard* kept accelerating and the corvettes continued to drop further behind her.

"The pirate ship is going active on her radar!" a signals-and-detection officer suddenly announced.

Handler cursed. That meant *Dragon Hunter* and *Amazon Warrior* would now be showing up on the pirate's radar. *No sense hiding now!*

"Okay…let's do the same and pass the word to *Warrior*. Weapons…stand by to fire four kinetics!"

"Standing by, Skipper!" the weapons officer answered. He had anticipated that order and had already selected missiles armed with collapsium-matter kinetic-energy penetrator rods which would use the speed of collision to punch their way into the ship, converting ordinary metal into super-hot plasma. While deadly to any crew in a room affected by the incoming round, it was meant to disable a ship rather than destroy it.

His orders were to try to capture the pirate if at all possible. They needed to find out who was behind the operation and where the other two freighter ships and their crews were. Or what had happened to them.

With active radar now turned on, the tactical display screen showed a new blip, a red triangle representing a ship deemed to be hostile.

He was expecting the pirate to fire at any second and was therefore surprised when the signals-and-detection officer signaled another incoming message and switched it to the overhead speakers.

"…to unidentified vessels. Repeat. TFNS *Valley Forge* to unidentified vessels. Identify yourselves. Be advised that you're interfering with a Terran Navy vessel engaged in anti-smuggling inspections." The message repeated one more time then stopped.

"Put me through to that ship, Johnson," Handler ordered. In about three seconds, the viewscreen at Tor's command station lit up with a white-haired man in a black FSN uniform looking at Tor in surprise.

"This is Senior Commander Tor Handler, in command of *Dragon Hunter* and *Amazon Warrior*. We are a privately-owned interplanetary craft owned by Interstellar Security, Inc. and are escorting the freighter *Vanguard* out past the no-jump threshold. Who are you?"

"I'm Captain Thoroldson. My orders are to inspect all outbound vessels for contraband. Your ships are in the way and I demand that you leave the vicinity at once!"

"Not so fast, Captain. First I want some questions answered: Why are you running without an active transponder, contrary to both standard civilian *and* Federation Naval procedures? Why haven't you informed the authorities on Valhalla that you're in-system, which is also contrary to established Naval procedures? Why have you threatened to fire on *Vanguard* when she has done nothing to warrant such extreme measures?"

"I'm prepared to answer all those questions, but not to you, Commander Handler. I'll only give those answers to that freighter's captain. Now… unless you want me to bring up charges of obstruction of justice against you personally and your company in my after-action report, I suggest you move away from this area immediately!"

Handler thought that over for a few seconds and then said, "Okay, look. I'm not an unreasonable person. Perhaps you have legitimate reasons for your outrageous actions. Here's what I'm prepared to do. My two ships will move up beside *Vanguard* keeping far enough away that you can safely rendezvous with her and carry out your inspection. I'm sure you won't find any contraband and then we can all be on our way. Surely you—"

Captain Thoroldson interrupted. "NO! That is completely unacceptable. I will not accept anything less than both of your ships leaving the vicinity immediately." He started to say more but this time Tor shut him up by cutting the connection altogether. Instead he contacted Commander Montoya.

"Did you hear that exchange, Commander?"

She nodded. "Sure did. Not very cooperative, is he?"

"No, he's not. This is what we're going to do. We will close in and match velocity with the *Vanguard*, then standoff at a reasonable distance—just as I offered. We will not respond to any further communications from the *Valley Forge*, but if she takes any hostile action against either *Vanguard* or our vessels, we fire back! Got that?"

"I got that, sir. For what it's worth, I agree."

"Okay. Then let's do that. Helm…go to maximum acceleration and adjust as necessary to match *Vanguard's* movements so that we're no more than five hundred yards away from her."

The helmsmen acknowledged the order and both corvettes started gaining on *Vanguard*. Tor switched channels to *Vanguard's* captain.

"Did you hear all that, Captain Anson?"

"I did. Do you want me to cut our acceleration?"

"Yes. Let's play along and see what that ship does. If you stop accelerating, it's going to be mighty hard for that Captain to argue that hostile force was necessary. Right?"

Anson nodded.

"If you're boarded," Tor continued, "keep a channel open to us at all times so that we can hear what's happening on your ship. If they really are pirates, they'll tip their hand soon enough and then we'll take action. I actually don't think it will get that far. If I was a pirate, I wouldn't try to board your ship unless I first scared our corvettes away. If I couldn't do that, I'd abort the interception and try to sneak away."

"I agree. I'm giving the order to cut acceleration now." The green symbol representing *Vanguard* on the Tactical Display, which up until that moment had shown a blue tail denoting acceleration, now showed no tail at all.

"That Navy ship is trying to contact us again," the signals-and-detection officer noted.

"Ignore them."

"Aye, aye, sir."

Tor watched the display carefully. The two corvettes were rapidly catching up to the now coasting *Vanguard*. Suddenly the now yellow triangle representing *Valley Forge* stopped accelerating, too. Tor held his breath. If that ship was planning on decelerating, it would need to rotate 180 degrees and in order to do that it had to shut down its Abbot lift-and-drive engines until the turn was complete. For a ship the size of the Navy cruiser, that would take about twenty seconds. Sure enough—after about 25 seconds—the symbol regained a tail that was pointing in the opposite direction, which meant that the Navy ship was now trying to increase the distance between it and *Vanguard*.

Tor smacked his fist against his station's armrest.

"If that's a Navy ship, I'll eat my uniform!" He hit a button and Commander Montoya appeared again on his screen.

"Commander, the enemy vessel is running away. We are going after her. Try to stay with me as best you can and take your cues from me. If I open fire, follow through."

"Understood."

Tor then ordered *Dragon Hunter* to pursue. The helmsman cut the acceleration, rotated the ship in far less time due to its smaller size and re-engaged maximum acceleration. *Amazon Warrior* didn't respond quite as quickly but she wasn't far behind. At this point, the pirate ship was actually still moving closer to the corvettes because her acceleration had been greater than *Vanguard's* and the fact that she was now decelerating simply meant that she was moving backwards at a progressively slower and slower rate.

With both corvettes now decelerating at 7.2 Gs versus the pirate's 5.5 Gs, the actual distance between them would continue to shrink even though at some point, both ships would start to move in the opposite direction. Even so, at this rate it would still take almost an hour for the corvettes to overtake the *Valley Forge*, which would make it impossible for the enemy ship to reach the hyperspace jump threshold. Tor didn't think Captain Thoroldson would allow that to happen without resisting and he was right.

As soon as it became obvious what both corvettes were doing, the signals-and-detection officer yelled out, "She's fired four missiles at us! Can't tell yet which ship they're locked onto."

Tor looked at his weapons officer who said, "Counter-missiles will fire automatically as soon as they have a lock!"

Even though the distance between the two forces was still almost fifty thousand miles, the *Valley Forge's* missiles were eating up the distance with impressive speed. The display estimated their acceleration at a rip-snorting 55 Gs! At first Tor thought that Thoroldson, if that was his real name, had made a mistake because the missiles would deplete their stored power source and be unable to maneuver by the time they reached their targets. However, when he queried the tactical computer about enemy effective missile range, he learned that even at this distance, *Valley Forge's* missiles could still make last minute course changes before impact.

The reason for their high velocity was that the missiles started out with *Valley Forge's* momentum, which extended their effective range, plus the fact that *their* targets were accelerating towards them, thereby bringing the interception point considerably closer. The reverse was not the case right at the moment; however in another thirteen minutes or so, *Valley Forge* would be in *Dragon Hunter's* effective missile range.

Handler shifted his gaze from the overall relative positions of ships and missiles to the upper right corner of the display which showed the estimated probability of counter-missiles successfully intercepting the incoming missiles if they were launched now, as well as time remaining to missile impact.

The probability number was less than thirty percent and climbing but it wasn't climbing as fast as the Commander thought it should. As he continued to watch it, it dropped suddenly to fifteen percent! Turning to his weapons officer he said, "Weapons! Why did counter-missiles hit probability suddenly drop in half?"

"The enemy ship has started emitting radar-jamming signals that are preventing my fire-control system from getting a good look at those incoming missiles!"

Handler noticed that the time to impact was now down to eight minutes and dropping alarmingly fast. He didn't have time to wonder how pirates had gotten control of a real Navy cruiser with missile launchers and electronic countermeasure capabilities. He decided he'd ponder that question later—if he was still alive.

Just as Tor was about to ask a question, one of the signals-and-detection officers yelled out, "More incoming!"

Another barrage of four missiles had just been launched towards them. He had to make a decision and *quick.*

"Weapons. Switch counter-missile strategy to continuous timed rate of fire and execute!"

His order was quickly acknowledged and seconds later *Dragon Hunter* began firing one counter-missile missile every ten seconds. With the hit probability now back up to just over twenty percent, there was an eighty percent chance the first counter-missile would miss but the chances that two counter-missiles would both miss was roughly sixty-four percent and for three missiles to miss was only fifty-one percent.

Between *Dragon Hunter* and *Amazon Warrior*, they had one hundred and twenty-eight counter-missiles which should be plenty, even if they had to fire five or six of them for each one of *Valley Forge's* missiles. And as soon as one incoming missile was taken out, the rest of the counter-missiles would simply switch to one of the other incoming missiles. *It should work in theory*, he thought to himself.

Provided that they didn't run out of time before those incoming missiles intercepted the corvettes.

If counter-missiles were fired more often, they might end up trying to hit the same target missile. If the first one hit, the next one might not have enough time to switch to another target.

The weapons officer pumped his fist into the air and yelled, "She's within our missile range now, Skipper!"

"Fire away, Weapons!" *Dragon Hunter* now fired its own salvo of two anti-ship missiles and seconds later, *Amazon Warrior* did the same. The tactical display was now starting to get crowded with overlapping symbols representing ships, missiles and counter-missiles.

He manipulated a control that made the display zoom in on the first wave of incoming missiles. With less than five minutes to impact, they were about to meet *Dragon Hunter's* counter-missile fire.

He watched as the first counter-missile reached the enemy missile wave and continued on past.

"A miss!" Weapons cried out.

He had to wipe the sweat off his brow.

Seconds later the second one missed, too! But the third one hit and surprisingly, the fourth one also hit. Then the next two missed, the one after that hit was followed by another miss and finally the last missile of the first wave was hit and destroyed.

Handler immediately ordered counter-missile fire to cease. The six counter-missiles that had already been fired and were still searching for targets, might be able to attrit the second wave but at that range the chances were slim. Better to let that second wave get closer so that additional counter-missile fire would have a better chance of hitting.

As expected, none of the counter-missiles already in transit hit any of the second wave.

Tor contacted Montoya. "Rachel, I want you to follow the same counter-missile strategy that I did for *Valley Forge's* first wave. Also, it's time to end this. I want you to prepare to launch sixteen offensive missiles at the same time that I do.

"We have to assume that the *Valley Forge* has her own counter-missile capability and we have to overwhelm it while we still have sufficient missiles to do so. After we launch an additional sixteen, we'll still have half our original load left if we need it. Let me know when you're ready, and fire on my command."

Montoya acknowledged.

Turning to his weapons officer, Tor said, "Did you hear that, Weapons?"

"Yes, Skipper, I'm preparing our own volley." Weapons paused, then said, "Ready to fire!"

The channel to *Amazon Warrior* was still open so Tor simply nodded and said, "Fire!"

Both corvettes vomited a total of thirty-two anti-ship missiles.

Almost immediately the Signals-and-Detection First Officer said, "Urgent incoming message from that ship, Skipper!"

"Okay. Let's hear what they have to say."

"We surrender, we surrender. Abort your missile attack!"

Tor turned to his Signals-and-Detection First Officer. "Has that ship stopped accelerating?"

"No, sir."

"Has she stopped jamming our fire-control radar?"

A different voice answered. "No, sir. She hasn't!"

"Is her second wave still locked on us?"

"Yes, sir. It is."

"Well then, let our missiles do our talking for us!"

Eventually the pleading stopped as it became obvious their offer of surrender wasn't being taken seriously. As the second wave of incoming missiles got close enough, *Amazon Warrior* began to spit out counter-missiles that eventually stopped them. To Tor's surprise, *Valley Forge* hadn't launched any more missile barrages. He watched in fascination as the four missiles launched by his two ships finally reached *Valley Forge*.

As expected, they were taken out by *Valley Forge's* own counter-missile fire. The range between the two sides was down to about thirty thousand miles when the thirty-two missile barrage reached their target. It made a valiant effort to stop them with counter-missile fire that hit almost half but the rest got through and almost all of those hit the ship.

Valley Forge's rate of acceleration immediately dropped from 5.5 Gs to less than 2 Gs. Clearly some but not all of her lift-and-drive units had been damaged. It wasn't long before he saw further reaction when acceleration dropped to zero. Realizing that the channel to Montoya was still active he said, "Rachel, does that look to you like she's giving up?"

"Yes, sir," Montoya answered. "Still, they might be trying to pull a fast one on us."

"They might at that. So here's what we're going to do. I'm going to broadcast a message to their captain that we will now accept their surrender. Furthermore, both of our ships will dock with theirs from opposite sides and that our boarding parties will be armed with instructions to fire if they even suspect foul play. I mean every word of that, too.

"Tell your people not to take any chances. A ship that size normally has a crew ten times larger than we do, so we can't let them take back the initiative."

"I agree, sir. What do we do with the crew after we've taken control of the bridge?"

Tor thought that over. "We immobilize them with wrist and ankle restraints and put them inside a room that has only one door which can be locked from the outside like one of their food storage compartments."

"Yes, sir."

Commander Handler sent the message to the *Valley Forge* and received a terse reply that the pirates would cooperate. With both corvettes now needing to match velocities with *Valley Forge*, it took an hour to accomplish that tricky maneuver.

By this time, *Vanguard* had sent a signal that it was across the no-jump threshold and was about to jump to hyperspace. Tor informed *Ouroboros II* of their situation and asked her to standby a while longer.

At last, both corvettes were carefully docked, one on each side of the much larger pirate ship. When both ships were ready to open their sealed hatches, everyone except for the helmsman and the weapons officer had donned combat armor and carried automatic shotguns with built in grenade launchers.

Before opening the hatchway that separated them from the interior of the *Valley Forge*, Commander Handler used the intercom to order the captain and his men to lie face down on the floor of the compartments that were on the other side of both his and Montoya's hatches. Anyone seen standing would be assumed to be hostile and would be fired upon without additional warning.

Captain Thoroldson agreed to comply.

He waited a few seconds, then ordered both hatches to be opened. He saw a score of men lying face down on the floor. No one was standing. The hatchway at the opposite end of the compartment was also open and beyond it were more prone bodies.

Eventually, all the pirates—the only one wearing a Navy uniform was Thoroldson himself—were fitted with restraints and moved to a storage room. Once that was done, Handler ordered Montoya to secure the ship's arms lockers, environmental controls and engineering control room while he sent his people to secure the bridge. They were able to use the ship's internal security system to verify that none of the pirates were hiding anywhere on the ship.

When it was clear that his people were now in complete control of the *Valley Forge*, Handler sat in the captain's command station and pondered his next move. His people were manning key stations on the bridge, but there were still two individuals on board each corvette. He had an idea.

"Is this ship carrying any smaller craft?"

"Ship's status indicators show that it has room to carry two pinnaces but isn't actually carrying them right now, Skipper," one of his signals-and-detection officers answered.

"Will our corvettes be able to fit into those berths?"

A quick check and the answer was, "Yes, sir. Schematics show that the pinnace berths have the necessary docking facilities and room to secure our corvettes."

"Good. Then let's get our corvettes inside, and then we'll decide where to go from here. While that's being done, I want to send a message to *Ouroboros II* and then another one to the Spaceport Authorities on Valhalla. What's the ship's status?"

"Sir, maneuvering capability is down to thirty-four percent of normal," Helm reported. "The Dillingham hyperdrive engines appear to be operational. Abbott lift-and-drive, pseudograv, power reactors, converters are all functional. Some damage to life support and there are a number of compartments that have lost atmosphere and are uninhabitable. Two missile launchers are inoperative and missile magazines appear to be completely empty."

Aha, that explains why they gave up so easily, Tor thought. They no longer had anything to fight with. It made sense. They wouldn't need a complete missile load if they expected to go up against a few unarmed freighters.

I

A short while later, *Ouroboros II* was in hyperspace on her way back to Poictesme with Tor's recorded message, while the *Valley Forge* was making her way back slowly to Valhalla Spaceport. The local Federation authorities had been notified of the whole operation and were standing by to arrest the pirates as soon as the ship landed. Handler had even managed to talk Asgard's chief legal officer into agreeing to offer a substantially lighter sentence for the first pirate who spilled his guts about who financed and set up this operation in the first place.

He was sure the pirates would jump at the chance to avoid the very harsh penalties that piracy carried under Federation law.

As the ship gently approached the spaceport landing area, he was in radio contact with the spaceport authorities.

"We see your ship coming through the cloud cover now, Commander Handler.

Our security people are standing by to take possession of that ship as soon as she lands. Arrangements for your crew have—"

"No," Tor cut him off. "Your people will *not* be taking possession of this ship. She is a prize ship that we captured and, as such, the *Valley Forge* is now Interstellar Security's property. I want that clearly understood and agreed to before we land."

"I'll have to discuss your demands with the Minister General."

After talking with his superior, the official finally caved in. When the ship landed at the spaceport, it was quickly surrounded by spaceport security personnel and vehicles. Handler ordered the large access ramp lowered to the ground. His people were waiting at the top of the ramp and led the security people to the holding room, where the pirates were promptly arrested and escorted out of the ship. With the ship powered down, he left the bridge and went outside.

He looked up at the hull of the *Valley Forge* and saw where some of the kinetic penetrators had gouged out scars in the collapsium armor from glancing hits. As his own people started coming out of the ship, except for the skeleton watch on the bridge, the head of spaceport security pulled up in a ground car and got out.

"Commander Handler?" he asked.

He identified himself with a hand gesture.

"Our Justice people will want to get statements from you and your people to be used as evidence against the pirates at their trials. I've arranged for accommodations for all of you unless you would prefer to stay aboard ship?"

He smiled. "I think I can speak for my people when I say that it would be nice to breathe some fresh air and see some open sky for a change, so we'll take you up on that offer. Some of my people will stay aboard the ship, but they'll be rotated out on liberty to give them a chance to relax as well. Do the accommodations you've arranged include some place where a person can get a stiff drink?"

The security chief laughed. "I know just the place!"

II

The *Valley Forge* and her new crew ended up spending almost a full week in Valhalla. Commander Handler allowed the Federation authorities on Asgard to send experts on board for short visits to confirm that the ship really was a Navy cruiser. In addition, the Terran Naval attaché determined that the ship's computer logs verified the pirate captain's belligerent messages, revealed data on the disappearance of *Pathfinder*—although no data was discovered about *Trailblazer*—and finally noted the location where both the *Valley Forge* and *Pathfinder* had jumped to after their capture.

That turned out to be a star system containing a large asteroid mining colony owned by a subsidiary of Terra-Baldur-Marduk Spacelines' parent company, Panstellar Industries. With no habitable planets in the Griffin Star System, the mining colony appeared to be involved with the pirate operation. This was corroborated when the prisoners were interrogated and revealed that they had been hired by individuals who had then sent them to a research facility owned by another subsidiary of Panstellar, which was located on the asteroid Ceres in the Sol System.

It turned out that Ceres was where the *Pathfinder* had been hidden along with another former Space Navy cruiser, the *Kursk*. Both cruisers had been decommissioned due to budget cuts and were then *lent* to the research subsidiary for purposes of testing advanced sensing and navigation equipment. The news of a second pirate cruiser was a shock, but it explained why the *Valley Forge* crew knew nothing about the disappearance of *Trailblazer*.

Handler asked the security chief if the pirates had revealed how the company behind the operation was able to obtain anti-ship missiles.

The security chief chuckled. "Who do you think makes them for the Navy in the first place?"

When the judicial proceedings no longer needed Commander Handler and his people, they got ready to head home with the damaged but still usable ship. Valhalla offered its shipyard services to help repair her, but Handler didn't want to stay any longer than he had to. He asked for and got copies of all recorded interrogations. He was sure company executives back on Poictesme would find them *most* interesting. Before lifting off, he also got permission from Valhalla authorities to return with two corvettes that could be stationed at the spaceport to escort other freighters out beyond the no-jump threshold.

Dragon Hunter and *Amazon Warrior* couldn't be left behind because their crews were needed to fly the navy cruiser back to Poictesme. The trip back was thankfully uneventful.

When *Valley Forge* emerged back into normal space in the Gartner Tri-System, it sent a signal to Poictesme. By the time it landed at the Barathrum Spaceport there was quite a crowd waiting for it. *Ouroboros II* had brought word of the battle outcome so that wasn't a surprise. The senior company executives and major shareholders, which he had overheard someone refer to as M-12, were quite surprised to hear the details behind the pirate venture.

When the briefing was over, Security Chief Tom Brangwyn escorted Tor outside the conference room and slapped him on the shoulder.

"Great Ghu, Commander Handler! That was a *fine* piece of work. Not only did you win the battle, but you brought back the pirate ship to boot. You and your people will be getting a hefty bonus as the company's way of showing its appreciation. In addition, I've been authorized to tell you that if the company gets any compensation from the Navy over the eventual return of the ship, ten percent of whatever the Navy pays will be divided up among yourself and the corvette crews.

"After you write up your report, we want you to take a couple of weeks off before reporting back."

He promised to have the report ready the next day. Then they shook hands and Tom went back into the conference room.

III

Once Senior Commander Handler had finished his briefing and left the room, the rest of the M-12 Group started chatting among themselves. Conn Maxwell felt a hand on his shoulder and turned to look at his wife, Sylvie. There was deep concern in her eyes. She leaned over to him and said in a low voice.

"What's the matter, Conn? You look like you've just killed your best friend."

Conn sighed. "In a manner of speaking that's true. I feel as though we've killed our son's future."

"How do you figure that?"

"For weeks now I've been trying to figure out why the Federation's decline was shifting from Merlin's slow, non-violent projection to the worst case, violent collapse scenario. The acts of piracy were the key catalyst that caused the shift, but I couldn't understand why piracy started so much sooner than Merlin predicted. How could Merlin have been so wrong? Now I know the answer: We caused it!" He almost shouted that last sentence and everyone around the table stopped talking and looked in his direction.

"We caused what, Conn?" his father asked.

Conn held up his left hand and ticked off his points on each finger in turn. "The Federation has jumped the slow-decline tracks and is heading for a cliff that will result in interstellar wars in less than a hundred years. The change in course is a direct result of the fact that piracy has started almost fifty years sooner than predicted. The piracy was not caused by planetary governments concerned about collapsing economies. It was caused by the greed and vindictiveness of our main shipping competitor. Why did they act that way? Because we disturbed the natural order of things by pursuing the Maxwell/Merlin Plan.

"If we had just left things to develop normally, Terra-Baldur-Marduk

Spacelines and their sister companies would not have set up this pirate operation! We've just accomplished what General Foxx Travis and his people swore an oath to prevent."

There was dead silence in the room as the shock registered on the faces of everyone around the table. His father recovered his composure first and said, "Are you sure about that, Conn? Isn't it possible that you're overstating the importance of the piracy as the main cause of the faster, more violent decline?"

"I'm sure, because Merlin is sure. I've asked Merlin that very question half a dozen different ways and the answer is always the same. Without the early piracy, people and planets maintain their faith in the Federation until the point is reached where planets lose the capability of building fleets of warships. With the piracy, people will start to think that the Navy can't or won't protect them and that they need to protect themselves, which means building their own warships. Later on these vessels are used for more aggressive actions. It doesn't matter that the first act of piracy was commercial empire-building instead of political empire-building. The result is still the same."

Conn noticed that Planetary President Kurt Fawzi, whose obsessive hunt for Merlin had been the key to its discovery, took the news particularly well. He didn't appear to be the same old Merlin idolater of old. It was getting more and more difficult to pull him away from the capital for these board meetings.

Conn looked around the conference table at the others. Klem Zareff looked grim, while Judge Ledue looked puzzled. Conn was certain that most of this discussion was going over his head. Professor Dolf Kellton was nodding in agreement with Conn's train of logic. The two bankers, Lester Dawes and Jethro Sastraman, were a study in contrasts. Lester was clearly upset by the news. Jethro looked like he was trying to figure out how to exploit the news. When Conn looked at his wife, he saw that she now understood his anguish and shared it. Their three-year-old son, Foxx Maxwell, might very well live long enough to see the start of the interstellar wars that his father and grandfather had helped to bring about.

The implications of what they had done were so terrible that Conn had to get up and leave the room. Sylvie followed him and after a few seconds, so did his father. They found him leaning over a balcony overlooking company headquarters, peering down at the hum of activity in the spaceport. Sylvie put her arm around Conn's shoulders and hugged him.

When Rodney Maxwell came up to Conn on the other side, he said, "Conn, you said inside that it was the perception that the Navy couldn't or wouldn't protect people from pirates that starts the slide into war and collapse. What if a privately owned company worked to supplement the Navy's anti-piracy actions? If piracy can be kept under control and not allowed to become endemic, wouldn't that help to prevent the worst case scenario?"

Conn thought about that before answering. "Maybe. I really don't know. I'll ask Merlin the first chance I get. Dad, how would we get around the prohibition of having armed warships?"

His father shrugged and said, "Same way we did it now. Unarmed freighters carrying armed interplanetary ships that aren't hyper-jump capable."

Conn felt the heavy weight of guilt start to lift. "That might work," he said. "I'll get my assistants at Force Command to start formulating the question."

"Good. After you do that, how about coming back into the Board Room and letting everyone else know about this, okay?"

Conn nodded, saying, "Fine. You go on back inside; I'll be there in about five minutes."

Sylvie put her arm around his waist. "Don't fret. What's done is done. You and your father will work something out. Right?"

Conn nodded distractedly, while he used his datapad to work up some numbers. "I'm going to make a quick call to Force Command. I want to put my team to work on dad's idea."

Sylvie smiled and gave him a hug. "I know they're all depending upon you, Conn. And, I know it's not fair. But I knew the two of you would come up with something."

When Conn returned to the conference room, the rest of the members of M-12 were noticeably relieved to see him. As he and Sylvie took their seats, the others were trying to get Conn to guarantee that the anti-piracy plan would put the future of the Federation back on the least disruptive path of decline. Conn held his hands up and waited until everyone quieted down.

"Okay, I want to be very clear on the anti-piracy plan. First, I don't know if Merlin can answer the question of whether a concerted effort by us to smother the smoldering fires of piracy will make any difference at all. Second, even if Merlin can answer that question, we still may not like the answer. Third, let's say Merlin tells us that we can make a worthwhile difference. That doesn't necessarily mean that we can actually pull it off. To do it successfully might just be beyond our material, financial and manpower resources. So I caution all of you not to get your hopes up until we have answers to those three questions."

There were murmurs of agreement.

Kurt Fawzi stood up and asked for quiet. When everyone had quieted down, he said, "Thank you, Conn for explaining that to us. Naturally we're eager to hear what Merlin has to say and, hopefully, you'll be able to tell us that soon."

Conn nodded, saying, "I've already contacted Force Command and my assistants are already doing the preliminary work now."

"That's good to know," Fawzi replied. "In the meantime, I think we should continue with the agenda that we have before us. We still haven't decided what to do about our captured pirate ship and the other pirate ship that's still on the loose. Rod, you want to say something?"

Rodney Maxwell nodded as he stood up. "I've been giving a lot of thought in terms of what to do next ever since the *Ouroboros II* brought back the news that our ships won the battle. Here are the things that I believe we're legally or morally obligated to do: First, we need to contact the nearest Navy base and let them know everything, including the fact that we consider the *Valley Forge* ours by right of conquest. However, the Federation Space Navy can have her back if they make us a decent offer of compensation.

"Second, we still have two of our ships and their crews missing. From what Commander Handler told us, there's a good chance that our people who were on the *Pathfinder* and *Trailblazer* are still alive. So, we need to find them and secure their release as soon as possible."

There was a ragged cheer around the table over that.

"We should have word on that pretty damn quickly, or we'll light a fire under their collective rear-ends."

Now there was a real cheer.

"You tell 'em, Rod!" Old Klem shouted, while banging the table with the head of his sword cane. Stonewall leaped off his shoulder and onto the table, where the Fuzzy was jumping up and down and yeeking.

Rodney used a calming gesture to quiet the room. "However, there's still at least one other pirate cruiser out there. Our next two corvettes are just about ready and *Ouroboros II* can carry them while escorting our freighter *General Travis* on her regular run to Tiamat. Now, the *Valley Forge's* captain said, in his recorded interrogation, that *Pathfinder* was taken to the mining colony on Griffin, which is apparently being used as a supply base for their pirate operation.

"Our two missing ships and their crews might still be there. We owe it to them to go there and ask some tough questions. With *Ouroboros II* tied up protecting *General Travis*, and our next large hyperspace ship not due back for another four weeks, I suggest we use the *Valley Forge*. We can repair the damage she sustained during the two week leave that Handler and his people have earned. I propose that we also fill up her missile magazines, too, for good measure."

"Damn straight," Klem shouted.

There were nods of agreement from around the conference table.

He paused to collect his thoughts and then continued. "We also need to decide on a response to the fact that Terra-Baldur-Marduk Spacelines, or companies affiliated with that company, have essentially declared economic war on us. You heard the testimony of the pirates. That ship was handed over to the pirates at a facility that was owned and controlled by a Terra-Baldur-Marduk Spacelines' parent company. Now, as you know, our shipyard on Koshchei is almost finished building another medium-sized freighter.

"I propose that we cancel our plans to use her for another short-range trade run and instead send her on a special trip to Terra, with someone versed in the law, who will represent our company and who will seek either a court-ordered payment to compensate us for our losses or perhaps reach some kind of settlement with the Panstellar Industries group of companies."

He turned to look at J. Fitzwilliam Sterber. "John, how would you like to visit Terra on a trip paid for by the company?"

"I don't think my wife would let me. Even if the ship takes a direct route with no intermediate stops, it's still four months each way plus the time required on Terra."

Rodney Maxwell interjected. "Okay, then. Take her along. The company will give both of you a generous spending allowance while you're there. Think of it as a very long second honeymoon."

Everyone including Sterber laughed.

"Well, if you put it that way, she may just go for it. I'll ask her."

The group voted approval of Rodney Maxwell's proposition and the meeting adjourned.

I

Conn Maxwell sat in his personal programming station, going over the latest output from Merlin. It was early evening and the rest of the programmers had left hours ago. Ever since the pirates had begun abducting their ships, he'd found himself spending more and more time working at the computer. The only time he could program the supercomputer in private was in the evening or late at night, away from his family. Sylvie understood the importance of his job, but little Foxx was feeling neglected.

To compensate for his graveyard shift, he'd started coming in to work on alternate days so that he could spend more time with Sylvie and his son, and to that end had temporarily taken Foxx out of nursery school. It was the six-hour journey back and forth to work every day that was the biggest problem. They had even refurbished one of the Force Command barracks and turned it into efficiency apartments for those staffers who were willing to stay there during the week. Many of them chose to do so, rather than suffer the long drive back and forth between Force Command and Litchfield.

Conn noticed that most of them who lived in them were single. A few young marrieds opted for the apartments, but Sylvie had her own work and put the kibosh on that arrangement. Besides, there were no children at the compound and Foxx would have been too lonely.

After working with the super-computer for half a decade, Conn had developed a feel for the way the machine *thought.* It only answered questions that were put to it; it interpreted those questions in the most literal way. If the question wasn't *phrased* just right, or if Conn asked the wrong question, then the output was not going to be useful or valid. In that way, it reminded him of talking with his son.

This time around, he had asked the machine if the Federation's decline could be slowed if the number of pirate attacks stayed below various levels. The answer was yes, if the number of attacks stayed at less than five per year, then their impact on the larger trend would diminish over time.

Next he asked the computer what the best way was to keep the number of pirate attacks down.

The answer was to station armed interplanetary ships, like the modified ammunition freighters used by Commander Handler, on dozens of key planets that were the most likely candidates for piracy. That seemed like a daunting project unless those worlds were willing to pay for protection, then it could turn out to be very lucrative. But Conn couldn't shake the feeling he had that he was not asking the right questions.

Something was missing. It was something important, and it was staring him right in the face, but he couldn't see it.

He decided that he needed to summarize what he knew by writing down the key points:

1. Terra-Baldur-Marduk Spacelines, and/or companies affiliated with it, reacted to increased competition resulting from the Maxwell/Merlin Plan by:

a) Filing a legal trade complaint with the Federation Office of Interstellar Trade.
b) Setting up a highly illegal covert pirate operation apparently aimed solely at Poictesme's shipping company, Tri-System & Interstellar Spacelines.

2. Someone, almost certainly acting on behalf of Terra-Baldur-Marduk Spacelines or their parent company had attempted to exploit the fallout from the trade complaint action in order to gain control of the holding company that controlled the Maxwell/Merlin Plan. That suggested a long-term strategy due to the distances involved between Terra and Poictesme.

3. The economic viability of Poictesme's shipping company was being gradually impacted by the loss of ships, crews and cargos to piracy.

4. As a result of this blowback, a series of dominoes was starting to fall that would eventually lead to the complete breakdown of Federation authority and then to interstellar war.

5. Interrupting the fall of the dominoes by keeping piracy at low levels of intensity, would cause the decline in the Civilization Index to level out until it merged with the original, non-violent projection.

Conn looked at his list, particularly points one and two. He couldn't understand why the decision makers behind the trade complaint would also later on decide to take the very risky step of engaging in the illegal action of piracy, which had to have been expensive to set up and had only a limited impact compared to the much more effective trade complaint. Why bother?

Then Conn remembered one of the things he had learned during his six years of study at the University of Montevideo. If your conclusions don't make sense, then maybe your assumptions are wrong. Okay, so which of his assumptions needed to be changed?

His first assumption was that the individuals who decided to initiate the trade complaint were also the same people who decided to initiate the pirate operation. What if they were two different groups? What if the pirate operation was the brainchild of a rogue group within Panstellar that had its own agenda independent of the trade complaint?

That was starting to make some kind of sense, but, on the other hand, the impact on Tri-System Interstellar Spacelines was only significant if a lot of ships were captured. He sat back and took a deep breath. *Is that the assumption that needs to be changed? If so, let's turn that assumption on its ear.*

If the impact of a few ships being captured was significant, just what is it supposed to be affecting? The only thing Conn could come up with was the impact on the Civilization Index which represented a slide down the slippery slope of decivilization and eventual collapse. The only way someone would know about that was if they knew about Merlin's projection about the coming end of the Federation, which would be kick-started by space piracy. Conn was as certain as he could be that *that* particular secret was secure.

But wasn't that just another assumption. If that assumption wasn't true, then one of two alternatives had to have happened. Either one of the M-12 Group had intentionally, or accidentally, let the secret out. Which was a possibility since Morgan Gatworth had provided the enemy with intelligence; however, Conn had a hard time believing that was the goal of the enemy agents who were trying to buy up company stock. From what Klem had been able to learn before he killed the intruder, it appeared that the focus of their efforts was gaining control over Tri-System Investments, Ltd., their holding company.

That assumption also appeared highly unlikely since said person or persons would personally suffer both financially and otherwise from such a move. While Gatworth had been willing to help scuttle the holding company, he would have wanted some compensation. And he was too smart a cookie to cut his own throat.

Or someone else got the information from Merlin. However, since access to Merlin was physically limited to a very small group of people who were monitored all the time, the second assumption was also highly unlikely.

Conn sighed.

Okay, he thought, *let's take this train of thought to its ultimate end. If none of the M-12 group let the secret slip and no one got the secret from Merlin directly, then what other possible explanation could there be?*

After racking his brains, he was left with only one other possible alternative. There had to be another Merlin somewhere out there and someone was using it to push the Federation into a chaotic collapse for their own nefarious reasons. The explanation was so bizarre, so ludicrous that Conn was tempted to dismiss it out of hand, but his intuition told him that he was on to something.

It was now 0200 hours and everyone but the caretakers had left the office long ago. Conn called Sylvie and told her he'd be late. "Later than usual, that is."

"I'm not surprised," she said on the viewscreen. "You're like a dog worrying a bone over this piracy thing. Maybe a good night's sleep is all you need."

He shook his head. "I wish it was that simple. I've got an idea, but I have to work it out in private, just me and Merlin."

"Why, darling?"

"If I'm right, the answer is too explosive to be shared with the staff."

Sylvie shivered. "Be careful, Conn. Remember, it's not your job to save the Federation. On Terra there are a half a million employees who are paid to do that job."

He laughed. "God help us, if we have to depend on *them*."

II

Conn had a quick snack at the almost deserted commissary, then he returned to the main programming port. Using machine language, he asked Merlin: "How likely is it that another Merlin-type computer is being used to divert the Federation's decline from its original path?"

Merlin did its usual light blinking and machine spinning. Six hours later he had an answer: *The probability of another Merlin binary being used to speed up the Collapse is eighty-nine percent.*

Conn was stunned. Someone, somewhere, had built another Merlin!

That was a mystery all by itself. Merlin was made of special computer components that had been custom-designed and made in a purpose-built facility, like the one the Federation military had constructed on Panurge, an airless planet at the fringes of the Gartner Tri-System. If someone had restarted that factory and manufactured the parts for a second Merlin, then maybe there would be records of where those parts had been sent. If the M-12 Group knew where the second Big Brain was, there might be a way to disable or destroy it.

A Merlin binary in the wrong hands could easily lead to complete disaster. The fact that someone else could potentially release news of the Federation's inevitable decline was too horrible a risk to ignore. Keeping the news of the Federation's decline from triggering the worst-case scenario was the whole reason why the M-12 group had been formed in the first place. All their hopes and plans for the future would be gone if knowledge of the coming decline were to spread throughout the Federation.

By this time, it was past midnight. Conn destroyed all records of his activities and made preparations to go to bed. In the morning, he would have more questions for Merlin; but he was already thinking in different terms. *We can't outthink the other Merlin ourselves. We have to use* our *Merlin to outthink theirs. Like a grand game of chess, move and countermove.*

Their opponents had the advantage of knowing where the original Merlin was located, although they had no way to contact it. The planet would have to be invested to gain control over Force Command. However, Conn did have one key advantage: the opposition side didn't know that the existence of the Merlin binary had been uncovered. M-12 would have the element of surprise. Now, they had to figure out how to make the best use of that precious commodity.

Conn decided to call his father on the viewscreen.

His father swore a blue streak as he pulled himself out of bed, and he could hear his mother complaining in the distance.

"Sorry to wake you, Dad. But this is *really* important."

His father started to reply, then his mother started in on one of her tirades, and he switched off the small bedside screen.

Conn imagined his father slinking out of the bedroom to his office viewscreen. A few moments later his father's face appeared back on-screen.

"Dad, can we find out if that computer manufacturing plant on Panurge has been used since it was claimed eleven years ago?"

His father was still brushing the sleep out of his eyes. "Sure. I suppose I can have Barton-Massarra make some inquiries. Is it important?"

Conn nodded. "I wouldn't wake you up this late, otherwise. I'm going to stay here at Force Command for a few more days. I'll fill you in on all the details when you can arrange to get away and visit me here." He wasn't about to discuss his fears over the comm line—secure or not. "Can you also have them check into the arrival and system departure times of all ships belonging to Terran-Baldur-Marduk Spacelines?"

"I'll try to have an answer for you in a few days. That'll take some research."

After his father signed-off, Conn left for the small compartment that he used when he spent the night. *I've been doing that a lot lately*, he mused. If he knew his father, he was already back in bed and asleep. His father was the lucky one. If he knew the twisted trail of thought that was snaking its way through Conn's mind, his father wouldn't be able to sleep a wink, either.

I

Three days later, Rodney Maxwell took the unusual step of flying down to Force Command Duplicate to bring Conn the results of the investigation in person rather than pass it on by a viewscreen call. As Rodney settled down in one of the comfortable chairs in Foxx Travis' old office, he pulled out a printed report and handed it over to Conn. It was the results of his search regarding the computer plant on Panurge and a list of all Terra-Baldur-Marduk Spacelines' comings and goings for the past six years.

Conn was disappointed to find that as far as anyone knew, the factory on Panurge had never been reactivated. The salvage claim on it had expired two years ago due to inactivity. As far as the schedule of arrivals and departures of the Terran-Baldur-Marduk Spacelines, there was nothing that stood out as unusual or suspicious other than the fact that one of their ships, the *City of Amenhetep*, had stopped coming to Poictesme about two GS years ago.

Conn remembered that at the time that ship had made its last trip here, its captain had let it be known that due to the increased competition from Tri-System & Interstellar Spacelines there wasn't enough cargo to make further trips profitable.

Conn leaned back in his chair and puffed on the cigar that his father had brought.

Rodney Maxwell blew out a lungful of smoke, asking, "Well…what's the bad news that you didn't want to tell me over the phone?"

Conn took a deep breath and said, "The reason why I asked if the computer factory on Panurge had been reactivated, is that Merlin is eighty-nine percent certain that someone has built another super-computer somewhere other than Poictesme and is using it to figure out how to accelerate the collapse of the Federation."

It took Conn's father almost a whole minute to finish cursing. When he finally calmed down, he said, "If Merlin is that certain, then we can assume it's a fact. But for the life of me, I can't see why anyone would want the Federation to go through such an ordeal." He shook his head. "We're talking about millions of people dying, maybe billions, and the complete collapse of civilization. That seems like an insane thing to do!"

"I thought so too at first," Conn agreed, "but then I thought about it carefully on the way home and decided there may be a more rational motivation. We know that Terra-Baldur-Marduk Spacelines itself, and/or companies affiliated with it, are involved in the pirate operation as well as the tariff/takeover gambit. Let's say that someone in a position of authority in that corporate group, maybe even the guy at the top, has learned that we've been using Merlin to boost Poictesme's economy."

"So they want one of their own to compete with us?" his father asked.

"Not exactly. Think about it, we've never tried to hide Merlin's existence. So let's suppose that this person, or persons, decides that having their own Merlin would be a good thing for the company and would enable them to counteract our shipping advantage. Let's also assume that somehow, they get their hands on another Merlin-type super-computer. How I don't know.

"We know that the plant on Panurge hasn't been reactivated, so then where would they get the parts from? The only other possibility I can think of is that during the war, Foxx Travis or Federation High Command had two super-computers manufactured. Merlin I being assembled here at Force Command Duplicate, while the unassembled components for Merlin II were kept in storage somewhere else as a backup in case the System States Alliance managed to bomb this Merlin out of existence."

His father leaned back in his chair, crossing his arms. "That makes sense, Conn. So, if this person discovered the location of the second Merlin's parts, knowing about our own success with Merlin I, he would have had them assembled hoping for similar results. It's possible that when he asked Merlin II how to cope with what we were doing, it told him about the best and worst case scenarios for the Federation as a whole."

Conn leaned forward and said softly, "That's exactly the conclusion I reached the other night. Now, father, put yourself in the position of the president of Terra-Baldur-Marduk Spacelines' parent company, Panstellar Industries: You're personally responsible for trillions of sols worth of shareholder investment and over hundreds of thousands of employees. Then you learn that in the future the best your company can hope for is to slowly wither on the vine in an ever deepening economic slump. How would you react to that news?"

His father thought about that for a while. Finally he said, "I think I'd be tempted to take advantage of the decline in order to grab whatever profits or assets I could before things went to Nifflheim in a basket!"

Conn nodded. "In other words, that's exactly the same kind of 'beggar thy neighbor strategy' that we were worried would be taken by planetary governments once they knew the collapse was coming. As soon as it's common knowledge that central authority is on the decline, then illegal activities like piracy suddenly look a lot more tempting. General Shanlee warned us of something like this when he said that Merlin couldn't predict what you or I would do, but could only predict the behavior of the masses. Whoever is the brain behind this piracy, he's beginning to look like that unpredictable exception that Merlin couldn't pin down."

Rodney Maxwell put his face in his hands and said, "Great Ghu! You're telling me that there's a totally immoral egomaniac on the loose with his own private Merlin to advise him how to destroy civilization. And there's not a damn thing we can do to stop it because we don't even know who or where he is."

He looked up at Conn. "We need to let M-12 in on what's going on and then figure out how to neutralize this threat."

Conn didn't say anything, but put out his cigar in the ashtray.

His father asked him point-blank: "Son, I get the suspicion that you don't think we should tell the rest of the M-12 Group about this. Why not?"

When Conn finally answered, he spoke slowly. "I agree that our ultimate objective has to be neutralizing this new peril. Merlin II not only threatens our own economic miracle, but the whole of civilization. But telling the M-12 Group? I'm not convinced that's the wisest course to take, and here's why: M-12 is essentially a committee. You and I know that committees in general are notorious for taking forever to make decisions.

"If we try to play this chess game against one individual—who may not need to consult with anyone—then we'll be at a big disadvantage. Take the reaction to the news about the tariff as an example. M-12 reacted immediately with what seemed to be a good strategy.

"But if we had known that our opponent had his own Merlin advising him, we might have wanted to consult our own Merlin to see what the other side's counter-response would likely be. It's entirely possible that we did exactly what the other Merlin predicted we would do, which, if true, means we did the wrong thing because our opponent will have already taken action to counteract it."

His father let his half-smoked cigar drop into an ashtray, then cradled his head as if he had the mother of all headaches coming on.

"I referred to this as a chess game." Conn continued, "because that's how I believe we need to think of it. We have to get our Merlin to outthink their Merlin. That may involve actions that may not be popular with some of the members of M-12. Suppose the majority of M-12 refuses to go along with Merlin's moves? Tell me what alternatives we have then?

Rodney shrugged. "We're up a creek."

"Exactly," Conn replied. "I've given this a lot of thought. Suppose you and I take a step back from M-12 and think of it as a tool or weapon in *our* chess game against this egomaniac?"

"I don't know about that," his father said. "You, me and our friends, we're all involved in this up to our eyebrows!"

"Dad, we have to keep this knowledge about the Merlin binary to ourselves. At least, for now. We need to figure out our best strategy using Merlin, and that includes figuring out what to tell M-12 to get them to do what Merlin thinks we should do."

"In other words, lie to them?"

"Maybe. We did it at the beginning, remember? If we had told them the whole truth back then, we probably never would have found Merlin, nor would they have supported the Maxwell Plan. There's one more reason for keeping this to ourselves. If the other side continues to believe that we don't know about the other Merlin, they might become overconfident and therefore more prone to making errors."

"I hope so," his father said.

"We've already gotten to the point where M-12 is juggling more secrets than is healthy. We've already had one serious leak. Some of them, like Klem, mean well, but are hotheads. People who lose their temper easily can be manipulated and used."

"I agree," his father said. "The more people we tell about the second Merlin, the more likely it is that word will eventually trickle back to the other side. They've already successfully infiltrated our inner circle, once. I'm sure they'll try again with spies or paid informers. Even with the distance involved in sending information back and forth, it could pay tremendous dividends. We already know with virtual certainty that the other side has been sending people and money to Poictesme in an attempt to engineer a corporate takeover of our holding company."

"Good," Conn said, letting out a cloud of smoke. "I'm glad we agree. If we view M-12 as already compromised, we can use that to our advantage.

Once the programming staff leaves tonight, I have a whole list of questions to ask Merlin. One of them is asking for an estimate of the probability that one or more members of M-12 is secretly working for the opposition and"—he held up his hand to prevent his father from interrupting—"what false information we could give to M-12 with the idea that it would eventually find its way back to the opposition and cause them to make a strategic blunder that we could use to our advantage."

"I can see the advantages of that strategy. Although I never was as good at chess as you are, son, I do see your point. Okay, then. For now we keep this information to ourselves. Who else knows?"

"No one. I've kept my assistants and programmers here at Command Force Duplicate in the dark. I haven't told Sylvie anything yet, but, as you know, she's an intelligent woman and I wouldn't be surprised if she figures it out for herself. Besides yourself, she's the only one who knows about the hyperdrive improvements that her father's team developed."

"Have you questioned Merlin about the impact of cutting hyperdrive travel times in half?

Conn shook his head. "There have been too many other damn variables popping up lately. By the time Merlin finished the Year End Projections, we were faced with the Gatworth Leak and their ramifications. Then we were working on our anti-piracy strategy. Now, we've got this hot potato to deal with."

His father held up his hands, palms facing outward. "I hear you, son. I was just wondering what the machine had to say about all this."

"Sylvie came up with the best idea. She believes we should share hyperspace drive improvements with the Federation Navy people. Let them deal with it; that way everyone will have the same advantage."

"Damn, just on principle, I hate to give something like that away to our competition. But, I'm sure Merlin will agree. By Ghu, if a little bit of piracy can send the Civ Index tumbling, our using the travel time advantage for ourselves could knock it head over heels."

"Exactly," Conn said.

"Well, it sounds like your wife's already part of our inner circle. How about you tell her that you've invited me for dinner tomorrow tonight. We can brief her on the Merlin Binary then."

Later the next evening at their home, Conn and his father told Sylvie the news. She was quite shocked, but understood why they wouldn't risk entrusting that knowledge to M-12. It was too clumsy and vulnerable a decision making body to trust with this latest development. She promised to keep their secret.

SIXTEEN

I

Over the next several weeks, as the *Valley Forge* was repaired and sent out with a larger crew for the trip to Griffin, Conn worked long hours each day trying to ask the right questions of Merlin and come up with a strategy that would put them ahead of the game, instead of playing catch up. He tried to imagine that he was the President of Terra-Baldur-Marduk Spacelines' parent company, Panstellar Industries, and wanted to exploit the collapse of the Federation for short term financial gains. So what would be the best way to go about that?

When Merlin provided the answer, it was chilling: Engage in pirate activity. Use the proceeds from captured ships to secretly finance the establishment of a shipbuilding facility that could also manufacture conventional and nuclear weapons. Offer to sell warships to planets as a defense against further piracy. Bribe the Navy to look the other way as more pirate attacks were arranged. Establish a "pirate-free zone" where planets would pay for anti-pirate defenses and are dominated economically through Terra-Baldur-Marduk Spacelines' monopoly on shipping.

When Federation authority collapsed, their shipyards could build whatever kinds of armed ships it wanted and sell them to any planet that could pay for them.

Next, Conn asked Merlin to list the locations where a remote shipbuilding facility could be built or established, Koshchei was top of the list. It was the only planet that had all of the necessary shipbuilding facilities and infrastructure already built in. Plus, it was located at a star system that didn't have a Federation Naval base that could keep an eye on whatever activities went on there.

Koshchei was the "King chess piece" that Panstellar had to capture.

The obvious next question was how? Merlin's answer was that Panstellar should undermine the economic basis for Poictesme's prosperity by arranging for punitive tariffs, then offer to remove the tariffs plus other additional incentives as a way of acquiring control of Koshchei Exploration & Development.

Conn was impressed with the cunning of that strategy. For purposes of boosting Poictesme's economy, their shipping company had already acquired just about as many ships of various sizes as they were likely to need for a long time. The shipbuilding and industrial facilities on Koshchei had pretty much served their purpose and, while nice to have, they weren't necessary for the long-term economic prosperity of Poictesme.

Regaining access to markets on Terra, plus regaining ownership and control of the local and interstellar shipping companies that the M-12 Group had rushed to allow Panstellar's agents to gain control of, or at least a major stake in, would make the members of M-12 very wealthy. Therefore, it would be very hard for them to say no to this offer.

As it turned out, Conn realized he was right in thinking that M-12's corporate maneuvering was in fact a strategic error, but that was water under the bridge.

Conn then asked Merlin what the biggest threat to that plan would be and what would be the best way to eliminate that threat. The answer was the industrial and military assets owned by the Poictesme companies behind the Maxwell/Merlin Plan, i.e., the M-12 Group. The best way to eliminate M-12 would be a sneak attack on Force Command Duplicate! At a single stroke, Panstellar would eliminate Merlin and cripple the opposing side's ability to anticipate and outthink the other super-computer.

Force Command Duplicate was remote enough that civilian casualties, outside the facility, would be virtually nil and therefore there would be no *witnesses* to the actual event. Anyone ruthless enough to use violent force in that manner wouldn't hesitate to arrange for the disappearance of the individuals who actually carried out the attack at a later date.

Conn, for the first time, began to realize he was fishing in not only deep, but dangerous waters, as well. If this cabal was willing to murder everyone in Force Command Duplicate, just how far would they go to achieve their goals? It might be harder to cover up, but it wouldn't be that difficult to kill everyone in the M-12 Group, especially since most of them lived and worked in Litchfield.

I'm going to have to get the Home Guard and Planetary Armed Forces involved, Conn decided. *I'll call President Fawzi and Chief Tom Brangwyn tomorrow. But first, I'll need a cover story. That's easy: Merlin warned me of a possible attack on M-12. Everyone believes Merlin's infallible so that should suffice.*

The next step was to ask Merlin what the opposing side's best countermoves might be if they were unable to dispatch M-12. Merlin's answer was: "threaten retaliation against the Koshchei facilities." In other words, a Mexican standoff. He asked more questions about possible moves and countermoves. The end result was an arms race where both sides had fleets of armed ships figuratively glaring at each other across the breadth of the Gartner Tri-System.

One final question: How to break the deadlock? Answer: Hire the best military genius that money can buy and win a decisive victory.

II

When Conn briefed his father several days later, Rodney Maxwell turned pale, then shook his head, saying, "Great Satan, son! If we didn't have Merlin to keep track of all these moves and countermoves, we'd be hopelessly outmatched."

Conn nodded. "That's why Merlin is the King chess piece in this game, and the one piece that *we* must protect while we try to neutralize the other side's king. I've come up with a list of things that we need to start doing now.

"First, when the offer for Koshchei Exploration & Development comes, we'll try to get the M-12 Group to turn it down. However, if we can't prevent that, then it's important financially that all twelve members vote to accept the deal, so that everyone gets their share of the purchase price.

"It does you and me no good if we refuse the offer and Wade Lucas and the others, who aren't as dedicated to the cause as we are, get most of the money. You know Wade will see that windfall as an opportunity to bring cheap healthcare to Litchfield. We'll need our share of that money to have any chance of fighting back."

His father agreed.

"Second," Conn continued, "we quietly transfer all nuclear weapons that are now on Koshchei to the Barathrum Spaceport so that they're under our control and we then dismantle some of the key equipment that's needed to make more nuclear warheads. This will take Panstellar Industries time to fix.

"Third, we—again quietly—move all of the finished interplanetary ships that are still stored on Koshchei to Poictesme. The reason for this is that without Koshchei's steel mills supplying steel, our spaceport won't be able to build anything. If we're really desperate for steel, we can scrap those ships to get it and at the same time we're denying the use of those ships to the enemy. One of our holding companies can buy them for a nominal one sol from Koshchei Exploration & Development *before* we accept Panstellar's offer, of course.

"Fourth, we get our Planetary President and the legislature to approve the establishment of a Poictesme Navy that can lease ships and crews from our companies. That will take some of the financial burden off of us. Our economy is good enough now that the Planetary Government is actually running a budget surplus so we may as well use it. It also means that if the standoff turns into a shooting war, it'll be between a corporate entity and a sovereign planet instead of two corporations shooting at each other.

"Fifth, we recruit as many ex-Navy personnel as we can so that our force will be more professionally trained than theirs.

"Sixth, we find out which Navy Officer is the best at combat tactics and we make him or her an offer they can't refuse. If money won't convince them to leave the service, then maybe we'll have to bring them into the inner inner-circle and hope that their sense of duty wins out. If Foxx Travis is still alive, maybe he'll help us in that regard if we can contact him.

"Seventh, we hire private investigators on Terra to snoop around and try to identify the mastermind behind this and the location of the other Merlin. Once we have that information, our Merlin can calculate how best to respond. If our Merlin is vital to our cause, then it stands to reason that the Merlin binary is vital to their plan."

Conn stopped and sat back to allow his father to absorb all that information.

After a short time Rodney Maxwell said, "That's all very well thought out, Conn. But how are we going to afford to build the kind of massive military force that you're talking about? Panstellar's financial resources are about thousand times larger than ours."

Conn nodded. "That's true, but irrelevant. Panstellar is publicly owned. If we assume that the president of the company is the mastermind, he still has to be careful about committing too many of the company's resources to this undertaking, or else the shareholders will become upset with him. Once we reestablish profitable trade with Terra—the revenue that brings in, plus what we're taking in from the local trade routes we've developed—will provide enough income to cover our operating costs.

"If the Poictesme Planetary Government leases the ships and crews from us that will help our balance sheet, too. The spaceport in the Barathrum volcano has all the equipment we need to build our own combat ships as well as additional hyperspace freighters if we decide they're necessary. It will take Panstellar at least two years to even begin to build armed ships on Koshchei. We already have a nucleus of an armed force with our converted ammo freighters and we can build more over the next two years.

"The biggest problem I foresee is that our Barathrum Spaceport has far less capacity for shipbuilding than the yards on Koshchei. We have to engineer and win a decisive confrontation before their greater shipbuilding capacity overwhelms us by sheer weight of numbers."

"But if our ships arc patrolling the Gartner Tri-System, how will we deal with the threat of increased piracy?" his father asked.

"Well...if we can put enough pressure on their forces here in Koshchei, they may not be able to divert any ships to conduct piracy."

His father sighed. "Son, that's a big *if*."

Conn agreed. "We'll have to start arming more ships, too. That way if the piracy continues we'll have the ability to strike back. If it gets too bad, we may have to hit Terra-Baldur-Marduk Spacelines directly."

"You mean, we create our own pirates to prey on their shipping?"

"No, these will be privateers engaged in lawful retaliation. They will be fully authorized by the Planetary Government of Poictesme to reply in kind to any so-called-pirate attacks on our shipping fleet."

"That's something to consider very carefully, Conn. I don't know that we have enough hard evidence to convince a Federation court that the Terra-Baldur-Marduk Spacelines is behind the piracy attacks. The last thing we want to do is start an actual interstellar war, unless we absolutely have no choice. And, most importantly, whatever we do: we need to keep the Federation Space Navy out of it."

"If the Federation Navy won't protect its Member Worlds," Conn replied, "then maybe it's time they protected themselves."

"That's awfully close to a declaration of secession, Conn. We're going to have to be careful how we present this to the Federation authorities if our fight with Panstellar comes to actual blows."

"I know," Conn said. "The alternative is to see all our work and efforts go down the drain, and in a few decades—the Federation with it."

"I get what you're saying. I just pray it doesn't come to that. Meanwhile, I'll get started with the transfers of the nuclear weapons and the inactive interplanetary ships. Where we'll put them all, I don't know but we'll figure something out."

I

The next morning, right after breakfast, Conn screened President Fawzi and told his executive assistant that he needed to talk with the President immediately. It took almost ten minutes of waiting before Fawzi came on-screen.

"What's going on, Conn?" President Fawzi asked. Fawzi actually looked almost a decade younger these days; Conn wondered if he'd undergone some cosmetic surgery. "I've got a busy schedule laid out for today."

"I got some *very* interesting news from Merlin yesterday. It's not something I can talk about over the screen."

Fawzi nodded. "Understood. I can squeeze a meeting with you at 1400 hours this afternoon."

"Good," Conn said. "Make sure that Tom Brangwyn is there, too."

"Really? This must be important."

"It is, trust me. It is."

Conn rode his aircar to Storisende and arrived at the Presidential Office right on time. Security Chief Tom Brangwyn was seated in the anteroom and stood up when Conn entered.

"Hi, Conn. Do you know what this special meeting's all about?"

He nodded. "Did you bring your sensor wand with you?"

"Of course," Tom said. "You want me to check the President's office?"

"Yes, and from now on we need to make sure every place the members of M-12 meet is clean."

"Okay, I know just the guys to do it."

"Good."

A few minutes later they were ushered into President Fawzi's office. It was completely unlike Fawzi's former office in Litchfield, a place of quiet dignity with minimal lighting and an overall feeling of gentile civility. The Presidential office had a Tri-D picture of Fawzi that covered most of one puce-colored wall; the rest was filled with trendy, postmodern—a Terran style of the previous decade—furnishings, with odd geometrically-shaped couches and chairs and arty pseudogravity modules hanging in the air.

Tom made a quick sweep of the room, only pausing when he heard a distinct and angry buzz when he ran his wand over the edge of Fawzi's desk.

"What's that noise?" Fawzi sputtered.

"It's a bug," Tom said. He got down on his knees and looked under the desk table edge. He nodded, as if verifying his own thoughts. Next he removed a penknife from his pocket and pried something small off the underside of the desk.

After putting it on the parquet floor and squishing it with his heel, Tom said, "A tell-tale transmitter."

"I can't believe it," Kurt Fawzi said, shaking his head. "I wonder how long it's been there."

"Too long," Conn said. "We're going to have to be more careful from now on."

Both men nodded in agreement.

"Is this what you called us together for?" Fawzi asked.

"Partially. I'm going to give you some news that I don't want you to share with anyone."

Tom Brangwyn drew back. "What about M-12?"

"Not even them. They're already keeping too many secrets as it is."

"Okay," Fawzi said, "Out with it."

"First, according to Merlin, there's an eighty-nine percent probability that the opposition has a Merlin binary."

Fawzi's jaw dropped open, while Brangwyn's face blanched.

"Another Big Brain?" Tom asked.

"Yes, and this means nothing but trouble. We're not only going to have to keep one step ahead of Merlin II, but outwit it as well."

"What does that mean to the Merlin/Maxwell Plan?" Fawzi questioned.

Conn held his hands out. "It means that if we don't stop this power grab, there will be no plan and, if I read it right, no Poictesme."

"It can't be that bad," Fawzi said, shaking his head in wonderment. "Maybe we can come to an accommodation."

"If I read this correctly, someone like the president or the chairman of the board of Panstellar Industries, Inc. is behind all of this. I doubt that the shareholders have any idea of what's going on. Just a few of this rogue executive's agents."

Brangwyn frowned. "Why don't we find out who he is, then terminate him? That would solve the whole problem."

"No, no," Conn said, shaking his head. "The cat's out of the bag. We'd not only have to kill the man in charge, but his primary agents. How would we know who or where they are? Also, we'd have to take out the super-computer doppelganger and we don't have a clue as to where it is or even on which planet it's hidden. It could be anywhere."

"Then we're doomed," Fawzi said, his face sagging, suddenly showing all its worry lines.

"No, we've still got a few cards to play. First, our most important job is to protect the members of M-12." Conn went on to tell them how Merlin had speculated that their opponents might try to dispose of them all out at once or individually, like they'd tried with Klem Zareff.

"That's diabolical," Fawzi muttered. "Tom, you're already Chief of Interstellar Security, so I'll put you in charge of protecting the members of M-12. Some of them won't like it, but it has to be done."

Tom nodded, saying, "Klem is going to jump out of his tree!"

"I'll have Dad explain it to him," Conn said. "They've always gotten along well. Plus, Klem will derive a certain kind of joy out of learning that his paranoia—for once—is justified. None of us are going to be happy with this until this plot is stopped."

"I'll make sure the M-12 security team goes through a veridicator before I give them their assignments," Tom said. "Plus, I'll assign a squad to protect the president and make sure his office is swept daily."

"Good idea," Conn replied. "I don't think the enemy's had time to establish a strong intelligence network on Poictesme, but they probably have a few agents with more on the way." He pointed to the squished telltale on the floor. "There's evidence that we've been infiltrated, right there."

That was a fact no one could deny and both men nodded their accord.

"Now, for the big picture." Conn went on to explain what he and his dad had discussed about creating a planetary navy and protecting Merlin. It took him most of the afternoon to give them all the details and answer their questions.

"It looks like we don't have any choice, but to go on the offensive," President Fawzi concluded.

Chief Brangwyn said, "I agree. We've worked hard for what we've gotten and I mean to see that we keep it."

"It's going to cost like Gehenna, though, to build our own space navy. I can hear my constituents bellyaching already."

"Well, they'll bitch even more if the economy tanks again like it did after the Big War," Conn concluded.

On that they all agreed.

II

A week later, a lot of things happened at around the same time. The hypership *Genji* arrived and Rodney Maxwell went out to the ship to brief the crew about the tariff and how it was expected to affect the run to Terra. The next day *Ouroboros II* arrived back from their ferry trip to Zarathustra and forty-eight hours after that, the *General Travis* arrived back from Tiamat with news that no pirates were encountered. The two corvettes taken there by the larger ship, remained behind as per the plan which was progressing nicely.

Two more corvettes were ready to be loaded aboard *General Travis* and they would head out as soon as the medium hypership freighter *Vanguard* returned from its run to Agramma and was loaded for a return trip. The clincher was the return of *Valley Forge* from the Griffin asteroid.

The trip was even more successful than expected. Commander Handler briefed M-12 by radio as the ship was still coming in. By the time *Valley Forge* had arrived at the Griffin asteroid, the Navy was already there. When the pirates at the mining colony realized the jig was up, they surrendered and spilled their guts. Not only that, but the crews of *Pathfinder* and *Trailblazer* were still imprisoned there and were released from captivity. A bonus no one had expected. There were some anxious moments when *Valley Forge* arrived and Commander Handler had to prove that she wasn't still under pirate control, but eventually that was cleared up to the Navy's satisfaction.

The icing on the cake was that the other pirate ship, *Kursk*, arrived unaware the Griffin base was now in Navy hands. With two navy ships plus the *Valley Forge* threatening a deadly missile barrage, the *Kursk* surrendered, too. This time the Navy took possession of her directly. The senior Navy officer in charge had tried to get Commander Handler to allow the Navy to retake control of *Valley Forge* but Tor stood his ground and convinced the Senior Captain that Interstellar Security would be glad to hand her back as soon as the Navy recognized and dealt with Tri-System and Interstellar Spacelines' claim to her under the Federation's recognized laws of salvage.

The released crews were allowed to board *Valley Forge*, and the trip home was full of celebratory parties. Her arrival and touchdown on Poictesme was broadcast planetwide and President Kurt Fawzi announced a Day of Celebration in honor of the homecoming of the captured crews. News of the elimination of the pirate threat caused the stock market to spike. Even Conn Maxwell took a day off from working with Merlin to bask in reflected glory. Commander Handler also brought back word that the Navy had been able to determine where *Pathfinder* and *Trailblazer* were now, based on records and testimony from pirate personnel at the Griffin mining colony.

The two ships had been renamed and given new transponders, sent to new destinations that were capable of buying the cargo that they were carrying and then *sold* to Terra-Baldur-Marduk Spacelines for hefty sums of money that T-B-MS had arranged through bank loans. Where that money went to wasn't known, but since T-B-MS had been involved in the whole operation to begin with, its purchase of the two ships was also illegal and fraudulent.

Someone high up in Terra-Baldur-Marduk Spacelines' management would face criminal charges for the whole sordid mess. Handler was assured by the Navy people that a report of all their findings would be sent to Navy HQ on Terra with a request that it be shared with the legal representative from Poictesme, J. Fitzwilliam Sterber, Morgan Gatworth's replacement and new member of the M-12 Group.

III

Two days after *Valley Forge's* arrival, Conn, his father and Sylvie met over dinner at Senta's restaurant again. Senta herself, dressed in one of her patented outrageous red and purple floral dresses, greeted them at the door. The dress camouflaged her bulges and matched her larger than life personality.

"Things must be going well," she said, with a big smile. "I haven't seen this much of the Maxwells since Conn's return. Where's that cute little boy of yours?"

Sylvie took a few moments to narrate Foxx's latest escapades, one of which involved secretly adopting a neighbor's cat and naming him Stonewall. Everyone cooed over that.

"I think that horrible old man should give Foxx his Fuzzy instead of keeping him for himself," Senta said, her voice booming.

Knowing Senta's temper, Rodney quickly defused the situation. "Klem's a lonely old man. Stonewall Jackson's practically his only friend; it would be criminal to take him away."

She graciously conceded that might well be true and asked what they were having for dinner.

After giving Senta their dinner orders, Rodney took out his surveillance wand to make sure there weren't any nearby listening devices. Fortunately, he was unobserved by Senta who would have taken immediate umbrage at the fact that he dared to impugn her restaurant's security.

Once he was satisfied the area was clean, Rodney said, "Conn, as you know, the *Ouroboros II* is sitting idle at Storisende Spaceport. You and I talked about hiring private investigators on Terra to identify the mastermind and locate his Merlin, and also recruit ex-Navy personnel. And maybe even talk to Foxx Travis. It seems to me that the only way to make sure all of that gets done, the way we want it done, is to send someone to Terra who knows the big picture."

Conn was silent for a while, then nodded. "Sterber is already on his way to Terra, but he doesn't know anything about this latest development. I agree someone needs to go, and the choice of who should go is obvious. It has to be me."

Sylvie was stunned. "Why does it *always* have to be you?"

Conn looked at his father for support.

His father took out a cigar, and while removing it from its wrapper, said, "Think about it carefully, Sylvie. It has to be someone we can trust, someone who knows the whole score as well as someone who is familiar with what the other Merlin would look like, where it's likely to be and how to operate it if that opportunity should present itself. Also, Conn has already met General Foxx Travis, back when he was at the university on Terra. Having already met him, Travis is much more likely to see him again versus someone he's never met before.

"What it boils down to is it has to be one of us three. After all, we are the only ones on Poictesme who know about your father's hyperdrive advancements. One of us has to personally ferry that data to Navy Headquarters on Terra and make sure it doesn't fall into enemy hands. I can't go because of my corporate management responsibilities and you can't go because your son needs you here and it's too dangerous for you to take him with you. Conn is the only one of us who can go on this mission."

Sylvie said nothing, which was as close to agreeing as Conn figured she could manage.

The rest of the dinner was spent discussing what Conn needed to take with him, which of his assistants—he chose Myra Atherton—should be put in charge of Merlin and what his father and the rest of the M-12 Group needed to do while he was gone. He made sure his father had his proxies for all of the stock in the various companies that he owned.

The biggest problem they faced was deciding what cover story to tell the rest of M-12. They finally decided on a version of the truth. Conn was going to see Foxx Travis one more time, before he died, to get his advice on how to keep the Federation from collapsing into wars and revolts.

They hoped the members of M-12 would not question the wisdom of Conn being away for a good part of a year just to ask that question of a man who might be dead by the time Conn arrived. It would have to do. His father arranged for Conn to take along a sizable stack of Federation sols plus authorization to tap into the Terran bank accounts of Tri-System and Interstellar Spacelines, if need be, once he arrived on Terra.

The *Ouroboros II* would also be carrying its usual cargo of melon-brandy, Poictesme tobacco and some other products unique to the planet. The ship would unload their goods into bonded warehouses on Terra that would not attract the tariff as long as the cargo remained in the warehouses.

If at some point the tariff was removed, then the cargo could be sold profitably. If not, the brandy and tobacco would only get better with age.

When the day came for departure, there were tearful goodbyes from Sylvie, little Foxx, his sister and mother. Even his father's voice was filled with emotion. In some ways it was like going off to war. Naturally there were some others there to see him off as well. Klem Zareff, with Stonewall Jackson by his side, Tom Brangwyn, his brother-in-law Wade Lucas, Professor Dolf Kellton and Lester and Anse Dawes.

When the ship lifted off, Conn settled down for the second longest journey of his life. Not in terms of actual days, weeks and months, but on a subjective basis. The longest trip of his life would be the return trip.

I

Because the *Ouroboros II* was not making any intermediate stops, it emerged from hyperspace into the Sol System four Galactic Standard months later. For Conn it wasn't a moment too soon. He was sick of carniculture steaks and algae bread and soy cakes. It didn't help that the ship's recycled air was beginning to get ripe. The six hundred-and-fifty light year trip could have been cut in half with Jacquemont's hyperspace improvements which were looking better and better all the time. He was beginning to think that not putting them into production while he was gone might turn out to have been a big mistake.

When the ship finally touched down at the La Plata Spaceport, it was almost like being reborn when Conn stepped down the ramp. It had just rained and the air smelled fresh and clean. His legs wobbled and trembled as they got used to normal gravity and not having to adjust to the constant compensating movements they performed aboard the spaceship under pseudogravity.

The spaceport itself was surrounded by the usual ground-hugging buildings, mostly warehouses and storage cubicles. Montevideo's thousands of collapsium towers and apartment spires stretched into the sky as far and as high as the eye could see. All around, over and through the shimmering stalks buzzed tens of thousands of aircars and taxis, which from the spaceport looked like flying insects. He'd forgotten this part of Terra, just how busy it was and how many teaming billions lived under her stars.

He wondered what it had been like before World War III had destroyed most of the Northern Hemisphere.

Conn had a lot of luggage this trip and he arranged for everything, except the briefcase containing the bundles of Federation currency, to be carried for him.

He kept a tight grip on the briefcase. After saying goodbye to the crew that he had gotten to know and like on the trip, he flagged down an airtaxi and told the robo pilot to take him to one of the skyscraper hotels that had a good view of the spaceport and the city. It wasn't long before he was settling into a comfortable suite in the Montevideo Hilton with a great view of the spaceport.

The next morning, he had a good breakfast in his suite and got started. First he deposited the Federation currency he was carrying into a personal bank account. Next he did some digging about who the most reputable and discreet local private investigative firm was and set up an appointment to see the owner. Then he hired a discreet law firm to learn everything that was publicly available about Panstellar Industries' and its subsidiary companies' senior executives. Last but not least, he checked to see if J. Fitzwilliam Sterber was still on Terra.

To Conn's surprise, Sterber was gone. That meant he had only stayed on Terra for less than four weeks before presumably heading back to Poictesme.

When his screen beeped, he turned it on only to see the *Ouroboros II's* captain's face.

"I've got some good news, sir."

Conn visibly relaxed. "I can use some."

"I was checking in at Federation Off-World Customs, when they told me that the tariff on our goods had been lifted on a provisional basis three weeks ago."

"That is good news, Captain."

"I've got more. The shipping agent told me that the last two Tri-Systems & Interstellar Spaceline hyperships, that arrived after the tariff had been imposed, had also transferred their cargo to bonded warehouses. So there is a *lot* of brandy and tobacco sitting on the ground right here and now."

Conn thanked him for the information. After signing off, he contacted their shipping agent, identified himself and produced documentation attesting to his right to take control of the bonded cargo and instructed the agent to sell the cargo for the best price he could obtain. With the amount of money that the agent believed he could sell the warehoused goods for, plus the cash that Conn had brought with him, the *Ouroboros II's* cargo, plus the money already in the company's Terran bank accounts, he would have almost fifty million sols at his beck and call.

Some of it would be used to buy goods that could be sold profitably on Poictesme. Still, the remaining cash at Conn's disposal was considerable, far more than he had ever had responsibility for in the past. Also, on the plus side was the fact that the *Ouroboros II* would be heading directly back to Poictesme, so they could fill the cargo holds to the gunwales. The profit on this trip would be a big boost to the company's coffers.

When Conn queried the shipping agent as to why the tariff had been provisionally removed, he was told that Sterber had managed to negotiate a deal with Terra-Baldur-Marduk Spacelines, the details of which he didn't know but apparently the removal of the tariff was part of the deal. Keeping it off was contingent on the deal being accepted by the company on Poictesme. Conn started a report for his father detailing the first part of what he'd learned in the short time he'd been on Terra.

The next day, Conn met with the head honcho of Kraken Investigations in their downtown office. Devlin Kraken himself invited

Conn to sit down in a comfortable chair, offered him what turned out to be a glass of Poictesme melon-brandy and a cigar made from Poictesme tobacco.

Conn didn't bother to ask him how he knew that Conn was from Poictesme.

After lighting his and Conn's cigar, Kraken said, "So Mr. Maxwell. What can my agency do for you?"

Conn waited until he'd taken a puff from his cigar, then took a document he'd put together on the trip to Terra from out of his pocket and handed it to Mr. Kraken.

"I'd like your agency to keep a careful eye on these individuals and tell me where they go, who they see and, if possible, anything you can find out about their internal company communications. Naturally, it has to be done *very* discreetly."

Mr. Kraken raised his eyebrows as he looked at the list. "Naturally."

He paused momentarily. "Mr. Maxwell, you do realize that this will involve a lot of manpower and other resources, and therefore will be quite expensive?"

Conn nodded and said, "I expected that it would be. If you'll provide me with a weekly tally of the cost that will help me to determine how long this surveillance will continue."

Kraken said that could be arranged, then asked if there was anything else that Conn wanted him to do.

"Yes. I would like your people to do some research for me. I'm interested in any information that involves large computer centers being built or the hiring of computer technicians that specialize in large computers. This activity could have taken place any time from four years up until to about one year ago."

"Would this computer activity be connected to those executives you want us to keep an eye on?"

"Possibly, but not necessarily."

"I see. Well, I'll have my people start work on this immediately. How often would you like to see the surveillance reports?"

Conn thought about that. "Let's try daily, and see how that goes. I'm only planning on being here for a short time. No longer than a week or two. You can contact me at the Hilton."

"Fine. Anything else?"

"Actually there might be something else. I'm in the market for individuals who have hypership technical and operating skills. It occurs to me that with the Navy decommissioning some of their ships, there would be a number of former Navy personnel who have been discharged and perhaps are looking for work in the private sector. Can you recommend a reputable employment firm that would know how best to find these people?"

"That's an interesting question. I'll have to consult with some of my colleagues and get back to you later today."

"Fine," Conn replied. "I believe that's all I needed to discuss with you. I look forward to the first surveillance report."

As Conn got up to leave, Devlin Kraken said casually. "Is there something in particular…some kind of behavior that you're looking for from that list of individuals? It would help us if we knew what to look for."

"Anything unusual…for example a pattern of regular trips to some location that would be out of place for a corporate executive. Maybe something that suggests that the individual in question is trying to hide something."

Kraken nodded slowly. "I see. Very well, I'll make sure my operatives are aware of this information."

II

When Conn got back to his hotel suite, he called room service and had a meal sent up. After eating he took a short nap and set the alarm for nightfall. When it was quite dark outside, he activated his suite's viewscreen and placed a person-to-person call to General Foxx Travis (ret.) on the moon.

The call was intercepted by a woman who was clearly a nurse. After a several-second delay, she said, "I'm sorry, sir. General Travis isn't taking calls these days. He requires a lot of rest."

Conn asked if he could leave a message.

The nurse agreed.

"Tell the General that Conn Maxwell from Poictesme is here on Terra and would like to speak with him. Please also tell him that Merlin sends his regards. Here's my number in case the General wants to reach me."

Conn gave her his viewscreen combination and she signed off.

Sure enough, two hours later, a call from Luna came in. The man on the viewscreen was clearly General Travis but he looked even frailer than he had twelve years before. He only had a couple of wiry white-hairs left sticking out of his skull-like head. The skin covering his face was so thin it was almost translucent and he could see the tracing of veins beneath the flesh. Travis had spent the last thirty years living in Luna's low gravity; he'd have died decades ago living in Terra's gravity well.

"Hello, General Travis. It's good to see you again, sir." Conn had to remind himself about the three second lag as the signal traveled to the moon and Travis's response traveled back to Terra.

"Well, well," he said, his wrinkled face breaking out into a smile. "If it isn't Conn Maxwell. I never expected to see you again, son. Naturally General Shanlee sent word to me about the...resolution, shall we say...of the situation on Poictesme a while back. How is Shanlee these days?"

"I'm sorry to have to tell you this, sir, but General Shanlee died from a stroke two years ago."

Travis nodded, his expression unchanged. "That's a shame. So many good men and friends gone...I was sure he would outlive me, not the other way around. So what is it that you wanted to talk to me about, young Maxwell?"

"I have a couple of things I need to tell you about. It would be much better if we met again in person."

"How important are they?"

"Very."

The old general nodded and a strong light illuminated his eyes. "You're damn right. I'll tell these busybodies, who are already writing my obituary, to see that you have the clearance for a short visit."

"Thank you, sir."

NINETEEN

It took two days before Conn was authorized to board a shuttle to Luna. It was a short flight but it provided a beautiful view of the blue pearl that was mankind's original home. He noted sadly that even now most of the Northern Hemisphere was covered with a thick ice sheet, a remnant of the glaciation that followed the atomic winters of World Wars III and IV. He wondered how many centuries it would take for the Terran ecosystem to restore itself.

Once at Bullialdus Station—located in the crater Bullialdus just in front of the central peak—Conn was run through exhaustive fumigation and search procedures, even more painstakingly complete than at his previous visit. After the decontamination procedures, he was cleared and led into the large half-domed room that served as the General's living quarters, displaying a big slice of the sparkling black sky with the huge blue-white orb of Terra in the background. For the most part, the room was as spartan as Foxx Travis himself. The former general was almost one-hundred and twelve years-old; however, Travis' eyes still showed an active light, although the color was almost completely absent from the pupils.

"How are you, young man?"

"I'm doing very well, General. Since we last met, I've married and have a wonderful son, Foxx Travis Maxwell, who—of course—was named in your honor."

The old man actually beamed. "Good for you. I'm both honored and pleased that you thought enough of me to name your son after me."

Conn took a few moments to bring out his pocket recorder and show the general a picture of Little Foxx.

"Looks like quite a handful," Travis said.

Conn nodded.

"And it must have taken something very important for you to leave him for a visit to see me."

"You're right, General. You don't mind if I use this, do you?" Conn asked, pulling out a pen that created a six-foot radial surveillance blanket. "This will insure that what I'm about to say stays between the two of us."

"You think I'm being monitored?"

Conn shrugged. "I wouldn't be surprised. I don't believe—if you are being watched—that anyone is stupid enough to let you in on the fact. However, this device will ensure our privacy."

Travis frowned, his entire forehead a washboard of wrinkles, before replying, "If you think it's necessary."

"I do, sir. Let me get down to brass tacks. One of our engineers, a hyperdrive specialist, has found a way to pretty much double hyperspatial speed."

"What!" Travis exclaimed. His face blanched and for a moment Conn thought he might be having a heart attack.

One of the medical devices at the counter began to beep insistently, and seconds later a medic rushed into the room. He immediately put a medpack on the General's arm and began to run a series of diagnostic tests.

Foxx Travis tried to brush him off in a cranky sort of manner. "I can take care of myself, young man!"

The doctor shook his head, then looked at Conn menacingly.

Conn held up his hands in surrender.

The device stopped its beeping and color returned to Travis' face. "Leave us alone, Brent. It was just a hiccup in the system."

The doctor scowled. "I don't need to remind you that at your age a hiccup can be fatal, now do I, General? As for you young man, I don't know what you've been telling the General, but keep it light. Is that understood? If not, you can depart right now."

It was obvious the doctor was a military man and his rank was that of colonel, or above.

"Yes, sir," Conn replied, all but saluting.

"Sorry about that," Travis said after the medical man departed.

"I'm the one who's sorry. I didn't mean to spring it on you like that, but there's no soft way to peddle this message."

"Does anybody know?"

Conn shook his head. "It's top secret. The only people who know about it are my father-in-law, head of the hyperspace team, and the team members themselves. I put the lid on it as soon as I learned about it."

"Have you isolated the team?"

"You can't get much more isolated than the airless ball they're living on. They're working on Koshchei."

Foxx Travis nodded, which shook his entire body in the lunar low-gravity. "That's good. I remember that chunk of rock. A damn good place for secrets to die."

"We've cleaned it up and restarted most of the robotic factories. There are over fifty thousand people living at Port Carpenter. There was no directive to improve the Dillingham drives. My father in-law, Yves Jacquemont, took it upon himself to look into it. Previously, he was a retired hyperspatial engineer. Had some ideas he wanted to check out and didn't bother to notify anyone off-world."

"Probably bored to death on that rust ball. I know living there would have driven me to drink."

Conn nodded. "What I need from you, General, is some advice on how to deal with this unexpected *windfall*."

"Windfall," the old man chortled. "Disaster might be a better name for it. This wouldn't have been a problem before the War; the Federation always had a team of top-notch men looking for ways to improve the Dillinghams. Whenever there was any real improvement, the specs were published throughout the Federation to ensure that everyone had a level field to play on. I suspect your folks wouldn't be interested in such philanthropy."

Conn snorted. "I wish! Most of them have anger issues with the Federation, dating back to the end of the War and what we like to call 'The Abandonment.'"

"That I can understand. We did leave in a god-awful hurry, but you couldn't know the political pressures we were under. We may have won the War, but now we are losing the peace. The end came at too high a price, whole worlds bankrupted or torn asunder for vital resources. I bet you don't know that there was a large party of worlds in the Federation Executive Council that wanted to end the war, even if it meant allowing the System States to break away."

Conn shook his head. He did know that it was the twelve civilized worlds of the Executive Council that called the shots, not the Planetary Assembly of Member Worlds. Nor the Federation president.

"Well, things were that bad." The General was puffing louder.

He didn't want the machine to start beeping again. "Let's take a moment to relax, General. No one's blaming you, but the people I represent blame the Federation for all of the problems of the last fifty years—fairly or not. The problem is that Pandora's Box is now open and I don't know how long I can keep it contained, but you have my word that I will not spring it on the Federation."

"Maybe you could sell it to them, then they could disseminate your findings."

"I'd rather give it to them in exchange for good will, General. And one of the reasons I brought it up. I thought you might know the best way to present this news."

"That was smart of you." The General's head bobbed up and down. "Damn straight. I'll have a few people that I trust over and we'll figure something out."

"Thank you, General." Conn felt as though the weight of the world had been lifted off his shoulders.

"Anything else, young man?"

"Well, sir, yes there is. I wanted to ask you about a certain piece of wartime equipment that helped you win the war against the System States Alliance. I think you know which piece of equipment I'm referring to. Specifically, I wanted to ask you if it were possible that another copy of that equipment might have been manufactured and stored somewhere else?"

General Travis' expression remained blank far longer than could be accounted for by a recall lag. Conn was beginning to fear that the General's memory had failed him.

Suddenly his eyes widened and he smiled. "Great greasy comets! Yes. You're quite right, young man. There were two identical machines manufactured, and one was indeed kept as a backup in case the first machine was damaged or destroyed. I had forgotten all about that."

He stopped talking and a peculiar look came over his face. Conn didn't say anything. Finally Travis said in a low, slow voice.

"Now why…would you come all this way just to ask me about something that you couldn't possibly have known unless…. Oh God! Is someone using the other machine?"

"Well, sir…it's looking more and more like that is the case. Unfortunately, whoever is using the second super-computer does not share the same benevolent interests that you and I have in our hearts towards the Federation."

Travis' expression became very grim when he heard that response.

"I'm very sorry to hear you say that, Conn. Do you have any idea who this other person or persons might be?"

Conn nodded. "We have a strong suspicion, which I'm trying to confirm, that it's someone at or near the top of the management of Panstellar

Industries or one of their subsidiaries. I'm also here to recruit some ex-Navy personnel because our magician friend has predicted a high probability of hostile action against himself in the not too distant future."

Travis sat quietly; the General was obviously thinking and Conn didn't want to interrupt him. His eyes were starting to flutter as though he could barely keep them open. Finally he said, "This is damn serious news, son. I'm going to make some calls to people who are in a position to help you. It might take a few days."

Conn checked his watch. "My return flight is in an hour." The fiat had come down from on high; he'd only been given two hours with the General. At that, he'd been given a big favor—even if it was at Foxx's instigation. *Somebody must think we're important. They don't know the half of it.*

"It'll take a bit of time. When you get back to Terra, sit tight, young man. I or someone else will be calling you soon."

I

Early the next morning at 0200, Conn got a call at his hotel suite. A visibly fatigued Foxx Travis exchanged greetings, then said, "You're going to get a call this morning from a General Frank Curtis who used to be in military intelligence. He was one of my junior staff officers during the war and he knows all about…our magician friend. Unfortunately, I'm too old and tired to be able to help you any further. Good luck to you, Conn Maxwell."

He broke the connection and, in spite of the early hour, Conn was unable to fall back asleep. So when the call did come shortly after dawn, Conn was bleary-eyed and groggy from lack of sleep. He turned on the viewscreen and saw the face of an older man, with silver hair, but with strong features that had not been eroded by the passage of time.

"Conn Maxwell?"

"Yes, sir, that's me," he replied.

"General Frank Curtis, retired. I believe that General Travis told you to expect my call."

"Yes, sir, General."

"Good. It so happens that I was coming to Montevideo today anyway. As soon as I arrive, I'll make arrangements for us to meet. If you have to leave your suite in the Hilton between now and then, please let the hotel people know where they can reach you. Is that agreeable to you?"

"Completely."

"Fine. Until then."

II

A few hours later, Curtis sent an aircar that took Conn to a nondescript office complex. He was shown into an equally nondescript office occupied by the General. Curtis got right down to business.

"First, I want you to know that even though I'm retired from active service, I have contacts in the Space Navy and Federation Army. Only a select few, less than the fingers on one hand, know about the Merlin Operation and why it has to remain secret. General Travis told me the basics of the current situation. I'm asking you now to fill me in on the whole story. After you've done that, I'll be in a position to determine how best to help you."

Conn took a deep breath and spent the next half hour briefing Curtis on the piracy, the attempted stock takeover and Merlin's latest predictions.

When he was finished, Curtis said, "Amazing. I had no idea that Merlin could detect the operations of another machine by indirect means. Let me now brief you on what you don't know. Through my contacts, I've found out that Navy HQ has received reports concerning the incident at Bifrost and at the Griffin mining base. Furthermore, your lawyer, J. Fitzwilliam Sterber, has managed to negotiate compensation for getting the *Valley Forge* away from the pirates at ten percent of the original cost of that ship which works out to twenty million sols.

"Navy Intelligence is preparing a criminal complaint against Terra-

Baldur-Marduk Spacelines, Inc. and, I can assure you, that they will investigate that company right down to its bootstraps. If the mastermind behind all this is in T-B-MS, they'll find him. Based on what you've told me, I somehow doubt that he'll be caught that easily. I'll ask my intelligence contacts to make discreet inquiries as to when, where and how the super-computer binary was acquired. If we can track down where it went, it may lead us to the ring behind this chicanery."

He paused to lean back and take a sip of coffee.

"I appreciate your help, General."

Curtis nodded. "General Travis told me that you're going to recruit ex-naval personnel. I can arrange to put the word out that your company is hiring. You've already told me about the private investigators that you've hired. What else do you need?"

"Merlin has informed us that it's quite possible our adversaries are interested in taking possession of the planet Koshchei."

The General nodded. "I've been briefed so I know that it holds considerable military assets as well as the facilities to build many more."

"According to Merlin, the only way to upset our adversary's plans is to defeat any arriving out-system military force before it reaches Koshchei. In order to accomplish that, we'll need the best tactical combat talent that's available on Terra. It would help if we knew who that person was so that we could approach him or her and try to recruit them."

Curtis nodded, turned to the viewscreen behind him and punched in a combination. The dark-skinned woman who appeared on the screen wore a Navy uniform. "Hello, Frank. It's been a long time, sir. Is this a social call?"

"Afraid not, Maria. Strictly business and *very unofficial*, if you know what I mean."

"I understand, sir. What can I do for you?"

"I need to know the names and current status of the ten officers with the highest tactical combat ratings."

"Okay. Give me a minute to execute a computer search."

A minute later she said, "I have that list."

"Does anyone stand out above the rest?"

Maria nodded. "The top three are in a class by themselves. Top of the list is a senior lieutenant who is currently on the cruiser TFSN *Resolute* out near the Edge. The second best is in command of the Home Fleet and the third is a staff officer in Logistics at Navy HQ, a Captain Valentina Koslova."

Curtis frowned. "How is it that the Navy's third-best combat tactician is a staff officer in Logistics? Why isn't she commanding a cruiser, for Ghu's sake?"

The woman on the screen shrugged. "I don't know the answer to that off-hand, sir. Give me a second and I'll take a look at her personnel file."

She turned her attention back to the screen and after a few moments, she said, "Well…from what I see here…and reading between the lines, it appears that Captain Koslova, while very talented in certain areas, also has a distinct lack of tact when it comes to keeping her unflattering opinions of senior officers to herself."

"Thank you, Maria. Do me a favor please and send a copy of that list to me here, would you? It was great seeing you again."

She smiled and said, "You bet, Frank. Good to see you, too."

General Curtis turned to Conn, saying, "Well, what do you think?"

Conn smiled. "Koslova sounds exactly like what we need. When can I talk to her?"

Curtis also smiled. "I thought you might like her profile. I'll arrange for you to get an appointment to see her. Now, is there anything else that you need?"

"Nothing that I can think of at the moment, General."

"All right, then. Here's how you can reach me if you need something else. Can I trust you to share whatever information you get from your sources with me?"

Conn nodded. They chatted for a few more minutes before he left.

III

Conn Maxwell could tell at the beginning of the interview that Captain Valentina Koslova didn't like being told by her superiors to meet with unknown off-world civilians. From Koslova's service record, he knew that she'd had to struggle her entire career to advance within the Navy in spite of her obvious gifts. It was quite clear that she herself didn't have the kinds of connections that would smooth her way up the command ladder. She'd had to make her way through her own natural ability and perseverance and now she was stuck in a career cul-de-sac.

Conn couldn't help but notice that Valentina Koslova was as striking in appearance, as she was on paper. She had ebony-colored skin and high cheekbones that looked like they could cut paper. Her hazel eyes were her most arresting trait; they studied everything like a security scanner.

"Please be seated, Mr. Maxwell. What can I do for you?"

He hesitated a moment before speaking. "Captain Koslova, I'm here from the Gartner Tri-System and the planet Poictesme. Have you heard of it?"

She nodded. "Of course, Poictesme was where Five-Star General Foxx Travis and the Third Fleet-Army Force were stationed during the War. Before my time, of course, but I'm well aware of Poictesme's strategic importance to the System States War effort."

"Good," Conn said. "Well, we have a problem there that can only be solved by someone with your qualifications. General Frank Curtis tells me that you are exceptionally good at ship-to-ship and multi-ship combat tactics."

She nodded, letting him know that she was aware of her gifts.

"I represent a company, Interstellar Security, based on Poictesme. We will be acquiring a number of armed interplanetary ships, which are perfectly legal under Federation laws, and we want to offer you overall command of those ships."

Conn was taken aback when Koslova started to laugh.

When she finished laughing, she said, matter-of-factly, "Now, what makes you think that I would give up a twenty-year career in the Federation Space Navy to go all the way out to the Gartner Tri-System to command a bunch of amateurs pretending to be a private navy?"

Conn squirmed in his seat. "Well…first of all, we expect that the planetary government of Poictesme will shortly establish its own naval force and our company ships will be leased to the government. So, while you may start out working for a private sector company, you'll quickly become a planetary naval officer and quite likely *the* commanding planetary naval officer."

"But I'm already a Federation naval officer. It seems to me that you're asking me to go from the big leagues to the minor leagues. I'm still waiting for a reason why you think I should do that."

Conn leaned forward. "I've been told that you commanded a light cruiser at one point, Captain. What I'm talking about will start out as a squadron and could eventually turn into several squadrons. Are you likely to get that kind of opportunity if you stay in the Federation Navy?"

He could see that his question had hit home.

"I'll concede that you have a point there, Mr. Maxwell. I'm still not convinced, but you have managed to intrigue me a bit. Go on."

"There are things that I'm not at liberty to disclose at this point, but let's just say that Poictesme wouldn't bother with the expense of setting up its own planetary navy unless it felt there was a real need for it—and I'm not referring to mundane needs like customs inspections. My planet is facing a serious problem that could very well turn into a shooting war with a well-organized and ruthless opponent. If things develop in the way that we expect, you'll find this job to be anything but boring."

Koslova laughed again. "Surely you're exaggerating, Mr. Maxwell."

Conn didn't return the smile. "No, I'm not exaggerating. Do you know General Frank Curtis?"

"General Curtis. Yes, I know of him. Haven't met him personally, though. Why do you ask?"

"Two days after I arrived here, I visited General Foxx Travis and he put me in touch with General Frank Curtis, who made some private inquiries, which is how your name came to my attention. Both Foxx Travis and Frank Curtis are retired and yet they both felt my mission here was serious enough to warrant taking action. Do you think they would bother to do that if they didn't consider my planet's situation serious?"

"You actually met with General Travis," she said, looking surprised. "Rumor has it that he's ill and barely hanging on in his Luna refuge."

"True," he answered.

"How and when?"

"I had previously met him in person, when I was studying at the University of Montevideo. I had some important news for him, and he agreed to see me at his home in Bullialdus Station."

"That's most interesting," she said.

He could almost hear the gears clank in her mind as she mentally revised her image of the young man facing her. General Travis, the most decorated military man in Federation history, had been in seclusion for several decades and had limited contact with anyone but a few old service buddies. If *he* had wrangled a personal invitation to see the General, he was a lot more important than he appeared.

"Okay. I'm intrigued enough to pursue this further," she said. "You were talking about a squadron of ships. What kind of ships?"

"Interstellar Security, the company that would be hiring you, has taken control of twenty abandoned Army ammunition ships. They're one hundred and fifty feet in diameter, collapsium-armored, with four 115mm rifles and two internal missile launchers. We're upgrading them by adding ground-based missile launchers to their cargo decks. Some of those ships are earmarked for deployment on nearby planets that Poictesme trades with in an anti-pirate role. That's what will be available in the short run."

Koslova looked a little deflated. Conn suspected that the idea of her taking command of task force of patrol boats didn't sound very interesting or challenging.

"Go on," she said.

"Longer term, a sister company has claimed an abandoned shipyard/spaceport that is completely capable of building new ships from scratch and we intend to build custom-designed defense ships, whose design by the way, you'll have a lot of input on."

Koslova shrugged. "Building ships, even planetary defense ships from scratch is going to be expensive. How can you afford that?"

"To begin with, all the construction equipment is basically there for the taking. Mostly war surplus the Third Fleet-Force Army left behind when the System States War ended. The only real expenses are salaries which we can cover from other profitable operations."

"But what about raw materials? They're the biggest single cost of a ship."

Conn hesitated. "For the time being we have plenty of raw materials from abandoned mines and processing plants located on another planet in the Gartner Tri-System. If we lose that source, we can recover raw materials from the almost four hundred interplanetary freighters that the Federation abandoned after the War. Which we've claimed and now control."

Koslova's eyes got huge. "You've got four hundred transport ships sitting around doing nothing?"

Conn nodded. "Yes. We've put twelve of them back into operation for trips between planets in the Gartner Tri-System. The rest aren't really needed. Have we overlooked something?"

"Well, I'm not sure. How big are these surplus transport ships?"

"They range in size from three to seven hundred and fifty feet in diameter."

Koslova was silent for a few seconds, then activated her viewscreen and called up what looked like ship design schematics.

Turning back to Conn, she said, "When I got shuffled off to Logistics, I had the chance to work in the Design Bureau for about a year. Before the budget cuts put an end to it, the Bureau was working on an experimental concept that involved a large, hyper-capable ship, carrying up to half a dozen smaller ships of about two to three hundred feet in diameter. The project looked at two variations. One was where those smaller ships had their own internal missile launchers while the other variant involved the smaller ships deploying semi-autonomous missile-carrying drones that could be launched en masse.

"The idea was that the mothership would leave hyperspace at the edge of a star system, deploy the smaller ships that could maneuver closer to enemy targets, launch their missiles in synchronized barrages, return to the mothership and hyper back out again."

"I'm not sure that would help us," Conn said. "Our strategy is strictly defensive and that system you're describing sounds like it's technically quite complicated. I think it would take too long to develop a working prototype. We need something that's simple to build and operate, and can be built relatively fast."

Koslova looked back at the screen while she digested his comments. "I see. Well, how about this concept, then?"

The schematic on the screen changed to one in which a large globular ship looked like it was wearing a giant belt of bullets.

"The main drawback with internal missile launchers," she said, "is that you need complicated loading mechanisms to take missiles from storage and insert them into the launch tubes. Those loading mechanisms can be knocked out of commission by relatively minor damage. But if all of the missile tubes were attached to the outside of the ship, which means that they would only be able to fire once, you could still pack a hefty punch because of the large circumference of a ship, even one as small as a three hundred-footer. Now, the drawback with this system is that the ship has to go to a depot in order for the missile tubes to be reloaded one at a time from the outside."

She paused to view her datapad. "The advantage of this system is that it's relatively easy to do and from your point of view, you can quickly turn your freighters into missile carriers. How much internal cargo capacity do they have?"

Conn knew that data by heart and told her.

"Well now...that's very interesting. The Navy at one time experimented with modular hyperdrive units that could be installed in a cargo hold smaller than that. The design for the hyperdrive units isn't classified. I can get it for you. If you can build them, we can turn those four hundred interplanetary freighters into four hundred hyper-capable missile cruisers."

Conn was both excited and confused. "I like the idea of external single-shot missile launchers but why bother with installing hyperdrives? All the action will be local and aren't armed hyperships illegal anyway?"

Koslova was smiling now. "This is why I'm the tactical genius and you're not. The Gartner Tri-System is composed of three stars, each of which has its own planets. Each planet has its own no-jump zone but that still leaves huge volumes of space where short, microjumps are possible. Having a squadron or two of hyper-capable missile cruisers could give your side a decisive edge. And as for the prohibition against armed hyperships, what I'm suggesting might be a technical violation. The fact is that both the missile tubes and hyperdrive units could be removed later which can be used to argue that these ships aren't really hyper capable warships."

Conn Maxwell smiled. "I understand. So does this mean that you're willing to take our offer?"

Koslova laughed. "You haven't *made* an offer yet. All you've done is tell me that you want to make an offer. Once you make it, I'll give you an answer."

"Okay, Captain. Here's our offer. If you agree to take charge of our off-planet defense forces, we will pay you the same salary as a TFSN commodore and when you do decide to retire, your Navy pension will be topped up to equal what a rear admiral receive."

"That very tempting, but here's my concern. You told me that the planetary government would be establishing a planetary defense force. What if they won't agree to the terms that you've just outlined?"

Conn smiled. "I happen to know the Planetary President *very* well and I can guarantee you that his administration will agree with these terms; however, just in case for whatever reason they decide not to match those terms, Interstellar Security will make up any shortfall out of its own pockets."

"And I get to run my operation any way I see fit?"

Conn nodded.

"Okay, I will have a talk with General Curtis and, if he confirms the seriousness of your situation, we have a deal. Where are you staying?"

"At the Hilton."

"Good. I'll get back to you within twenty-four hours."

They stood, shook hands and Conn Maxwell turned and left her office.

Back in his hotel suite, Conn ran over his conversation with Valentina Koslova. He was a little intimidated; it had been a while since he'd met someone with such a formidable intellect and presence.

She was the perfect candidate to head up Interstellar Security and later the planetary force he and his father envisioned. He hoped her talk with General Curtis went well.

TWENTY-ONE

I

After Conn Maxwell left her office, Captain Koslova looked up Curtis' screen combination and dialed it.

"Ah, Captain Koslova, I presume?"

"Yes, that's right. I'm sorry to bother you, sir, but I've just had a very interesting conversation with a young man who claims that he's spoken with you."

She was about to say more but Curtis interjected. "Conn Maxwell. We had a nice little talk. Did he make you an offer you couldn't refuse?"

"Let's just say that his offer is very difficult to refuse, but my answer depends on what you tell me about how serious the situation on Poictesme is now, or is likely to become. And what the Navy thinks about all this."

Curtis stared at the screen pickup for what seemed like a long time. "Captain Koslova, as a military officer, you understand that operational security sometimes demands that the people who need to do the heavy lifting can't be told everything. This is one of those situations. Just believe me when I tell you that in my opinion, your participation in the security of Poictesme will do far more to help the Federation than anything you could do in logistics or any other staff position. Does that address your doubts, Captain?"

"Yes, it does. Thank you, General." Koslova cut the connection and sat back in her chair. This was clearly something *Big*. She started thinking of who to recommend as her replacement.

II

Conn Maxwell sat at a desk in his hotel room looking over the first surveillance report from Kraken Investigation's firm. Nothing jumped out at him as being unusual or suspicious. The report had one shocking piece of information added at the end. Apparently a Senior Vice-President of Operations at Terra-Baldur-Marduk Spacelines had committed suicide, with a note admitting to having instigated the entire pirate operation on his own initiative. The company had agreed to pay a fine and to return the two ships that had been purchased in good faith under different names, but were now believed to be *Pathfinder* and *Trailblazer*.

The Navy investigators were satisfied that the investigation was now closed. Conn didn't believe it was that simple. *Some poor bastard was ordered to fall on his sword. I wonder what they had on him?*

What about the other Merlin? Was the offer for Koshchei that was on its way back to Poictesme just a coincidence and not part of a master plan at all? He put a call in to the general. When he got through, he expressed his doubts that the whole thing was over.

General Curtis agreed. "I'd say it's just a little too convenient that the senior executive in charge of the piracy operation is dead and can't be questioned. I've been talking with a very senior intelligence person, who knows all about our magician friend and in his opinion, there's at least a fifty/fifty chance that the real mastermind is still alive and had a patsy terminated to deflect attention away from himself. The investigation into the piracy is officially closed, but the unofficial investigation into the second machine is still ongoing.

"What we know so far is that after the Big War, the binary's machine parts were shipped back to the Sol System and stored in a Navy depot on Luna. It appears that four years ago, a lot of material dating from the System States War was declared surplus and sold for scrap, including the parts for the second super-computer. How *that* happened no one seems to know or will admit to. The parts were supposedly shipped off to the scrapper, but whether they were actually scrapped or not is impossible to determine at this time. Any leads from Kraken Investigations?"

Conn told him that initial reports showed nothing unusual.

"Okay, then. Naval Intelligence will keep searching for those missing parts. If I hear anything, I'll contact you. I'll expect the same from you," Curtis finished, signing off.

III

The next day Conn got several calls. Most importantly, Captain Koslova had accepted their offer and was putting in her retirement papers with the Space Navy. She was preparing to leave for Poictesme as soon as passage could be secured. Unless an unscheduled Poictesme ship arrived unexpectedly, that would be in about four weeks, when the next Terra-Baldur-Marduk Spacelines ship was scheduled to begin its circular route to Odin, Poictesme, Aton and back to Terra.

According to the employment agency he'd hired, ex-Space Navy personnel were starting to respond to the hiring call. They'd already had over a hundred queries since yesterday afternoon. After the System States War both the Federation Space Navy and Army had both downsized, more than once, both restructuring and eliminating personnel. There were a lot of naval officers and spacemen who were cut from the rolls and were now out of work, or dissatisfied with civilian life.

He received official notification from the Space Navy that Tri-System Interstellar Spacelines would be getting *Pathfinder* and *Trailblazer* back which would restore their trade routes to nearby inhabited planets. Terra-Baldur-Marduk Spacelines had shrugged its corporate shoulders and paid a fine, which amounted to a slap on the wrist, and the pirate trail had gone cold.

Conn spent the rest of the day doing research on Panstellar Industries and trying to figure out where they might strike next. The question now was from what angle the next attack would come from. He knew full well there was a lot of unemployment on Terra and lots of criminals, many of them unemployed naval veterans with few other skills than killing people and damaging things. It wouldn't be that hard to set up a new pirate crew secondhand, or even third hand, that would be almost untraceable since Terra-Baldur-Marduk Spacelines wasn't concerned about profits in the usual sense.

Now that their subsidiary had been linked to the pirates they were going to have to give that gambit up.

After dinner, Conn received another report from Kraken Investigations. Still, no smoking gun. He sighed, put down the report and got up to look out the window of his hotel suite. It was late at night. He could see the lights of some of the hyperships in the foreground at the spaceport, which was where recent arrivals landed. As Conn continued to watch, he noticed a light coming on in one of the ships at the back of the spaceyard where mothballed ships were stored.

Why is there any activity at this time of the night on a mothballed ship? he asked himself. Conn grabbed the high-powered electronic binoculars that he sometimes used to watch the spaceport during daylight hours and examined the light source. Even with the binoculars, he was only barely able to make out that a hypership had one of its large cargo doors open and a small vehicle, most likely an aircar, was flying into the ship, with the cargo doors closing immediately afterwards. The light suddenly winked out and Conn was left looking at blackness. He visualized in his mind where the light had been and made a mental note of the locations.

When it was light again, he would try to figure out which ship he had been looking at. Then he would get Kraken's people to keep an eye on that ship. It was a long shot but he had a gut feeling that he'd just witnessed something important.

IV

Identifying the ship turned out to be easy. At that bearing, there was only one ship in the mothballed section. She was a recent arrival, the *City of Amenhetep*, and she used to be part of the Odin/Poictesme/Aton/Terra milk run. She was also owned by Terra-Baldur-Marduk Spacelines. Conn asked Kraken to have his people keep a close eye on her and sure enough, a day later, reports started coming in that there was regular traffic to and from that ship involving small numbers of individuals, including some late at night.

Kraken called and asked if Conn wanted those individuals watched as well and Conn said, "Yes, keep them under surveillance."

More days passed. More surveillance reports that showed nothing suspicious from Panstellar's or T-B-MS executives and the *City of Amenhetep* traffic, while unusual in and of itself, did not lead back to either Panstellar or T-B-MS.

Kraken's people were still trying to get information on why men were visiting the ship on a regular basis, but so far the only thing they had on these people were a few names and addresses, nothing more.

Then, on the seventh day of Conn's stay on Terra, two pieces of information arrived that felt like a breakthrough. One of *City of Amenhetep's* regular visitors was identified as a recent graduate of the University of Montevideo's Computer Program. That got Conn's attention. The other piece of information was that one of the ship's regular visitors had left late the previous evening and been picked up at the base of the ship by an airtaxi, which had taken him to the head offices of Panstellar Industries.

Conn quickly crosschecked the whereabouts of senior Panstellar executives for the evening in question. Three of them had been working at the company head office when the ship's visitor had arrived. That suggested to Conn that one of those three was the mastermind. The three were the president, the company treasurer and the senior personnel officer.

Conn immediately contacted General Curtis and passed on the news.

"Now why would T-B-MS need a computer graduate to make regular visits to a mothballed ship?" Curtis asked.

"There's only one reason I can think of, General, and that's to take a regular shift operating a very large computer system that was installed in the cargo hold of that ship."

Curtis' eyes widened in sudden comprehension. "You're saying they may have assembled the Merlin binary inside that hypership!"

Conn nodded, it made perfect sense. "A ship that size has huge cargo holds totaling millions of cubic feet of space. Why build a new building to house the other Merlin, where it would be tied to one location, when you could put it inside a hypership which could be moved whenever the need arose?"

Curtis smacked his right fist into his left palm. "It all fits! I'll get Navy Intelligence to pick up that computer grad and question him."

When Curtis signed off, Conn was sure that they would at the very least be able to deny the opposition—whoever that was—the use of the second Merlin, which the Navy would confiscate. Once they figured out who the mastermind really was, the Navy could pay him or her a discreet visit and politely but firmly *insist* that the mastermind cease and desist from any further moves that would destabilize the Federation—or else.

TWENTY-TWO

I

Twenty-four hours later Curtis called back with disappointing news. The second Merlin wasn't in the *City of Amenhetep* at all. The computer grad had been picked up and questioned. He claimed that he was hired to watch over some valuable cargo that was being stored in the ship temporarily until other arrangements could be made. He had taken that job because no one was hiring computer grads at the moment.

He then offered to take Navy inspectors with him on his next shift, which they did. The inspectors searched the ship very thoroughly and found nothing that even remotely resembled a large computer and the cargo holds were indeed full of non-electronic cargo of various kinds.

The clincher came the next day. After a meticulous investigation, undeniable proof had been found to confirm that the Merlin binary really had been scrapped four years ago. General Curtis was both relieved that the threat had gone away and embarrassed at having raised the alarm over what turned out to be a red herring.

Conn called off the Kraken personnel from further surveillance. All the available evidence now pointed to the fact that Merlin had misinterpreted the evidence pointing to a second super-computer. Eighty-nine percent wasn't one hundred percent; this time Merlin had missed the boat.

So it was with great surprise that Conn received a call from a woman who identified herself as the senior administrative assistant to the president of Panstellar Industries, Inc. "Is this Mr. Conn Maxwell?" she asked.

"Yes, this is he."

"Can I see some identification?"

He held up his Terran Federation Member Citizen ID for her to scan.

She returned to the screen a few moments later, asking, "Would Mr. Maxwell be willing to meet with Panstellar President, Howard Tarkington, at 1000 hours tomorrow morning?"

Conn paused to think it over for a bit. *If I do go, I'm a great hostage. But if I don't go, I'll never forgive myself.*

"Yes, I can make that appointment," he finally said.

"Good, I'll inform President Tarkington." She then gave Conn directions to Panstellar's offices, which Conn knew anyway from Kraken's reports and instructed him to check in at the main desk on the hundred and forty-fourth floor.

Conn immediately called General Curtis and told him about the invitation, asking how Tarkington had found out about Conn's activities.

Curtis snorted and said, "I wouldn't be surprised that when the whole thing turned out to be a wild goose chase, someone in Navy Intelligence happened to mention it to someone else who told someone else who knew Tarkington. He probably got a good laugh out of it and wanted to meet you in person to check you out."

"Should I go? What if he's angry and wants to get even?"

Curtis chuckled. "You mean, arrange for you to disappear permanently?"

Conn nodded.

"I doubt very much that he would be so obvious about it if that's what he really intends. Let me put it this way. If something happens to you tomorrow, we'll know where to start looking, won't we?"

Conn conceded the point, but it didn't make him feel any safer.

"Go talk to him and if he says anything interesting, let me know." Curtis signed off.

II

The office of Panstellar Industries' president was huge and the panoramic view of Montevideo out the large windows was impressive. As Conn was ushered in by his secretary, the man himself got up from his large desk and came to meet him.

Tarkington was a bald professorial-looking type who wouldn't have looked out of place in tweeds rather than the finely tailored sheen-suit he was wearing. He wore an anachronistic pair of thick glasses with a light gold frame. His skin was fair and he looked as if he hadn't spent any time under the sun in decades. Not the sort of man Conn would have called a mastermind.

"Mr. Maxwell, I'm Howard Tarkington. It's a pleasure to finally meet you in person. Let's sit over here by the coffee table where we can be comfortable."

The two of them sat down where Tarkington had pointed. "Can my robot-tender get a drink for you, Mr. Maxwell?"

Conn smiled and said, "Melon-brandy if you have it."

Tarkington smiled, too. "We do. I can also offer you a cigar made from Poictesme tobacco." He opened an ornate box that was sitting on the coffee table.

Conn took a cigar and used the filigreed gold lighter sitting next to the cigar box. Tarkington called over his robot-tender, ordering two melon-brandies that arrived by the time both men had gotten their cigars lit.

"I asked you to come here today, Mr. Maxwell, because I've gotten word that Panstellar's recent scrutiny by Naval Intelligence was instigated at your request. I wanted to find out why you think my company has done something illegal."

Conn thought about his reply very cautiously. It was vitally important that he not give any of their plans away. "Well…as I'm sure you're aware, I represent a group of companies on Poictesme that are trying to boost the local economy by exporting our brandy, tobacco and other products via our own ships. And we were doing just fine until one of your subsidiaries, Terra-Baldur-Marduk Spacelines, filed a trade complaint that resulted in a punitive tariff on our shipping. On top of that, we lost two freighters to pirates in raids that were organized by one of your company's executives. I'm sure you can understand why we might be in a position to have some concerns when it comes to Panstellar Industries?"

Tarkington laughed and nodded. "Yes. I can definitely understand a little healthy paranoia. But let's look at the facts objectively, shall we? The piracy was the act of a rogue executive, not the deliberate act of the company as a whole. The aforementioned rogue has committed suicide and T-B-MS has paid a fine for not preventing his crimes as well as agreeing to return the two ships you've lost.

"As for the tariff, that's been negotiated away in a deal that is waiting to be ratified by your company's Board of Directors and involves terms that I dare say will be quite profitable to your side. From where I'm sitting, your side hasn't made out too badly at all."

Conn took a gamble and said, "Except that you're proposing that we turn over all our facilities on Koshchei to Panstellar's control."

Again Tarkington nodded. "So you know about that. That's correct. The mining, industrial and manufacturing assets on Koshchei are the key component in our strategic plan to take maximum advantage of the approaching economic boom that your Merlin has been predicting."

The mention of Merlin threw Conn for a loop.

"You know about Merlin?"

"Of course. You haven't tried to keep its existence a secret since you rediscovered it six years ago. We were pleasantly surprised when we heard about Merlin's prediction of a boom because up to that point, we were convinced that the Federation was in the initial stages of a long-term economic decline."

"What made you think there was a 'long-term decline' ahead?" Conn asked.

Tarkington waived the question aside with his cigar. "Oh, it's very obvious if you know what to look at. You see, Mr. Maxwell, my company has some very smart analysts working for us, and all they do is gather data, make charts and analyze trends."

He took a puff on his cigar, and then said, "Here, let me show you." He got up, walked to his desk and touched a button. Conn then realized that the corporate logo on the wall behind the desk was actually a giant wallscreen when it morphed into a chart.

Tarkington gestured to the chart, saying, "This is a long-term chart depicting average per capita Gross Interstellar Product. You'll notice that the four centuries prior to the System States War show a definite uptrend even though there are the usual cyclical ups and downs. The trend levels off before and during the War, which is no surprise, and then drops at the end of the Big War as a lot of planets in the Systems States Alliance suffer economically from the defeat. Not to mention those Federation planets that had their own economic dislocations, either from war damage or changes to trade and economic policies brought about by the war. Again, no surprises there. As you can see, in the almost five decades since the war, the overall trend, again subject to temporary ups and downs, is now down.

"We can see the same kind of trend change when we look at almost any other parameter that we measure, especially when it comes to things like the volume of goods shipped between planets, which to our shipping company Terra-Baldur-Marduk Spacelines is quite important. Even before we heard the good news from Merlin, we had come to the conclusion that for T-B-MS to continue to be profitable in the decline, it needed to get its cost of shipping down. The only way we could see that happening was if the company could acquire a new fleet of super-large hyperships, we call them VLFs for Very Large Freighters, at a very low cost of construction."

Conn was drinking his melon-brandy in gulps. Nothing had prepared him for this; Tarkington was giving away the house figures.

"Acquiring control of Koshchei facilities for a tiny fraction of their replacement cost would allow us to do exactly that. That fleet of VLFs will be ten times as profitable when the economic boom kicks into high gear and Koshchei will become a priceless asset that other interstellar shipping companies will be unable to match. We estimate that T-B-MS will completely dominate shipping throughout the entire Federation in another two, or at most three decades."

Conn was stunned. Panstellar had known about the overall decline in its most basic form, which was economic, even if they didn't know about the social and political trends predicted by Merlin. But if the economic trend was bad enough, Panstellar's long-term strategy to overpower its competition was precisely the same kind of grab-what-you-can-get approach that planetary governments would resort to if they knew of the inevitable decline.

Why hadn't Merlin taken this kind of corporate behavior into consideration when it was projecting the slow, peaceful decline over the next two centuries? Suddenly Conn understood why: Merlin could only predict what large groups were likely to do, not the actions of a relatively few senior corporate executives. And Foxx Travis and his military officers and computer techs weren't trained to think in commercial and economic terms, so it never occurred to them, or to Conn when they reran the projections six years ago, that the overall economic trend would become self-evident long before the decaying political and social trends became obvious.

The implications of this information suddenly hit Conn like a bolt of lightning. The slow, peaceful decay projection was therefore never really a likely scenario to begin with. Possibly, yes. Likely, no. That meant the best that M-12 could hope to achieve was to delay the onset of, and/or minimize the extent of violent action in the future. He had to get back to Poictesme as soon as possible to ask Merlin a whole new set of questions. Conn realized that Tarkington was patiently waiting for his response.

"What's Panstellar's fallback plan if the Board of Koshchei Exploration & Development won't ratify the deal?"

Tarkington's smile vanished and his voice took on an alarmingly sinister tone. "That would be viewed *very* unfavorably, I can assure you. For one thing, the tariff would be reinstated immediately. We would also take a very serious look at a Federation Supreme Court challenge to the legality of Poictesme's Abandoned Property Act of 867, which is the whole basis for Koshchei Exploration & Development's claim over those assets on Koshchei. In fact…I think my Board of Directors would even go so far as to insist that we send security forces to Koshchei to secure the facilities to prevent your people from removing or destroying valuable equipment, until such time as the Federation Supreme Tribunal renders its verdict, which my legal experts have advised me is likely to be in our favor."

So finally, the wolf is showing his true colors, Conn thought. "Do I understand your use of the term 'security forces' to mean armed troops backed up by what—contragravity tanks? Gunboats? Warships?"

Tarkington was now smiling again in an evil kind of way. "All of the above, Mr. Maxwell. We will not hesitate to spend millions to protect billions of sols worth of assets. Your companies and the inhabitants of Poictesme will end up without access to markets for your products and you won't have Koshchei either in the final analysis. So I sincerely hope for your sake that your board—or M-12 as you call them—ratifies the deal. Young man, it's in your best interest to give our proposal some hard and deep thought."

"We've spent five years rebuilding and retooling the shops on Koshchei, and spent millions of sols doing so. Plus, better than fifty thousand of our citizens live there now."

The Panstellar President paused to inhale, leaned back and visibly relaxed, before saying, "I'm sure we can find work for them. But, really, it's a moot point. You see, your counselor, J. Fitzwilliam Sterber, seemed to be convinced that it was a good deal when he left here on one of our regularly scheduled runs to Poictesme by way of Odin, so even if you felt inclined to want to persuade your board not to take the deal, you still wouldn't be able to get back in time for the vote."

Conn tried not to let the shock and dismay he felt color his expression.

Tarkington put down his glass of brandy, stubbed out his cigar. "Well, this has been a most enlightening chat, but I do have other things that I need to attend to and I'm sure you do, too. Good day, Mr. Maxwell."

Conn took the hint, finished off his drink, and taking his cigar with him, got up and left the room.

TWENTY-THREE

I

When Conn got back to his hotel suite, he called General Frank Curtis and told him about Panstellar's strategy for Koshchei.

Curtis was less than sympathetic. "Listen, Maxwell, you sent us on a wild goose chase when you convinced me that there was another Merlin in operation. What you're telling me now is that you want the Navy's help to undermine a perfectly legitimate and legal company strategy just because you believe that it will have the same long-term impact as if Merlin's predictions become common knowledge. Sorry, but I don't buy it. I've got egg on my face, thanks to you, because I got our intelligence people to chase their tails for nothing! What exactly do you want me to do, anyway?"

"I was hoping that I could hitch a ride on a Naval ship back to Poictesme in order to get there in time to try to get our Board to turn down the negotiated deal."

General Curtis snorted. "Assuming for a moment that I believed your paranoid scenario about Panstellar's strategy, if I got the Navy to do that for you and Panstellar found out about it, they'd sue the Navy for billions in damages! So my answer to that is no."

Curtis hung up before Conn could say another word.

II

The next five days were very depressing for Conn. There was no longer anything for him to do. The agency Conn had hired to recruit ex-Navy personnel was doing its job and his participation wasn't required. No one was being watched by Kraken's people any longer and Captain Koslova was ready to leave at any time. Then Lady Luck stepped into the picture.

The company shipping agent called Conn to let him know that Tri-System Interstellar Spacelines' ship the *Wayfarer* had just entered the Sol System and would be landing in about thirteen hours. She hadn't been scheduled to return so quickly and he was concerned about not having enough cargo lined up to satisfy her captain. Conn told the agent not to be concerned about cargo as that ship would be lifting off again in less than thirty-six hours. He instructed the shipping agent to have the captain call Conn as soon as the ship touched down and was secure.

Panstellar had been in a hurry to get J. Fitzwilliam Sterber back to Poictesme so they had decided to skip the dozen intermediate stops between Terra and Poictesme, which would cut the journey down to four Galactic Standard months. Since the lawyer had left Terra over six weeks ago, Conn wouldn't be arriving until long after Sterber had already informed M-12 of Panstellar's *deal*.

Three hours later, the captain called. "Captain Jonathon Dietrich, *Wayfarer*. I understand you wanted to speak with me on an urgent matter, Mr. Maxwell?"

"Yes, Captain and thank you for calling so promptly. I need to get back to Poictesme as quickly as is humanly possible. How soon can your ship be ready to liftoff again? And don't concern yourself with cargo."

Dietrich rubbed his chin as he thought about that. "Well, we just landed. We like to give our crews at least a few days to stretch their legs after being cooped up in the ship on a long journey, but aside from that, if we absolutely had to liftoff as soon as possible, we could do that in forty-eight hours. Other than refueling, refreshing our hydroponics and carniculture vats, and airing out the compartments, we're ready to go."

"Fine. I have the necessary authorization from the Company to make a course change. Please be ready to leave in twenty-four hours. You can promise your crew a bonus to make up for the quick turnaround. It's urgent that we arrive on Poictesme as soon as possible."

Captain Dietrich asked, "Is this a secure line?"

Conn nodded. One of the first things he'd donc aftcr his arrival in Montevideo was have Kraken's people install a secure line to the outside, one that bypassed the hotel's usual communications system.

"Your father thought speed might be of the essence, which is why we arrived so soon. He had the *Wayfarer's* Dillingham drives upgraded on Koshchei with the new modifications. Yes, I know we were supposed to wait for the Federation, but Mr. Maxwell decided that you might need to get home in a hurry."

"Well, Captain, he was right. If those modifications can cut our travel time in half—"

"They have. We left the Gartner Tri-System just over two standard months ago."

"Phew!" Conn felt his heart begin to race. "Captain, this is wonderful news. We stand a good chance of returning before it's too late."

As soon as the connection was broken, Conn screened Captain Koslova.

"Hello," she answered.

"Hi," Conn replied. "Can you be ready to liftoff in forty-eight hours?"

"I can put my kit together in half that time."

"Good. One of our ships, the *Wayfarer*, just landed at the Montevideo Spaceport and I want to return to Poictesme as soon as possible."

"I take it things are not going smoothly."

"You could put it that way. I'll fill you in once were aboard the *Wayfarer*."

Koslova nodded. "I've got a dozen good people, all ex-Navy officers, who'd like to sign up. Can I bring them along?"

Conn smiled. "The more the merrier."

"I've worked with most of these people and I believe they will prove invaluable. Most got cut in the latest round of Naval layoffs…."

From the tone of her voice, Conn suspected she had expected to be cut in the next round herself, which probably explained why she'd taken their offer and left the Space Navy. "Good. I talked with the recruiting agent earlier. He has a list of eighty or so names of ex-Navy personnel. I'd like for you to go over the list and vet them. I'd like to bring as many of them with us as possible."

"I'll do what I can in the short time I have before departure," she said, her brow furrowed. "Have him send me the list immediately. Anyone who I don't know, I'll have a *friend* in personnel do a deep background check on."

After signing off, he called the shipping agent and finally General Curtis, who was not available or had decided not to answer. Conn left him a message explaining that he was leaving in less that forty-eight hours and thanked Curtis for his assistance.

III

Two days later, Conn was all packed and ready to checkout of the hotel when a Navy courier knocked on his door and handed Conn a sealed envelope, which Conn had to sign for. He opened it and it read:

I just learned about this and thought you should know about it. Good luck to you.

General (Retired) Frank L. Curtis.

Below the message was a report from Currency Export Control, which monitored the amount of physical currency arriving on or leaving the planet. It was dated the same day that J. Fitzwilliam Sterber had left Terra and it stated that Sterber had declared that he was taking five million sols worth of

Federation currency to Poictesme. Attached to the report was another piece of information (source unknown) that indicated that Terra-Baldur-Marduk Spacelines had withdrawn five million sols in cash a few hours earlier on the same day.

The implication was obvious that T-B-MS had given/paid Sterber five million sols for some unknown reason. *Bribe* was the first thing that popped into his mind. Still, Conn hoped the lawyer had a legitimate reason for accepting that money. He carefully packed the envelope and its contents away and called for the robot bellhop to carry his things to the airshuttle for the trip to the spaceport.

When he arrived at the base of the *Wayfarer*, he found about fifty or so ex-Naval personnel and Captain Koslova waiting to board. Some of the Space Navy recruits hadn't been able to leave Terra on such short notice, but they could be picked up on the next ship leaving for Poictesme.

Koslova walked up to him as he exited the airshuttle. "Please tell me I'm not making a huge mistake by going with you, Mr. Maxwell."

"I'm not promising you anything, Captain Koslova, but I'm convinced that we are headed for an armed confrontation with Panstellar's mercenaries, probably sooner than later. That's why I have to get back to Poictesme as soon as possible."

"I hope you're right, for both our sakes. I've some bad news, too."

Conn went rigid. "What is it?"

Captain Koslova said, "General Foxx Travis passed away last night on Luna at 2305 hours. I just thought you'd want to know."

"I do," Conn said before quoting a line from *Hamlet* he'd memorized in grade school: "'He was a man, take him for all in all, I shall not look upon his like again.'"

Koslova wiped at her eyes with her sleeve. "You're right. Without the General, who knows how much longer the System States War might have lasted or how many more might have died…."

Once it became clear that no one else was coming, the *Wayfarer's* captain allowed the passengers to board. Conn made sure his luggage was stowed securely, but he kept the bank draft for twenty million sols, which represented the money from the sale of the warehoused cargo, with him in his briefcase.

The loudspeakers announced that liftoff was imminent.

I

The journey back to Poictesme was uneventful. Captain Koslova turned out to be an excellent chess player, and Conn even managed to join in a few poker games with the ex-Navy people. When the *Wayfarer* emerged from hyperspace in the Gartner Tri-System two months later, Conn insisted on sending an encoded message to his father, asking him to delay any meeting concerning any negotiated deal with Panstellar if by some chance J. Fitzwilliam Sterber had beaten him home.

They were still far enough out that any reply would take minutes to reach them. Another microjump brought the ship much closer to Poictesme.

When the reply did finally arrive, Conn was relieved to find out that Sterber's ship hadn't yet arrived. His father was at the Storisende Spaceport to meet him when the ship touched down. It was just after midnight local time and

Conn guessed that was why no one else was there.

On the way down, Conn had asked his father to arrange for accommodations for the ex-Navy people, and he arranged for their transportation to one of the better hotels in Storisende. Once all of them including Koslova were taken care of, Conn and his father had an opportunity to talk privately.

"Dad, first of all I want to thank you—"

"What for, son?" his father interrupted.

"For having better foresight than I had, and having the *Wayfarer's* Dillinghams upgraded."

Rodney Maxwell nodded. "Since you were already delivering the new modifications to the Federation, I didn't think anyone would complain if we started modifying our own fleet. Plus, I had a strong suspicion you might need to return in a hurry. I had the *Wayfarer* sent to Terra as soon as the refitting was finished and tested out. So, what did you find out that brought you back so soon and why the urgent message to delay a vote on Sterber's negotiated deal?"

Conn took a deep breath. "Great Ghu, I don't know where to begin!" He paused while his father waited. "Okay. First of all, Counselor Sterber is bringing back a deal that is so good that it will be hard for M-12 to turn down. But we have to convince them otherwise, because the deal involves handing our Koshchei facilities to Panstellar Industries. Panstellar Industries will then use them to build very large freighters for practically next to nothing, just as we did, in order to put their competition throughout the Federation out of business.

"I have to check with Merlin, but my gut tells me that will not be good for the Federation's long-term prospects. Furthermore, it will leave Poictesme dependent on Terra-Baldur-Marduk Spacelines for our shipping needs as well. As if that isn't bad enough, I found out that T-B-MS handed over five million sols in cash to Sterber the day he departed and that he's bringing that money back with him."

"What!" his father cried. "Five million sols…is that our Judas's price?"

Conn shrugged. "I don't know. Maybe he's holding it as a good faith payment from Panstellar Industries."

"Yeah, sure. It's a good thing Klem Zareff isn't around to hear this; he'd have Sterber tarred and feathered within five minutes of his arrival!"

"I know, I know," Conn commiserated. "That's why we have to keep it to ourselves for now. My information about the negotiated deal didn't include any cash payment. I hope it's not a bribe, but we have to consider that a possibility."

Rodney looked worried. "Sterber's always been a straight shooter, but five million sols is a lot of temptation for anyone. Look what happened with Morgan Gatworth."

"You're right, Dad. But Morgan had gambling problems and serious debts. We thoroughly vetted Sterber on the veridicator—no secret debts, no hidden vices. I hope you're wrong in this case."

His father shrugged. Then changed the subject, asking, "How'd it go with General Travis?"

"I got to Foxx Travis, only days before he died—"

"Travis is dead? I can't believe the ground beneath our feet isn't shaking. General Travis was a giant among men; his passing marks the end of an era."

"I know, Dad. I was fortunate to see him when I did. The General put me in touch with some Navy people who helped me search for the other super-computer—"

Rodney slapped his leg. "You were right! I knew it."

"Yes, I was right. There was a backup Merlin, but I was wrong about it being put into service."

"What do you mean, Conn?"

"Further investigation by Navy Intelligence confirmed the fact that there was another super-computer manufactured at the same time as a backup; however, they discovered that it was scrapped four years ago. There's no doubt about that."

"Are you sure?"

"Absolutely. I saw the documentation."

"Well, for one, I'm damn glad they scrapped it," his father said. "But what does that do to your theory that some mastermind is attempting to cash in on the Federation's collapse?"

"That's a good question, Dad," Conn replied. "However, the answer is not a simple one. The pirate operation that captured our freighters *appears* to have been instigated by a rogue executive at Terra-Baldur-Marduk Spacelines, who was acting on his own. Or at least that's the snake oil they're selling."

"How convenient...."

"Yes, too convenient. I was able to arrange an appointment with Panstellar's President, Howard Tarkington. I believe he's our 'mastermind.'"

"The *President* of Panstellar?"

"Yes, he's a real piece of work. He flat out told me that they didn't need another Merlin to figure out that the Federation was in a long-term decline. It was obvious to the company prognosticators; after all, they were working from the same data base that Merlin was. Ironically, they're using Merlin's falsely optimistic predictions as one more reason for gaining control of Koshchei."

His father shook his head.

"But, here's the clincher. If we turn down their deal for Koshchei, Tarkington told me in no uncertain terms that Panstellar would use any means necessary, up to and including armed force, to take Koshchei away from us. They see Koshchei's manufacturing and shipbuilding facilities as essential to their plan to takeover interstellar shipping within the Federation."

"Can we stop them, Conn? They've got a hundred times our financial resources and the Federation Space Navy to back them up."

"I believe we can. For one, Koshchei's in our backyard, but four months travel time from Terra—that's a long supply line. We have the nucleus on Mothball Row of our own fleet. You saw those ex-Navy people I managed to recruit. One of them was the third-best combat tactician in the whole Federation Space Navy. Her career has reached a dead-end which is why she's here with us, but I had to make her some promises, which I'll tell you about later."

"At least you didn't come home empty-handed," his father said. "This is a lot to digest."

"Yes, and we're going to have to keep most of it to ourselves."

"Right. This is political dynamite in the wrong hands," his father said.

"You know about the rescinding of the tariff. I've also got a bank draft with lots of zeroes on it to turn over to the company. And that, in a nutshell, is pretty much it."

Rodney Maxwell looked disturbed. "That's plenty! I hope you're wrong about John taking a bribe, but we'll have to play that one very carefully. It wouldn't be fair to him to accuse him of financial malfeasance the minute he steps off the ramp. I have some ideas on how to handle this hot potato. As for the rest of it, how about you brief me in detail while I take you back to Force Command Duplicate so that you can start asking Merlin to substantiate what you've brought back."

Conn sighed. "Can we at least stop at home first so that I can say hello to my wife and son?"

His father agreed.

By the time they arrived at Litchfield, Conn was getting sleepy and his father agreed it was best to sleep on it. Sylvie was ecstatic to see her husband home so soon. Little Foxx was asleep and they decided to wait until morning to surprise him.

II

The next morning, after getting reacquainted with his family over a sumptuous breakfast, Conn flew over to Force Command Duplicate and surprised his staff who hadn't known that he was coming back today. They in turn astonished him. While he was gone, they had taken it upon themselves to program a translation capability that allowed questions to be put to Merlin and answers translated back into Lingua-Terra instead of in programming code, which would save oodles of time.

After congratulating them and promising bonuses, Conn got down to work. First he had to update Merlin about the circumstances surrounding the piracy and confirm that the Merlin binary had been scrapped four years ago. Next, he made sure that Merlin would take corporate strategies into account for its next projection as to how the Federation would fare.

Not surprisingly, Merlin predicted that the slow, more or less peaceful decay would soon change into an alarmingly more violent collapse, and Panstellar Industries—through the offices of Terra-Baldur-Marduk Spacelines—was the trigger. Its heavy-handed monopolizing of interstellar trade would inflame anti-Federation sentiment and make economic conditions on many planets worse as trade between worlds broke down. That would start a vicious cycle: less goods traded meant that T-B-MS would have to charge even more for whatever goods still were shipped, which would cause the volume of goods shipped to decline even more, resulting in even higher shipping rates, and so on.

With resentment against Terra-based corporate "carpetbaggers" soaring, Terra-Baldur-Marduk Spacelines' ships would become very tempting targets for hijackings and piracy. By this time, the Federation Space Navy would be a shadow of its former self and support for secession from the Federation would flourish, followed by renewed warship building and, soon after, interstellar warfare.

Conn's hunch that allowing control of Koshchei to change hands would drastically affect the future was confirmed. Now he asked Merlin how M-12 could prevent Terra-Baldur-Marduk Spacelines from monopolizing shipping. The answer was: retain control of Koshchei, and build lots of hyperships of various sizes. Sell most of them to other shipping companies and use the rest to compete directly against Terra-Baldur-Marduk Spacelines with subsidized shipping rates, if necessary, to promote trade not only from Poictesme to other planets but throughout the Federation. These strategies would delay the onset of conflict until the middle of the eleventh century A.E, almost a hundred and fifty years into the future.

It wasn't the slow, peaceful decline that M-12 preferred, but it was a lot better than the fast, violent collapse that Terra-Baldur-Marduk Spacelines' monopoly would bring about.

With his hunches confirmed, Conn called his father on a secure line later that evening and gave him the news.

Rodney Maxwell nodded solemnly and said, "So you were right. Koshchei is the key to a better future. We have to keep it in our hands at all costs. I talked to Captain Koslova. She's eager to get started, so I arranged for her to be flown to the Barathrum Spaceport to see what we're doing with the converted ammo freighters."

"Excellent," Conn said. "She's our hole card in this game we're playing with Panstellar over the future."

His father turned to one side to listen to a message, then turned back, saying, "Talk about timing. The *City of Asgard* just emerged from hyper-space and after three more microjumps will land in about thirty-six hours. Mr. Sterber is going to be watched very carefully when he disembarks. I've asked Lester Dawes to keep an eye out for a large cash deposit at Litchfield Bank and Trust when he's back on the surface. You'd better gather your data and get back here."

"I'm certain Sterber will want M-12 to meet as soon as possible," Conn said. "Considering what's at stake, I'm not sure if I want him to be bribed or not!"

His father nodded in agreement. "If he's been bribed and exposed, that will make it easier to turn down Panstellar's offer. I've known John for over thirty years and consider him a friend; I'd hate to think that he sold us down the river for five million pieces of silver."

Conn agreed and said that he would be back in Litchfield before the *City of Asgard* landed.

I

There was a noticeable tension in the air at Storisende Spaceport by the time the *City of Asgard* landed. All of the M-12 Group, except for President Kurt Fawzi, were there waiting for its arrival. Litchfield had its own smaller spaceport, one of the recent improvements, but Terra-Baldur-Marduk Spacelines did not use it. Litchfield Spaceport was used mostly by Tri-System and Interstellar Spacelines' ships and tramp freighters, who wanted melon-brandy, since the Gordon Valley was the heart of the planetary brandy business.

Standing at the arrival gate were half a dozen company police that Rodney Maxwell had requested. They stood to one side very quietly. Rodney and Conn were standing away from the rest of M-12.

Conn leaned over and said in a low voice. "Does anyone else know about the five million sols?"

"Only Tom Brangwyn, our security chief. I didn't have time to brief the rest of them. Just as well. We want John to be at ease. If he's carrying a briefcase, I'll try to get him to let me carry it for him and we'll see how he reacts."

"That should be telling," Conn answered.

Fifteen or so minutes later, the ship had touched down and the passenger ramp extended. Surprisingly, J. Fitzwilliam Sterber and his wife were the only passengers to disembark. Sure enough, he was carrying a silver metal briefcase with a coat folded over it so that it's handle and his hand were hidden. As the Sterbers approached the group, everyone was all smiles and friendly greetings, including Rodney and Conn Maxwell.

John was gushing about how he had great news for the group, regarding both the tariff and a settlement with the Navy over the return of the *Valley Forge*.

As the group turned to leave the terminal, Rodney stepped up to Sterber and reached out to take the briefcase from him, saying, "Here, John. Let me carry that for you. It looks heavy."

Before the lawyer could stop him, Rodney had lifted the coat and everyone saw the security chain attached to both the case and Sterber's wrist. He pretended to be surprised.

"Great Ghu, John! What have you got in that case? A small fortune in Federation bills?"

Everyone except Rodney and Sterber laughed.

Sterber looked pale, saying, "No, no…nothing like that. Just the contracts relating to the negotiated deal with Terra-Baldur-Marduk Spacelines—that's all!"

Rodney clapped his hands. "Great! Well let's see them!"

"No," he declined. "I'd rather not get them out now. I'm kind of tired and we still have an eight-hour flight back to Litchfield. We can talk about this tomorrow."

Sterber started to edge away, but Rodney grabbed his arm, saying, "But I insist, John. Open the briefcase."

He said it in a low, non-threatening way but Tom Brangwyn and the company police came closer and Sterber swallowed hard.

"Okay," he said reluctantly. Sterber turned towards the nearest counter and laid the briefcase on its side on the counter top. He then unlocked the chain from his wrist and slowly manipulated the combination lock.

Even though they didn't know what was going on, everyone gathered around. They were all quiet, and even Klem Zareff didn't have anything to say. It was obvious that this was a moment of high drama.

Sterber's wife was looking alarmed.

John hesitated, popped the top, then stepped back, saying nothing.

Rodney Maxwell stepped up to the counter, looked into the briefcase. Inside were neatly stacked bundles of wrapped hundred-sol notes.

Conn heard a few gasps.

Rodney Maxwell turned to Sterber. "I don't see any contracts here, J. Fitzwilliam. A *lot* of money, but no contracts. If you have an explanation, now's the time to offer it."

Sterber's shoulders slumped and his face blanched. He looked like he was about to faint. In a tired voice he said, "Terra-Baldur-Marduk Spacelines offered us a great deal. It really is. But they wanted a guarantee that I would support the deal, and do all I could to get it signed. I was intending to do that anyway, so I figured no harm done if I took the money they offered."

"Bribe, you mean!" Klem cried out.

No one said a word for what seemed like a long time. Rodney Maxwell turned back to the briefcase, closed it and handed it to Lester Dawes, saying. "Lester, until such time as we can figure out whether or not Sterber should be charged with taking a bribe, how about you take custody of this money and put it in your bank's vault for safekeeping? Is that a proper thing to do at this time, Judge?"

The old judge stepped forward and said, "Safeguarding evidence is entirely appropriate under the circumstances."

"Fine. John, these Interstellar Security people will go with you and ensure that both you and the money arrive at the bank safely."

Lester Dawes nodded and started walking away, followed by the security people. Everyone looked to Rodney for guidance on what to do next.

He said, "I think we should meet tomorrow afternoon and let Sterber get a good night's sleep. He can give us a detailed briefing then. In the meantime, we can all think about what that money represents and how we should deal with it."

There were a lot of unhappy faces and the group slowly broke apart as everyone went their separate ways.

II

The next afternoon, when the members of the M-12 Group met in the company boardroom, J. Fitzwilliam Sterber was subdued and somber. When everyone was present, Rodney Maxwell asked Judge Ledue to chair the meeting since President Kurt Fawzi was unable to attend. But this time Judge Ledue declined the honor.

"No, Rod, this meeting is clearly very important and I'm not as sharp as I used to be. Therefore I believe that you should chair this meeting. "

No one disagreed.

Rodney Maxwell nodded and looked around. "Fine, I don't mind taking on that responsibility. I propose that we ask John to talk about the settlement with the Navy first, followed by the details of the negotiated deal with Terra-Baldur-Marduk Spacelines. Does anyone disagree with that?"

Everyone shook their heads.

Rodney nodded to Sterber who got up slowly and, in an unusually subdued voice, described how the Navy had agreed with an amount of compensation to Tri-Systems & Interstellar Spacelines of twenty million sols in return for taking possession of the *Valley Forge*. Because that amount was within the range of possible offers that M-12 had already given him permission to accept, he had taken the settlement money and the sols had been deposited into a new bank account on Terra set up for that express purpose, the details of which Sterber would provide later.

"Next," Sterber said, his voice quivering a little bit. "Let me outline the proposed deal with Terra-Baldur-Marduk Spacelines. As a show of good faith, T-B-MS asked the Federation Office of Interstellar Trade to temporarily suspend the tariff on our cargos pending the outcome of the negotiations. In addition to permanently canceling the tariff, T-B-MS will exchange all the shares of Tri-System Investments that it owns, either directly or indirectly, for a minimum of fifty-point-one percent of the shares of Koshchei Exploration & Development. Terra-Baldur-Marduk Spacelines will also agree to stop competing for shipping business between Poictesme and Terra. Its ships on the Terra-Odin-Gimli-Poictesme-Aton-Terra run will skip the Poictesme connection altogether, giving Tri-System & Interstellar Spacelines a monopoly on all trade between those two planets."

Conn could tell that the other members of M-12, besides himself and his father, were impressed by the deal.

"In my opinion, as the Lawyer of Record for Tri-System Investments and Tri-System & Interstellar Spacelines, I believe it's a good deal for both the M-12 controlled companies and for Poictesme."

He looked around at his fellow board members to see if they agreed. Conn noted that Sterber would not meet his or his father's eyes.

Sterber slumped forward, saying, "I had already made up my mind to push for acceptance of this deal when the Controller of Terra-Baldur-Marduk Spacelines approached me with an offer of five million sols for my efforts."

"Oh, I bet you had, sonny!" Klem Zareff cried out. "A big bribe like that can really focus a man's mind." Stonewall was getting so excited he was jumping up and down and yeeking.

Sterber's face flushed, and he added, "At the very least, I should have admitted accepting the money when Rodney asked me what was in the briefcase, and then explained what it was for."

"What was it for?" Klem said. "A pay-off for railroading your friends—"

"Enough!" Rodney shouted, his voice ripping the air like a pistol shot. "Let John finish talking without interruptions, then we'll discuss what he did in detail and our response."

Sterber had the grace to look chagrined. "I would have abstained from voting either way on the deal. Believe me. You have my heartfelt apology for my lapse in judgment."

Klem said under his breath, "A convenient lapse, for you."

Rodney Maxwell thanked Sterber and asked him to leave the room so that the group could discuss what to do about the T-B-MS pay-off.

Sterber nodded and walked stiffly out of the room.

"That mealy-mouthed son of a bitch!" Klem snarled as he banged his cane's silver-headed handle on the boardroom table. "If I've told you all once, I've told you a thousand times: You can't trust lawyers, even if they do look like butter wouldn't melt in their mouths."

"That may, or may not, be true," Rodney noted. "But we've certainly learned we cannot *trust* this one."

Almost all of the M-12 members nodded in accord.

Rodney Maxwell looked around the conference table, saying, "I've been giving this situation a lot of thought since last night. As far as the deal is concerned, there's some important additional information that I'll ask Conn to brief everyone on. But, before we vote on the deal, I have a suggestion as to how we deal with Sterber.

"I've known John Sterber for over thirty years. Some of you have known him even longer. I've never known him to violate his ethics as a lawyer and have always considered him to be completely trustworthy. Before we judge him too harshly, I think we should ask ourselves what we would have done if T-B-MS had offered us a briefcase full of Federation currency to do something that we had planned to do in any case."

"I know what I'da done," Klem interrupted. "I woulda thrown that briefcase back as if it held all the hounds of Hell!"

"I'm sure you would have, Klem," Rodney responded. "However, not all of us share your moral rectitude." *Nor your paranoia*, he thought, *not that some of it wasn't justified after his run-in with Panstellar's hired gun.*

"I don't know that any one of us in this room would have been able to turn that offer down. So what I propose is that we offer Sterber a choice: The first choice is that he donates the five million sols to one of our companies to be used to promote our overall strategic agenda; if he does that, he'll be allowed to continue to participate in our group and we'll pretend this incident didn't happen. The second choice is that he can keep the money, but he has to sign over all his shares in all of the various companies that we have going, he no longer participates in any M-12 meetings, nor will we give him any more legal business. And he has to swear an oath that he will keep Merlin's secret to himself. If he violates that oath, we will pursue charges of accepting a bribe both in criminal and civil court.

"Now, once word gets around that Sterber is no longer getting legal business from M-12, it will negatively affect his legal practice, which means that he might be forced to retire from the legal profession. Of course, he'll have the five million sols to cushion the blow. What do you think of this solution?"

"I think we should shoot the rat-bastard," Colonel Klem Zareff declared.

The responses varied but by the time everyone had a chance to have their say, it was clear that no one objected to the proposal but Klem, and no one took his alternative seriously.

Judge Ledue said, "I'll go along with your proposal, Rod, but with one suggestion. Sterber should not be allowed to cast a vote for or against the deal, even if he gives up the money."

There was general agreement to that provision. Rodney went to the door, opened it and called Sterber back in.

Once Rodney explained the two choices, Sterber's expression changed to one of profound relief. "Of course, I'll give up the money; it doesn't mean anything compared to my good name and all of your friendship."

The response from the group was mostly positive, although the look on Klem's face spoke volumes.

TWENTY-SIX

Once the good wishes and pats on the back had subsided, Rodney turned to Conn and said, "Conn, why don't you brief everyone on what they need to know about the situation with Panstellar."

Conn nodded and stood up. "Before I left for Terra, I asked Merlin some questions about the piracy, where it was coming from and its impact on the future of the Federation itself. Some of these answers I found surprising, to say the least. The most surprising result was that Merlin was eighty-nine percent sure that another machine like Merlin had been constructed and was being used to deliberately cause the Federation to collapse faster and more violently than would otherwise be the case."

"Hot damn!" Klem Zareff cried out. "How come we weren't told before you left?"

Some of the others started to interrupt with questions of their own, but Rodney asked them to wait until Conn's report was finished.

"Because I didn't want anyone going off half-cocked, that's why." Conn stared directly at the Colonel so everyone got the picture. "I shared this information with my father and we agreed that someone had to be sent to Terra to try to find where the other Merlin was, and the only qualified person who could make important decisions on the spot was me."

There were nods of agreement up and down the boardroom table.

"Now you're probably asking yourselves why we didn't inform the rest of M-12 about the other Merlin; well, the blame for that rests squarely on my shoulders. I believed, and convinced my father, that the other side not knowing that we were aware of their Merlin was a priceless advantage. One that we couldn't risk losing by sharing that information with anyone else, even the members of M-12. Not after Morgan selling us out and learning that President Fawzi's office was being bugged."

There were several nods among the M-12 group, but Klem's face was a rigid mask.

"You all know what happened to Klem when that liquidator tried to break into his house."

They all nodded.

"Klem, even you must admit that if that murderer had gone after one of the other members, say a family man, things might have turned out quite differently."

Old Klem gave a reluctant nod.

Conn looked Klem straight in the eye. "My father and I talked it over and we decided it wasn't safe or prudent to entrust such an important piece of knowledge with twelve men, no matter how good and decent. So I went to Terra alone and hired a private investigative firm to follow the senior executives of Terra-Baldur-Marduk Spacelines and its parent company, Panstellar Industries. From all we've learned, they seemed to be the most likely suspects behind the scheme to derail the Federation and push it into a death spiral. We were convinced, and still are, that the majority of the company officers and stockholders had no idea of what a few misguided and rogue executives were up to.

"Our thinking was that whichever one of the companies contained the mastermind, he would lead me to the other Merlin. After my arrival on Terra, I contacted Foxx Travis, and he confirmed that a backup Merlin had been manufactured at the same time as our Merlin but it was kept disassembled in storage."

Several of the men's jaws dropped.

"General Travis put me in touch with retired General Frank Curtis who had connections with people still active in the military and they made inquiries as to the disposition of the Merlin binary. After following some false leads, we received confirmation that the backup Merlin had been scrapped four years ago and that the pirate attacks on *Pathfinder* and *Trailblazer* had been instigated by a rogue executive from T-B-MS who had been acting on his own."

"Horsefeathers!" Klem scoffed.

"Curtis and I both agreed that the so called 'rogue executive,' who committed suicide shortly after confessing, was most likely a convenient stooge."

Everyone in the room had something to say about that. "Isn't the Federation going to do anything about it?" the Judge asked.

Conn shook his head. "As far as the Federation officials I talked with are concerned the evildoer is dead. Most of the Fed officials I met were time-servers and mostly concerned about not making waves. When I got a call from General Travis telling me that he had conclusive proof that the parts for the Merlin duplicate had been destroyed…well, you could say my credibility with Military Intelligence went right out the space-lock."

"Yes, I can see their point of view," the Judge said. "You show up making all kinds of accusations against one of the most powerful corporations on Terra and just when they're starting to take you seriously, one of the most respected military men in the Sol System pulls the rug out from under you."

"That's it in a nutshell," Rodney Maxwell said, shaking his head.

"Frankly, I was shocked to find out that Merlin was wrong. But I saw the documentation and there was no reason for the Navy to cover it up at this point, since we already have possession of the original. This was later verified when I was contacted by the Chief Executive Officer of Panstellar who invited me to come to his office for a chat."

"President Howard Tarkington and I had a very interesting discussion. He showed me over four hundred years of economic charts and spreadsheets that clearly showed that the Federation was in the early stages of a long-term economic decline. He then went on to explain that Panstellar's way of coping with the new downward trend was to obtain control of the industrial facilities on Koshchei so that they could replace their fleet of freighters with ships that would be much larger and less costly to build, which they would use to force the other shipping companies into bankruptcy; thereby ending up with an effective monopoly on interstellar trade."

Even the Judge was taken aback. "He actually admitted this to you? What did he say when you accused him of having the duplicate Merlin?"

Conn shook his head wearily. "Tarkington all but laughed in my face. He pointed out that all this data was clearly available to anyone who wanted it and was willing to make the effort to extrapolate future trends from past events. They want the Koshchei mothball fleet and ship-building facilities for all the wrong reasons.

"When I asked what the response would be if we voted down the deal, he became very threatening. The tariff would be put back in place, T-B-MS would challenge the legal basis for all of our claims to the Koshchei assets and Panstellar would send mercenaries to physically secure all of the installations on Koshchei, with the excuse being that they were there to prevent us from destroying them, while the court challenge worked its way through the judicial system. Because he believed that there was no way I could get back to Poictesme before the vote on the deal was taken, Tarkington wasn't the least bit concerned that I knew their plans. It was sheer luck and my father's foresight that the *Wayfarer* arrived in time to bring me back here before Sterber arrived with Panstellar's deal."

"Now what are we going to do?" the Judge asked. "We can't afford to tie-up all the company's assets in a long drawn-out court battle."

"I know," Conn said. "That's one of the things Panstellar's President is counting on. I've had a chance to ask Merlin what the impact of Panstellar's slash and burn strategy would be; its answer is virtually the same as if news of the Federation's eventual decline were to become widespread. Merlin also confirmed that its original slow, more or less peaceful decline that represents the status quo was never really the most likely outcome, once the reaction of commercial companies like Panstellar were explicitly taken into consideration.

"The best that we can realistically hope for is to delay the ultimate breakdown of Federation authority, and the violence that will follow, until the middle of the Eleventh Century A.E. The only way that can happen is if we keep control of Koshchei and use it ourselves to keep interstellar shipping for the entire Federation as competitive as possible by building and selling cheap hyperships."

Nobody looked too happy at that announcement. It appeared that some of the Merlin faithful were losing faith in the super-computer's infallibility. Klem Zareff's face was scrunched-up like a crab apple.

"Just before I boarded the *Wayfarer*," Conn continued, "I received a message from General Curtis informing me that Terra-Baldur-Marduk Spacelines had paid J. Fitzwilliam Sterber five million sols. Which is how we knew what to look for when you came back, Mr. Sterber."

He nodded, casting his eyes down, as though studying the table top.

"Great Ghu, Conn. I had no idea of what they were up to," the Judge said. "Of course, we'll have to turn the deal down."

Conn said, "The *City of Asgard* has been ordered to wait at Storisende Spaceport for a maximum of ninety-six hours in order to bring back the results of the vote. If no vote is taken in that time, Panstellar will interpret that as a 'no' vote. I didn't mention it during my briefing because I assumed that we would be voting on the deal today, and therefore they would have their answer before the ninety-six hours were up."

Rodney turned to Conn. "Did you want to add anything else, son, before we discuss the deal and vote on it?"

Conn shook his head. Rodney asked the group if there were any questions.

There were none. Everyone at the table looked downcast.

Rodney, acting Chair, called for a vote. The vote was unanimously against taking the deal. Conn noticed that his father's expression was one of profound relief.

Discussion then turned to how they would deal with Panstellar's threats. With two thirds of the stock of Tri-System & Interstellar Spacelines under M-12's direct and indirect control, the original plan to allow the bank to repossess the hyperships for violating debt covenants was suspended. Tri-System & Interstellar Spacelines was now well-capitalized with the sale of the cargo brought back by the *Wayfarer*, plus the money on Terra for the *Valley Forge*.

Rodney had grounded all of the interplanetary ships owned by Panstellar's agents through Tri-System Investments and their crews had been transferred to a few of the interplanetary ships that had been moved from Koshchei to Poictesme and were now owned by Litchfield Exploration & Development, Ltd.

This meant that Panstellar would end up owning Alpha Interplanetary's fleet of grounded ships, but with no revenue coming in it would be pretty much a bust. Alpha Interplanetary still owned one third of Tri-System & Interstellar Spacelines, but that wasn't enough to exercise control.

"Now that we've defied Panstellar, the tariff on Terra will soon be reinstated," Rodney Maxwell said. "I now propose that the hyperships that were formerly used on the Terra-Poictesme run should be redeployed to Baldur, Odin, Aton and Marduk for starters. We'll just bypass Terra as a destination for as long as the tariff is in force."

Everyone liked that and the Judge made a toast, "To Merlin and free trade!"

"Down with the Federation!" Klem added, spontaneously, then looked around sheepishly.

When everyone had quieted down, Rodney continued, "Next, we should start designing very large freighters in our Koshchei spaceyards. Freighters that would be sold to all shipping companies *except* Terra-Baldur-Marduk Spacelines."

This led to more toasts to "Free Trade" and a "Down with Panstellar!" cry from Klem Zareff.

When the discussion turned to the Panstellar President Howard Tarkington's threat of military occupation of Koshchei, Conn informed everyone that he had recruited the Navy's third-best combat tactician and that she should be given operational control over all off-world armed forces.

"According to General Frank Curtis, Captain Koslova is just about the best tactician the Space Navy *had*. She even has a revolutionary idea for converting interplanetary freighters into hyper-jump-capable missile cruisers."

Klem Zareff and Tom Brangwyn were both enthusiastically in favor of the idea.

Rodney Maxwell said, "I'll put her in touch with our engineers at the Barathrum Spaceport. This is a project we need to start work on yesterday."

Chief Tom Brangwyn talked about integrating the ex-Navy personnel that Conn brought back into the rapidly expanding paramilitary force run by Interstellar Security.

He told the group that all twenty ammo freighters had now been converted into corvettes and eight were currently stationed on trade planets. Tom finished with, "Now that the pirate threat appears to have been dealt with, I wonder if we shouldn't bring those corvettes back to the Gartner Tri-System?"

It was a good question. Rodney put it up for comments and analysis. The general consensus was that it was a good idea. Kurt Fawzi, who'd just arrived from Storisende, told Conn that the legislature had approved a standing military force that would be leased from Interstellar Security and he then added, "Perhaps, one way of neutralizing any court challenge to the Abandoned Property Act of 867 would be if the colony on Koshchei declared itself to be a sovereign entity and annexed all former Federation facilities. It could then lease them back to Koshchei Exploration & Development for a modest annual fee in lieu of taxes."

"I'll second that motion," Rodney Maxwell said. "All in favor, say aye. Those opposed, say nay."

The ayes took it unanimously.

Conn nodded happily, since that would strengthen the defense against Panstellar's court challenge. It would also provide the legal justification for employing military force, if necessary, to prevent Panstellar's mercenaries from seizing control of those assets.

There was general agreement that Poictesme's planetary defense forces would be used to defend Koshchei.

When the discussion came to the last point, which was whether to advise *City of Asgard* of the results of the vote, Klem Zareff made the clinching argument. "I say we tell those jaspers that no vote has been taken, then stall as long as possible. If they have to leave after ninety-six hours, that's their problem. Yes, they say they'll interpret a non-vote as a vote against the deal. So what? That's what we've done anyway. This way they won't know what the vote is."

"I like that, Klem," Rodney said. "If they're not sure of the outcome, and if they think there's a chance of the vote going their way, they may not move against Koshchei right away. The extra time could be valuable to us."

"So I propose that we have J. Fitzwilliam Sterber contact the ship and tell the Panstellar rep that we haven't voted, and he doesn't know when we will vote."

Everyone agreed.

After the meeting broke up, Lester Dawes came over to Conn. "Conn, on behalf of the others I want to express our thanks for what you did by going to Terra and saving us from making a horrible mistake. If you hadn't told us about Panstellar's plans, I'm pretty sure we all would have voted to accept the deal."

"Believe me, Lester, when I say that no one is happier about how things turned out than I am," Conn replied.

That night when Conn got home to his family, he had the first really restful sleep in weeks. He took the next few days off and spent some time with his family. When he finally decided to go back to work, he found that a lot of things were in motion.

Under the authority of the act authorizing the establishment of a planetary defense force, President Kurt Fawzi appointed Valentina Koslova as the Planetary Defense Force's first director and also its first chief of operations with the rank of commodore. Her first act was to immediately delegate administrative responsibilities to Tom Brangwyn.

Koslova's next official act as director was to sign an agreement to lease ships and certain facilities from Interstellar Security and to pay them for the services of some of its people who were being seconded to Poictesme's Planetary Defense Force. The PPDF was well on its way to hiring most of the ex-Navy people away from Interstellar Security.

By this time, the *City of Asgard* had jumped out of the Gartner Tri-System and was on its way to Aton. Even if it cut their journey short, it would be at least sixteen to eighteen weeks before news could reach Terra, plus another sixteen weeks for any mercenaries to travel straight back to the Gartner Tri-System, plus the time in between to organize a paramilitary force. Conn estimated that it would be at least eight months, or more, before an attack could materialize.

The *Genji* had returned from the trade run to Bifrost with news that Terra-Baldur-Marduk Spacelines' crews had brought the two captured ships to Valhalla and informed *Genji's* captain that the ships could be reclaimed there. As soon as *Genji* was ready to return to Bifrost, she had embarked with the two hijacked ships' crews, who were eager to get their ships back. With all four large hyperships now on the ground at Litchfield Spaceport, Tri-System & Interstellar Spacelines was busy buying brandy and tobacco plus other cargo to send to Baldur, Zarathustra, Odin, Gimli, Aton and Marduk.

For the first time in a long time, Conn Maxwell wasn't spending most of his time in Merlin's hideaway. There was no time to second-guess their plans and, like many of the M-12 members, Merlin had lost some of its cachet when its prediction of a second super-computer turned out to be flat-out wrong. Things were now set in motion that no one person or thing could halt.

He was in his office at the Airlines Building when his secretary announced that his father was in the anteroom. "Tell him to come on in, Rita."

His father had bags under both eyes and his now almost all-gray hair was all messed up, like he'd forgotten to comb it. "Hi, son. I understand you wanted to see me."

"Yes, I want to send one of our ships back to Terra. They can use our remaining funds there to buy military equipment and supplies that we're having trouble manufacturing locally. I've got a list here of those items sent to me by Commodore Koslova."

"That's a good idea. I'm glad she's on our side."

"How about you, Dad? You don't look like you've been getting enough sleep."

"Probably not, it's your mother. She thinks I've been neglecting her again, so I'm burning the candle at both ends."

"We all are, I fear. It's either that or let Panstellar come in and call the shots."

"Oh, I agree. Win, lose or draw; it'll all be over before year's end."

With his worst fears about a second Merlin put to rest and the path ahead clearly laid out, Conn felt more confident and relaxed than he had in a long time. The *Ouroboros II* would very likely be the last Poictesme-based hypership visiting Terra for a long time. It would also be carrying official notification that the Koshchei Planetary Assembly had applied to become a Member Republic of the Terran Federation. The new government had annexed all the former Federation property on the planet and had the ability and will to defend its sovereign territory against armed aggression. If it were granted membership, the Gartner Tri-System would have twice as much influence in the Federation Parliament.

If Panstellar did challenge Koshchei's application and property claims in court, the ship also carried instructions to Koshchei Exploration and Development's legal firm on Terra, hired on retainer, as to how they should defend the case.

Preparations had already started on a monster two-thousand foot hypership freighter, which would be designed from the ground up to carry up to four five-hundred foot interplanetary ships if necessary. It would also be the first new ship outfitted with the hyperdrive improvements suggested by Yves Jacquemont. He had been testing them ever since Conn had left for Terra.

Three months later, a prototype modular hyperdrive and external missile pod were successfully tested on one of the many interplanetary ships left behind by the Federation. With robot factories able to manufacture both, Commodore Koslova was certain that at least one squadron of hyper-capable missile cruisers would be operational by the time a military response from Panstellar was likely to occur. That squadron would be kept out of any no-jump zones so that it could immediately microjump to Koshchei's aid if unknown ships approached that planet.

All the corvettes were back in the Gartner Tri-System. Half of the corvette force was based on Koshchei ready to be deployed on fifteen minutes warning. The rest of the corvettes were based on Poictesme to protect Merlin. The *Ouroboros II* had returned from Terra with cargo consisting of sophisticated detection systems, decoy drones and specialized electronic components that were required for missiles that couldn't be made locally, as well as another two hundred ex-Navy personnel that Koslova quickly added to the Planetary Defense Force.

Conn also received a recorded message back from General Frank Curtis.

It sounds like you people have things well in hand. I can tell you that Panstellar's unofficial inquiries to the Navy about assisting in the "securing of Koshchei assets" have been firmly rebuffed. Koshchei declaring itself a sovereign world and applying as a Member Republic of the Federation separate from Poictesme was a clever move. Navy Intelligence is hearing that Panstellar's board is now in a quandary over whether to go ahead with the military move at all. I doubt if they'll actually do it.

Because of your advance warning, Naval Intelligence agents are keeping a close eye on what that board and CEO are doing and if there's any hint of illegal actions like piracy, the Federation will take action. Good luck to all of you.

General Frank Curtis (ret.)

II

General Frank Curtis was wrong. The attack, when it came, occurred almost nine Galactic Standard months after J. Fitzwilliam Sterber arrived back on Poictesme. It was a very well-planned attack. Commodore Koslova's plan to have at least one squadron of missile cruisers proved to be overly optimistic. True, eight five-hundred foot interplanetary ships had been modified to accept external missile pods, but only four of them had been fitted with the modular hyperdrives and she had difficulty finding crews for those four. Each missile cruiser had the ability to launch onc hundred and fifty missiles, either as one single massive barrage or as a series of smaller partial barrages.

The total number of missiles compared favorably with the missile load of a twelve-hundred foot diameter Navy light cruiser.

Panstellar's attack force turned out to consist of three two-thousand foot diameter hyperspace freighters that between them carried twenty-four of the larger space-combat capable gunboats that at one time had been stationed on Poictesme but had been removed when the Federation pulled out.

Each of the one-hundred-and-twenty-foot diameter gunboats had two 120mm cannon plus four missile launchers each fed with twenty offensive missiles and twenty counter-missiles and were protected by collapsium armor.

Commodore Koslova's cruiser force was stationed just beyond the no-jump zone over Koshchei's north pole. As per normal operating procedures, she rotated one of her cruisers back to the base on Koshchei to rest the crew every two weeks, so she only had two cruisers fully manned and on station. Since the fourth cruiser was only partially manned, it was only available on an emergency basis but could be called into action on fifteen minutes notice.

Commodore Koslova was resting in her cabin, reading a book, when her intercom buzzed.

"Koslova here."

"Combat Control here, Commodore. Remote sensors have just detected three large ships emerging from hyperspace approximately thirty-five thousand miles outside of the no-jump zone and only slightly south of the planetary equator. The vessels are not squawking any transponder signals nor are they transmitting any communication or radar signals."

Koslova immediately jumped up and reached for her emergency pressure suit. "Okay. Go to General Quarters and make sure *Zhukov* does the same. Order *Yamamoto* to liftoff immediately and head to Point Baker! The corvettes on alert status are to liftoff immediately and head for the bogeys. Standby crews are to report to their corvettes immediately, but they are to remain on the ground until I order otherwise. Have them advise me when ready. I'll be in CC in two minutes. Maintain zero emissions as planned, Koslova out."

Koslova finished donning the pressure suit but left the flexible helmet off until it was needed, carrying it with her as she ran out of her cabin to the stairs leading to the room refitted for tactical combat control one level up. As she entered Combat Control, she wished for the nth time that this ship was a real navy cruiser, designed from the ground up for combat, rather than a civilian freighter with limited offensive and detection capability.

The room now used for Combat Control had been the officers' lounge. Interstellar Security's engineers had added large screens, target tracking and weapon stations, command and damage control stations but, nonetheless, it was still a jury-rigged set up.

She settled into her command station chair and looked at the main screen. The tactical display showed a small circle representing Koshchei, with a red ring around it denoting the limit of the no-jump zone.

A flashing red triangle, with the number "3" inside it, was outside the no-jump zone. The numbers next to it told Koslova that the three bogeys were barely moving relative to Koshchei.

She adjusted her controls so that the screen now showed the tactical situation from both *above* and from the *side*. The side view showed missile cruisers *Zhukov* and her flagship *Guderian* just above the no-jump circle over Koshchei's north pole. She started to give a command, "Astrogator, plot a microjump for both ships to put us 55 miles beyond the…."

Before Koslova could finish the command to jump behind the three ships, the screen changed. The three ships jumped away and left behind twenty-four very small craft that were now accelerating at 6 Gs towards Koshchei.

Damn, she thought to herself. *Whoever planned that operation isn't taking any chances. Jump in, launch these smaller craft, then jump away to avoid attack on the vulnerable motherships.*

"Let's try to identify those craft ASAP!" she snapped.

The main viewscreen now showed an additional five small craft moving from Koshchei towards the incoming vessels. Those would be the five corvettes on alert status for quick liftoff.

"Okay, now we wait," Koslova said to no one in particular. It had been decided that for legal and political reasons, the intruders would be allowed to fire first. Then the defending forces would have clear justification to fire back.

"Did we warn those craft off?" she asked. The answer was immediate.

"Yes, Commodore. As soon as we spotted them, Koshchei Space Control ordered them to leave the vicinity. No reply ye….wait a minute." The communications tech switched on the loudspeakers.

"…are here pursuant to an order by the Federation Supreme Court that permits Panstellar to secure all facilities and equipment on Koshchei, pending the outcome of Panstellar's legal challenge to the Abandoned Property Act of 867. We have been hired by Panstellar to ensure that company engineers on the transport ships can land safely. In order to accomplish this mission peacefully, all armed forces on or over Koshchei are ordered to stand-down."

The recorded message repeated itself. Koslova signaled the tech to cut off the message. The audacity of the message was breathtaking. The Federation Supreme Tribunal would not order the plaintiff of a pending case to take "possession" of disputed property. They might order the Navy to do so, but not a private company. It was a bluff designed to allow Panstellar's mercenaries to waltz right in without firing a shot.

"Tell our ships to ignore that stand-down directive," Koslova ordered.

Her directive was acknowledged.

When the Panstellar forces didn't get any response, they then issued a threat of their own: "If you do not stand-down, we are prepared to use force to compel you to. You have five minutes to comply."

The five minutes went quickly. According to the tactical display, which contained data relayed from Koshchei, the twenty-four Panstellar craft were now moving at eight-point-two mps. They were still far outside the no-jump zone and still a good distance from Koshchei. Since both the enemy ships and the Koshchei corvettes on alert had started accelerating from zero, it would be some time before either side was in missile range.

Commodore Koslova wondered what they could possibly do while still this far away. When the answer appeared to be nothing, she chalked it up to more bluffing. After ten more minutes passed, Koslova received word that the corvettes on standby status on Koshchei were now manned and prepped for liftoff upon her command. If she ordered them to engage now, and ordered the alert group of corvettes to reduce acceleration, the standby group could catch up by the time the range was down enough to contemplate missile fire.

Missile cruiser *Yamamoto* was still some distance away from rendezvousing with *Guderian* and *Zhukov*.

Is it better to keep the five standby corvettes on Koshchei as a reserve and let the five alert corvettes bear the brunt of the incoming attack or should I commit the reserve and give the alert corvettes a better chance of surviving the battle?

"Do we have *any* idea of what those craft are yet?" she asked in an exasperated voice.

Her tactical officer answered. "Based on radar reflections and acceleration, the computers think we're looking at twenty-four Sawtooth class gunboats. One hundred and twenty feet in diameter, two cannons, four missile launchers and collapsium armor." Collapsium armor meant they would be difficult to knock-out.

Koslova briefly considered, then discarded, the option of using nukes on them. That was an escalation that would be hard to justify. As long as the enemy didn't use nukes, she wouldn't either, although two could play at the bluffing game if things got scary.

That left kinetic-energy penetrator warheads, which meant lots of missiles attempting to overpower defensive counter-missile capability and hope for crippling hits. That meant the alert group's odds of winning this confrontation were much better if all ten corvettes were operating together. Koslova made a decision.

"Order the two corvette groups to rendezvous before they get into missile range."

By the time that happened, almost thirty minutes had gone by and both sides had covered about a third of the initial distance meaning that the distance between them was down to roughly fifty thousand miles and the opposing force's speed was now up to fifty-six mps. Missile range was coming into focus very fast.

Koslova looked at *Yamamoto's* estimated time to rendezvous. She was decelerating now so that she would come to rest where *Guderian* and *Zhukov* waited and that would be in about another fifteen minutes.

Still no further messages from the incoming force, which Koslova found very peculiar.

A ping from the tactical display notified Koslova that both approaching forces were now within missile range of each other but the gunboats weren't firing. *Why not?* she wondered. They needed all the time they could get to fire as many barrages as possible, given that they could only launch four missiles per gunboat at a time. *I'm missing something! What is it?*

She was just about to order the corvettes to commence firing when the tactical display gave a double ping and a new symbol appeared on the opposite side of Koshchei. A flashing red triangle with the number 3 inside it. The freighters had jumped back into the picture. Seconds later, the number inside the triangle started going up: five, eight, thirteen, twenty-one and then finally twenty-seven. Suddenly Koslova had it figured out.

The three freighters weren't big enough to carry forty-eight gunboats. But they could carry twenty-four gunboats plus twenty-four drones designed to act and give off radar reflections like gunboats.

The important question was this. Which group of twenty-four units were the real gunboats and which were the decoys? Koslova decided that security on the missile cruiser project had been sufficiently tight that it was unlikely that Panstellar knew she had a second backup force available.

Given that set of assumptions, it made far more sense that the initial group of twenty-four were the decoys deployed in such a way as to pull the defending corvettes away from Koshchei so that the real gunboats could charge in from the rear before the corvettes could reverse direction and come back. She made the decision to roll the dice with that assumption.

"Order the corvette force to fire one missile at each target. Let's see if they shoot back. Tell *Yamamoto* to forget about rendezvousing with us and to get outside the no-jump zone as soon as she can. Astrogator, how far apart are those motherships?"

Signals-and-detection answered, "Approximately five miles, sir."

"Fine. Contact *Zhukov* and *Yamamoto*. I want our ships to emerge from hyperspace not more than half a mile away from each of those ships."

Her astrogator looked at her in horror. No one expected jump accuracy like that. The risk of emerging inside another ship was too great.

Koslova nodded. "I know the risks. Do it."

The astrogator nodded and turned to his console. Koslova knew that her strategy depended on the motherships remaining where they were. If they jumped away again, she would go ahead with the same suicidally close microjump on the gunboats.

The tactical display pinged again. *Yamamoto* was accelerating again and would clear the no-jump zone in seven minutes. Her interception would be trickier than *Guderian*, or *Zhukov's*.

Both of those ships were more or less stationary and when they jumped, they would still be more or less stationary afterwards. *Yamamoto* on the other hand would have built up a considerable vector by the time she jumped and she would still be moving at the same speed and direction after she emerged from hyperspace. The astrogator had to take that into consideration when calculating the jump co-ordinates, otherwise Yamamoto might smash into one of the motherships if she emerged from hyperspace at the wrong point.

So far the motherships hadn't jumped away again. Koslova suspected that her counterpart was on one of those motherships and therefore needed to be close enough to the action to give orders if necessary.

Just then her corvette force fired a timed barrage of twenty-four missiles, one for each enemy decoy. With an acceleration of 55 Gs, those missiles would eat up the remaining 45,000 miles to target in a handful of minutes. Koslova was not surprised to see that the twenty-four targets were *not* firing back. Not even counter-missiles, which would have been the prudent thing to do—if they were in fact gunboats.

The further away you could intercept incoming missiles, the better because it gave you more time to fire additional waves of counter-missiles if needed.

She turned to her tactical officer. "Weapons, have a fire plan ready to execute the split-second we emerge from hyperspace. If those motherships are still there, I want each of our ships to fire thirty missiles at the nearest mothership. As soon as the missiles have been launched, I'll order another microjump to a distant point where we will prepare to jump back to within point blank range of the gunboats, and then we will immediately fire ten missiles at each gunboat. We'll save the remaining missiles for another attack if needed.

"Astrogator! Did you get that about jumping away again?"

"Got that, Commodore!"

Koslova turned to the viewscreen on her command station and programmed some calculations. If the corvette force turned 180 degrees and went to maximum acceleration, they would get back to Koshchei almost half an hour after the second—real group of gunboats—reached Koshchei and set up defensive positions that would be hard to eliminate without unacceptable collateral damage to facilities and inhabitants. Very clever plan.

She ordered all corvettes to return to Koshchei base as soon as possible.

By the time they slowed down to a complete stop in order to come back to the planet, they would have crossed paths with the decoys anyway and since the decoys weren't firing back at them, they could easily take them out. Her job now was to stop the real gunboats.

Yamamoto was less than a minute away from being able to jump. She heard her astrogator speak.

"Microjumps for all three ships have been calculated and loaded. Follow-up microjump is in the buffers. Standing by."

"Acknowledged! Weapons, are you ready?"

"Ready!" came the reply. The remaining seconds until all three cruisers could jump counted down quickly. When the countdown reached zero, Koslova waited another thirty seconds to be sure, then gave the command for a synchronous timed microjump by all three cruisers.

The microjump was virtually instantaneous. The tactical display went crazy with proximity alarms warning of possible collision. *Guderian* emerged from hyperspace only half a kilometer, less than the diameter of the Panstellar freighter itself, away from its target. Two seconds later, the Tactical Officer announced missile launch in a high-pitched voice. Two seconds after that, *Guderian* jumped back again to its previous location and the other two cruisers arrived in the vicinity at almost the same time. They were still able to get radar data relayed to them by Koshchei ground-based sensors.

It showed that the missiles fired at that insanely close range hit all three freighters before the targets had time to jump away. Sensors detected venting of atmosphere from all three targets. If those freighters had been armored warships, the point-blank attack wouldn't have worked because the collapsium penetrator warheads wouldn't have built up enough velocity to be able to punch their way through the equally tough armor. However, these were commercial vessels with ordinary metal alloy hulls and the missiles provided just enough kinetic energy to get through.

It was impossible to tell how much damage they had inflicted, but Koslova hoped that if nothing else, their hyperdrives would now be offline. If she could force those ships to surrender, they should be able to force

Panstellar to pay a hefty price to get them back. But she had no time to worry about that now. There were twenty-four gunboats racing towards Koshchei that required her attention.

She quickly moved over to the astrogator's station and motioned for her tactical officer to join her. She explained to both of them what she wanted to do. They nodded and got busy making the arrangements. The final plan differed somewhat from what she had originally been contemplating. *Guderian* and *Zhukov* could jump quite close to the wave of gunboats due to their relatively slow velocity. They could then fire a barrage of missiles that the gunboats would likely not have time to intercept with counter-missiles. Unfortunately, that meant her missiles wouldn't have time to build-up a lot of kinetic energy to be able to punch through the gunboats' collapsium armor.

If her ships jumped in and fired from further away, they would have the necessary kinetic energy, but the gunboats would also have enough time to intercept them. *Yamamoto* was the key. She already had almost four hundred miles per second velocity built up. That meant that any missiles she launched would also start out with that velocity. Even if she jumped to within one thousand, six hundred miles of the gunboats, she would overtake them in two seconds.

So the revised plan was for *Yamamoto* to jump about fifty-five miles ahead and about a thousand miles below the wave of gunboats. She would then fire five kinetic energy penetrator missiles at each gunboat and then immediately jump away. With almost no warning, the gunboats would not be able to launch counter-missiles in time. At that velocity, the damage done by the incoming missiles should be considerable.

As soon as *Yamamoto* was ready, Koslova gave the go-ahead. It was all over in less than ten seconds.

Sensors detected clear evidence of damage to each gunboat. Koslova ordered them to surrender and a half minute later, they did so. She ordered them to decelerate to zero relative motion if their maneuvering drives were still operating and if they weren't, then the crews had to abandon their gunboats.

Only five were able to slow down, the rest were abandoned. Precise measurements by Koshchei ground control showed that the abandoned gunboats would crash into Koshchei safely away from any inhabited areas.

As it turned out, one of the motherships was able to jump away and did so. The other two also surrendered. Two hours later, both motherships, the five maneuverable gunboats and the lifeboats from the abandoned gunboats were all being escorted to Koshchei by the three missile cruisers and the ten corvettes that had now made it back to the opposite side of the planet after destroying the decoys.

Over the next seventy-two hours, all of the passengers and crews of the hyperships and gunboats were interrogated. It was discovered that the three motherships were two mothballed freighters plus an active freighter that was pulled out of service. All of the captured personnel were sequestered in barracks that had been used by Federation troops during the War. Koslova was called back to Poictesme and given a medal. Everyone except Conn Maxwell behaved as if the whole thing was over.

I

As far as Conn Maxwell was concerned, the stakes were simply too high to think that Panstellar would give up now. Two weeks later, news arrived from Terra that the Supreme Tribunal had decided that possession was in fact one hundred percent of the law and, since the various properties had been abandoned outright, whoever controlled those properties had the right to keep possession of them.

If the attack had succeeded, Panstellar's mercenaries would have been in control. It was easy to confirm that the attack was dispatched from Terra immediately after the verdict had been released in the hope that control would have changed hands by the time the news had arrived.

Judge Ledue explained to the rest of M-12 that this meant it was open season on abandoned property in the Gartner Tri-System. Koshchei and even the spaceport and Force Command

Duplicate on Poictesme for that matter, belonged to their current owners for only as long as they could physically keep control of them.

The Merlin-12 Group decided to let the captured civilian participants leave as soon as T-B-MS arranged for transportation for them, if it bothered to do so. The mercenaries, however, were another story. Those who were cooperative were offered a position with Commander Koslova; those who refused were to be tried in Koshchei courts as common criminals.

With the first of the new very large freighters almost complete, and regular runs to Odin, Aton, and Marduk among other highly developed planets progressing smoothly, Tri-System & Interstellar Spacelines was again making a profit. When Koslova put forward the radical notion of converting both of them to missile battleships, able to carry up to six-hundred missiles externally as well as parasite craft internally, the two captured freighters were repaired, refitted and earmarked for trade runs. She also recommended that Poictesme's Planetary Defense Force ask for the development of missile-carrying drones that could also act as decoys if needed.

II

Howard Tarkington was mad as hell. The *City of Nefertiti* had just returned with news of the disastrous Battle of Koshchei. Two hyperships lost, hundreds of engineers and technicians that would have to be returned at company expense, lump-sum payments to the heirs of the dead mercenaries. The cost of the operation, which had been budgeted at fifty million sols, now looked like a loss of at least ten times that figure, when the write-off of the two lost ships were added to the cost.

The board would be furious. Panstellar's stock was already dropping on rumors of poor financial results for the fiscal year. When he entered the boardroom for the emergency board meeting, he could tell that he was now on thin ice. Board members who would normally be friendly were now being coldly polite.

After the Chairman called the meeting to order, they moved

immediately to the results of the Koshchei operation. Tarkington explained to the group as best he understood it of the actual events of the battle and the fact that Koshchei had jump-capable hyperships of unusually small size from the sound of them, that had upset the carefully laid plans which dozens of simulations had predicted would work. Unfortunately, the board was not in a mood for excuses.

After Tarkington finished his briefing, the Chairman said, "Howard... that explanation sounds quite logical; however, I'm afraid that it won't change anything. Most of us on this Board have been having informal discussions and we've reached a consensus.

"When word of this fiasco gets out, the financial press will crucify us if we don't take some action. The sad fact is that someone's head has to roll and it's our concerted opinion the head that has to roll is yours."

Howard clenched his fists, "It's not fair. You all backed my plan!"

"Of course it's not fair, life's not fair—you know that. You also understood when you were given the president's position that you might be required to fall on your sword. Well, that time has come."

Tarkington was defiant. "Firing me won't change the Koshchei situation. Without that planet under our control, Terra-Baldur-Marduk Spacelines' and Panstellar's prospects are pretty limited. If you fire me, who will you get that can accomplish that goal and how will they do it? I'm the only one who can! You need me!"

The Chairman shook his head sadly. "No, Howard. We don't." Turning to the rest of the Board of Directors, he said. "Do I hear a motion to replace Howard Tarkington as President of Panstellar, Ltd?"

One of the others put forward the motion. Another seconded it.

The Chairman called for a vote. The motion passed unanimously.

As Tarkington was being escorted out of the building, he took a deep breath and thought, *This isn't over, not by a long shot. By the time I sell my shares in Panstellar and make some discreet proposals to wealthy investors who don't care how they make their money, I'll have enough money to set up a pirate operation of my own. Then we'll see who has the last laugh.*

III

Conn Maxwell was eating breakfast with the family. While the robot-server was passing out the plates of food, he said, "I'm not used to having so much time on my hands."

Sylvie smiled, lighting up his day. "We like having you around, don't we, Foxx?"

Little Foxx looked up from his bowl of cereal and smiled. "Un-huh."

"I like being around, but it's the reason I have so much time that's bothering me," he said.

"What's that, dear?"

"Everyone around me, at least in M-12, appears to be living in Cloud Cuckoo Land; they believe that with one victory Panstellar is going to turn over on its belly and we've won the war. Now, there's talk of disbanding the Planetary Defense Force as an unnecessary expenditure."

"Well, it is costly," Sylvie said. "And we sure could use some of that money for the Litchfield School District."

"See, that's what I mean. After all the money Panstellar invested, first on the pirate attacks and later on the Koshchei invasion force, they're going to want some kind of dividend. The latest word from Terra is that Panstellar stock has taken a nosedive. I've met President Tarkington, and I don't believe he's the type that will 'forgive and forget.' But no one else in M-12 seems to get it."

Sylvia shook her head. "Maybe it's because you're beginning to sound a little like Klem Zareff."

"Great Ghu, I hope not. Still, Klem's paranoia paid off big time when that thug from Terra came knocking."

"Yes, but that's the first time it has since I've known him."

"True. I guess what's really bothering me is that no one is taking Merlin's predictions seriously anymore. Sure, they'll give me lip service when

I tell them that Merlin says there's better than a sixty-two percent chance that Panstellar or Tarkington will make another move against Koshchei and Interstellar Securities. But, instead of preparing for it, they want to layoff Commodore Koslova."

"You know," Sylvie interrupted. "She's really quite striking. Valentina was visiting the Mall last week and I saw her there. I introduced myself and we went to Senta's and had lunch. Valentina is really a beautiful woman, once you get her out of that uniform. Her eyes are almost emerald in color and her ebony complexion is flawless."

"Hmm, I must say I never noticed."

Sylvie laughed. "I can't say I'm surprised. If it isn't a computer or a robot, you don't really look very close."

Conn shrugged his shoulders. "You know me too well. Still, the current situation on Poictesme reminds me of the period in Terran history, right after the Third World War, when organized religion took a big hit. With most of the Northern Hemisphere radioactive slag, the survivors blamed god, and/or his earthly representatives. Almost every religion left on Terra lost a lot of followers. To this day, none of the major religions, at least those that have survived, have recovered even a tenth of their former worshippers."

"Ah," she said. "So you're saying that now, since Merlin's been proved fallible, that there's been a loss of faith in his predictions and Merlin-12's guidance."

"Exactly! Now don't get me wrong, I don't agree with bowing down to god-Merlin like some do, but at the same time we shouldn't discount its predictions because of one bad call. It's a tool, after all, maybe the best tool in human history."

"That's a good point," Sylvie said.

"What eggs my face is that the biggest scoffer of all is that former dedicated Merlinolator, President Fawzi. What a hypocrite! Now that he's fallen in with the First Families outfit, he's become a different person. One I don't like. You ought to see his Presidential Office; it's in worse taste than that old bordello that used to run itself out of the Litchfield Mall before it was rebuilt."

"Watch what you say, Conn. We've got little ears to watch out for."

He turned to see little Foxx suddenly alert with eyebrows raised.

"What did I miss, Mommy?"

"Nothing, dear. Daddy was just speaking out of turn."

Conn returned to eating his shovel-snout ham. After swallowing, he said, "I know I'm outvoted these days, but I have a feeling that bad times are on the way."

I

Commodore Koslova was nervous about the upcoming meeting at the presidential office in Storisende. It was now over six months since the attack on Koshchei and nothing had happened since then. She knew that one of the agenda items for this meeting of President Kurt Fawzi's cabinet was to consider how much longer the planetary government would continue to pay for a planetary defense force. Rumors of cutbacks or even outright disbandment of the entire force had been circulating for weeks.

She turned to Conn Maxwell. "Well, what's it to be? My head on a platter, or a brief extension?"

Conn shook his head. "I don't know, Commodore. I believe we need you and your team until we know just how things are shaking out on Terra. I find it hard to believe, after all their expenditures that Panstellar is just going to write this off."

"With my bonus and the severance package you promised, I'll be in fine shape," Koslova noted. "Like you, I'm just worried because I don't believe my job here is done."

"Unfortunately, my influence here has diminished in direct proportion to the President Fawzi's loss of faith in Merlin."

The Provost Martial said, "Please, come with me. The President is ready to meet with you."

They were led into an expensively appointed council chamber where President Fawzi sat in a high-backed chair raised upon a dias surrounded by his cabinet.

"Next he'll be wearing a crown," Koslova said sotto voce.

Conn just nodded, thoroughly disgusted. He noted that there was only one Litchfielder among the President's Cabinet, the rest were the usual Storisende political hacks that orbited around the office of president. Not a good sign.

When the meeting started, Koslova noticed that continued funding of Poictesme Planetary Defense Force was the last item on the agenda. It was almost two hours before they got to it and President Fawzi asked Koslova to express her opinion as to why the Defense Force should continue in its present form.

Commander Koslova had written and rehearsed a justification and started to go through the reasons why. Even as she ticked them off one by one, she admitted to herself that they sounded lame, basically amounting to "what if." As she was about to wind-up her presentation, the emergency communication device in her ear beeped three times, which was the code that meant she needed to communicate with PPDF Headquarters immediately.

She looked at the President and said, "President Fawzi, I've just received an emergency code requesting I contact my staff immediately."

Fawzi looked surprised, but quickly recovered.

"Well, in that case, we'll take a short recess while you speak with your staff."

"Thank you, sir." Koslova quickly left the boardroom and walked over to the nearest vacant office with a working viewscreen. She quickly punched in the combination for the Operations Center.

When she came back to the meeting a few minutes later, her expression must have indicated that something was amiss.

President Fawzi said, "I can tell you're not bringing good news. I presume it's something that we should know about?"

Koslova stopped at her chair but didn't sit down. "You're correct, sir. A few minutes ago I was explaining how the Planetary Defense Force needed to be kept at its current strength in order to be able to deal with unforeseen threats. Well…one of those unforeseen threats has just now reared its nasty little head. My staff have just informed me that two of our missile cruisers, the *Zhukov* and the *Nimitz*, have disappeared into hyperspace but, before they lifted-off from Barathrum Spaceport for what was to have been a routine patrol, they apparently loaded some twenty missiles, armed with tactical nuclear warheads, as well as a large supply of food. This was NOT authorized by me or anyone else; the fact that they have hypered away leaves me with only one conclusion—their crews have gone rogue."

Everyone was noticeably shocked.

President Fawzi asked, "How could that happen? That *is* disturbing. Do you have any idea as to where those ships may have gone?"

Koslova replied. "No, sir. They could literally be anywhere. The fact that they loaded additional food suggests that they were planning on either a long hyper-jump or a faraway deployment within the Gartner Tri-System. Might I suggest that I leave immediately for the Barathrum Spaceport to personally supervise the investigation. I'll provide you with a verbal briefing within twenty-four hours."

President Fawzi agreed.

II

The report the next day was not as illuminating as President Fawzi hoped. Koslova gave her verbal report by viewscreen to the president, his cabinet and the entire M-12 group.

"What seems to have happened is that the captains of the two missing ships presented bogus authorizations to have the nuke missiles loaded aboard at the last minute. Unfortunately, no one thought to verify those authorizations with headquarters. I'm not making excuses but this is the kind of snafu that happens when you have a force that's made up of half-professionals and half-civilians who don't take military protocol seriously."

Conn Maxwell bit down on the "I told you so" about to come out of his mouth.

"As you all know," she continued, "I've been pushing for months to have those nukes handled in a more secure manner. Why General Foxx Travis left them here for anyone to find when Third Fleet-Army pulled out, I'll never understand. It's like leaving a loaded gun lying around a children's playground."

She paused. "Now, getting back to the bogus authorizations, the fact is that they appeared to be genuine. This tells me that this hijacking was a well-planned venture, and that the captains, and at least a sizable portion of the crews of the two ships, were involved in the operation. Meaning this wasn't some last minute impulsive act, but rather a carefully planned conspiracy. One of the two captains was promoted to that rank when the previous CO died in a mountain-climbing accident on Koshchei. The other captain was also recently promoted when his CO suddenly, for no apparent reason, quit and left Poictesme on the very next passenger liner."

Klem snorted, "I told you, we should have vetted all these off-worlders—"

"Quiet!" the President roared. "Let the Commodore finish speaking before we open up the floor for discussion."

Koslova nodded, saying, "At the time, there wasn't any reason to suspect that these developments were anything other than isolated events. Now, however, it's certainly plausible that one captain was bribed to leave and the other was…murdered in order to put the conspirators into the positions where they could execute the theft of our ships. Under the circumstances I think we should immediately notify the Federation Space Navy to be on the lookout for these two ships."

There were nods of agreement from all those in the room.

"To prevent anything like this from happening again, I've ordered all remaining nukes to be locked away under guard. All remaining senior officers and NCO's are having their backgrounds checked as thoroughly as possible, including their banking records. If there are any inconsistencies, they'll be thoroughly veridicated.

"Are there any questions?"

President Fawzi looked over at Rodney Maxwell, who nodded back.

Rodney said, "Commodore, please bring everyone in the group up-to-date on the current status of the forces under your command."

"Certainly. In addition to the twenty corvettes, ten of which are stationed at the Barathrum Spaceport, the other ten stationed on Koshchei, we now have eight…no…six five-hundred foot diameter gunboats with jump capability. Plus the missile battleship *Lexington*, formerly the hypership freighter *City of Amenhetep*, captured during the attack on Koshchei. The *Lexington* and two cruisers are based on Poictesme and four more cruisers are based on Koshchei."

Rodney Maxwell nodded and then asked. "And what about the status of the missile drone project?"

Koslova cleared her throat. "The most recent tests were completely successful and the ramp-up to full-scale production was started two weeks ago. Once the production line hits its stride, we'll be producing one new missile drone every twenty-four hours. The schedule calls for all of our corvettes, cruisers and the *Lexington* to have a full load of missile drones within six months."

Rodney turned to President Fawzi and said, "I have no more questions for Commodore Koslova."

Fawzi asked if anyone else had any questions.

Klem Zareff nodded and rose up, using his silver-headed cane to brace himself. "Commodore, what's your best guess as to what the conspirators' next move is likely to be?"

Koslova paused before answering. She'd been wrestling with that question herself for the last twenty-four hours. Finally she said, "Good question, Colonel Zareff. If my assumption that the conspirators in the crews were bribed to do this, then someone else is pulling the strings. If it wasn't for the fact that Panstellar's former President Howard Tarkington is no longer running that company, I would bet my last sol that he was behind it. When M-12 heard that he had been fired, we arranged for Kraken Investigations on Terra to keep an eye on him; unfortunately, by the time they got that request, he had dropped out of sight—which on the surface is itself suspicious.

"If Tarkington is the driving force behind this operation, then I have to believe that he is angry with us for foiling the attack on Koshchei, which played a large part in his termination as president. That suggests that revenge is the motive. Although I wouldn't rule profit out, either.

"How Tarkington plans to get his revenge on us is hard to say. I can think of several possibilities. They are as follows: The bombardment of either Koshchei or Poictesme to inflict as much damage as possible. An attack on Panstellar/T-B-MS' assets, perhaps trying to make it look like M-12 did it. Or as a way of getting his hands on some armed hyperships that he can use to commit piracy, either for straight monetary gain, or because he wants to destroy Tri-System & Interstellar Spacelines as an economically viable company."

That got everyone's attention. Conn felt as if a black cloud had just dropped over his head. If whoever was behind the hijacking started committing acts of piracy in sufficient numbers, that could very well cause the recovering Civ-Index to nosedive again, pushing the Terran Federation into a violent death spiral.

President Fawzi said, "Thank you for the update, Commodore. I propose that we divert one of our smaller freighters to the naval base at

Sarpanitum with the news and they can spread it out from there. Under the circumstances I don't see how we can justify reducing the size of the Planetary Defense Force at this point in time."

The President turned to Conn Maxwell. "Conn, you should update Merlin on this development and find out what it means for the overall trend and also maybe what, if anything, we can do about it."

Finally! Conn thought. He nodded yes, and the meeting was adjourned.

THIRTY

I

Howard Tarkington didn't fully relax until the *Nimitz* was in hyperspace on its way to Terra. The previous twenty-two hours had been anxious ones. He had been smuggled to the Barathrum Spaceport and onto the *Nimitz* before liftoff. The last few minutes prior to departure were concerned with loading of the nukes plus enough high-end food supplies to last at least six months. Let the crew eat carniculture and hydroponic foods; not him. Even after liftoff, there was the chance that the other two missile cruisers and the ten corvettes based at Koshchei Spaceport would be alerted and would liftoff in pursuit, but that didn't happen. Once both ships were beyond the no-jump zone, they entered hyperspace.

Tarkington poured himself a drink from his personal liquor supply and sat back in the large comfortable armchair in the only first class cabin that was actually larger than the Captain's. The last six months had alternated between busy and stultifying. He replayed his steps over in his mind to double-check for the nth time that he hadn't overlooked something.

First he had liquidated his personal holdings of Panstellar stock. Compared to the market value of the company, it was small but it still amounted to some thirty million sols. Next he had contacted a few of the less scrupulous members of the board of directors, who he knew were not fussy about how they made their money and got them to unload their stock too.

The next step was very discreetly, through indirect means, to sell short massive amounts of Panstellar stock. With the overall economy nearly stagnant, it was unlikely that the company's stock would go up in the short run. His co-conspirators did the same. When that was accomplished, he arranged for a new identity. Nothing elaborate, just enough documentation to get aboard a freighter headed for Poictesme.

Once on Poictesme, he had set himself up very quietly in one of the better hotels in the capital with the large amount of Federation sols that he had brought with him. Then over the next two months, he had hired operatives to approach Defense Force personnel with bribe offers. It was unfortunate that one captain had decided to renege on his initial agreement to cooperate and had to be eliminated.

The other captain had simply been bought off and left. Now that he had his own fleet as it were, he could proceed with the next phase of the plan. Panstellar's shipyard in orbit around Terra's moon would be destroyed in a vicious attack. His operatives on Terra would do everything in their power to convince the authorities and the Navy that Poictesme's Defense Force had done it in a misguided act of revenge.

A few key people in the Navy had already been paid to push for the Navy to go to Poictesme and force the Poictesme Planetary Defense Force to ground or disable their cruisers and battleship. With one false-flag attack, Poictesme's military force would be crippled and Panstellar's stock would take a huge plunge. His short selling would make many millions in profits but that was just the start. After that attack, *Zhukov* and *Nimitz* would target T-B-MS' freighters, only this time they wouldn't capture the freighters outright.

He didn't have enough personnel for that. No, they would disable the freighters' hyperdrive, thereby making them useless to the company for all practical purposes and they would transfer any cargo of value that could be resold without any questions being asked. The additional hammer blows to T-B-MS and Panstellar would force the two companies' stock down even more.

Then the final phase, the endgame so to speak. Both cruisers would return to the Gartner Tri-System and confirm, via spies left behind, that Tarkington's bribed officials on Koshchei had ordered those annoying corvettes to leave the planet and that the missile cruisers and battleship had been neutralized. Then his two ships would land at Koshchei and very quietly take control of the colony government, which would then rescind the agreement to lease the industrial facilities to the Maxwell group of companies and Koshchei would effectively be his.

The final move in the chess game would be to offer the same leasing deal to Panstellar but only *after* Tarkington and his conspirators had cashed in their short position and bought as much Panstellar stock at rock bottom prices as they could.

The leasing deal would restore confidence in the company and the stock would go back up. With a little luck, Tarkington and his allies would together hold a controlling block of shares. He would then have himself reinstated as not only the president but the board chairman, as well. Being ten times as wealthy as before wouldn't hurt either. Once Panstellar had its administrative and security people firmly in place on Koshchei, their stranglehold on the colony government would be secured. Then Panstellar could proceed with the long-term plan to exploit the Koshchei assets.

II

Commodore Koslova felt a stab of nostalgia as the two Navy cruisers, *Waterloo* and *Midway* landed at the spaceport inside the extinct Barathrum volcano. She had once hoped to command a Navy ship like one of these two. Her one consolation was that technically she outranked both COs. The thought that protocol required them to salute her first was comforting. She wondered if they would observe protocol.

Once the two ships were on the ground and their boarding ramps were starting to extend downwards, she and her senior staff approached the ships in the small open low-speed ground vehicles used to move around the spaceport field. They arrived at the bottom of the boarding ramp just as the captain of the *Midway* stepped off it. He had his own people behind him.

Koslova didn't recognize anyone but did notice that their expressions were not friendly. This was apparently not a courtesy visit. Koslova stopped when she was about three feet from *Midway's* Captain. His name tag said Terrell.

She waited. Terrell said nothing but he looked around the spaceport with his hands on his hips. He finally looked at her and snorted, then gave her a very sloppy salute. His officers did the same.

Koslova took her time and gave them back a textbook perfect salute. When that was out-of-the-way, she said, "Welcome to Poictesme, Captain Terrell. I'm Commodore Koslova. What brings you to our fair planet?"

Terrell turned and pointed to the battleship *Lexington* that filled up one side of the spaceport and said, "That is what brought us here, Commodore. I have orders from the Terran Federation Space Navy HQ instructing me to see to it that all of your jump-capable military ships are either grounded or rendered incapable of hyperspace jumping. I hope I can count on your cooperation."

Koslova wasn't surprised. After hearing about the attack on Panstellar's shipyards and the buzz that Poictesme had been responsible for the attack, she'd suspected that something like this was coming. General Frank Curtis' message, which had arrived at the same time as news of the attack, had indicated that the push to blame Poictesme for the attack seemed to have been carefully coordinated and was surprisingly effective. Curtis even suspected that some key Navy personnel had been bribed.

Koslova had already discussed this possibility with the rest of the M-12 Group and knew exactly how to respond. "Well, Captain, I'm prepared to cooperate with any legitimate and legal directive, but I'm going to have to ask you to show me the authorization from your superiors before anything else happens."

Terrell was clearly not happy with that reply, but he didn't argue. He ordered one of his officers to go back into the ship. Terrell avoided looking at Koslova while he waited for his subordinate to return. When he did return, he carried a document which he handed to Terrell, who glanced at it briefly, then handed it to Koslova.

It was an official directive from the Command Council of the Navy stating that Poictesme's hyper-capable armed ships were in violation of the Federation articles that prohibited military forces capable of attacking planets in other star systems.

As Koslova continued to read the entire document, she heard Terrell say, "Well, Commodore. Are you satisfied that my orders are legit?"

When she was finished reading, she looked up and said, "Yes, Captain. I am. We'll cooperate with your people."

Terrell had a smug look on his face. "Glad to hear it, Commodore. Then, here's what is going to happen." He turned and pointed to the *Lexington*. "That ship and the other smaller cruisers are going to have their hyperspace drives crippled. My engineers have determined that a small explosion in the primary field chamber will prevent the drive from working and because of the nature and location of the damage, the drive will have to be completely removed in order to be repaired."

He was about to say more but Koslova interjected, "Not so fast, Captain!" She made sure that she emphasized his rank to reiterate the point that she outranked him.

"The *Lexington* started out as a civilian freighter. Her hyperdrive can't be removed because it was installed when she was being built. If you cripple the drive you'll turn a perfectly good interstellar freighter into a useless pile of steel. I'm not prepared to let your people do that. The cruisers are a different story. Their hyperdrives were modular to begin with and can be removed, but not the *Lexington's*.

"If we remove all of her armament that would convert her back from a military ship to a non-military ship and that would satisfy your orders."

Terrell looked like he was about to argue with her until one of his subordinates whispered something in his ear and he changed his mind. Koslova had a pretty good idea of what was said. The *Lexington* had been owned by Terra-Baldur-Marduk Spacelines and as long as she was capable of hyperjumping, it was worthwhile for T-B-MS to try to get her back somehow.

"All right, Commodore. But that ship doesn't go anywhere until all of the external missile launchers are removed."

Koslova agreed. They proceeded to do exactly that. It took a total of two days to cripple the cruisers because three of them were on Koshchei and had to space back to Poictesme.

It took several more days to remove all of *Lexington's* external armament. In the meantime, Terrell insisted that his officers check all the computer logs of all the cruisers and the *Lexington* as well, just to make sure that none of them was involved in the Panstellar shipyard attack or any of the Terra-Baldur-Marduk Spaceline pirate attacks that followed.

When all her jump-capable armed vessels had been crippled or disarmed, the Navy left with a stern warning not to reinstall the external missiles, or repair the hyperdrives.

It was two weeks later when the other *shoe* dropped. Conn was out at Force Command Duplicate querying Merlin, when a call came in from his father.

"Conn, we've got another problem."

"What now, Dad?"

"The Koshchei Planetary Assembly has voted to order all Poictesme Planetary Defense Forces, including the corvettes that have been stationed on Koshchei, to leave. No reason was given."

"Does everyone else know about it?" Conn asked.

"I got the message from President Fawzi. Afterwards, I called all the M-12 members in town and updated them on this latest development. The consensus was that someone, probably Tarkington, had bribed a few of the Assembly members."

Conn leaned toward the viewscreen. "This is one of the scenarios we discussed. I hope Commander Koslova has a backup plan."

The objective was obvious. With no local defense forces in place and no jump-capable ships left that could quickly move from Poictesme to Koshchei, that planet was now wide open for any outside military force that wanted to take it over. As Koslova had briefed them, stationing the corvettes permanently near Koshchei wasn't an option, either. The Federation Order to Leave had insisted that the corvettes stay at least ten light-minutes away.

Not only was that too far to be able to intervene if a hostile force did show up, but the corvettes weren't designed for long deployments in space and didn't have the necessary crew facilities or supply capacity for staying on patrol for long periods of time.

It only took a week for the inevitable to occur.

Conn Maxwell and the rest of M-12 found out later what happened. The missing missile cruisers arrived in Koshchei space and landed without fuss at the Sickle Mountain Observatory site. Both ships released scores of contra-gravity armored personnel carriers who swarmed over the main industrial and residential sites and took control. The Planetary Assembly voted to cancel the leasing deal with Koshchei Exploration and Development and approach Panstellar Industries with the same deal.

Poictesme received a radio message to keep all armed ships away from Koshchei or they would be fired upon without warning.

III

As soon as news of the missing missile cruisers' arrival had been received, Commander Koslova and her staff reviewed her tactical plan to retake Koshchei. When she was satisfied, she presented the plan to the M-12 Group, including Planetary President Fawzi, who approved it whole-heartedly. His actions of the last few months had left his administration holding the bag, so to speak, and he was getting a lot of heat from constituents.

The plan required three of the large freighters. The defanged *Lexington* and her sister ship the *Yorktown* were available, but the corvettes had to be modified, which took one week. The newly built *City of Litchfield* would have to be taken out of regular service in order to complete the plan. By then, all of the corvette and missile cruiser crews had been trained in simulations to a fine edge.

Operation Dropkick was about to commence.

I

The tactical display read that it was thirty minutes to Zero Hour. Commodore Koslova got up from the command station on board the *Lexington* and nodded to the ship's captain that he now had command of the ship. She left the room without another word and headed down to the main cargo hold where Corvette Squadron Alpha was waiting. Most of the rest of the corvette crews were already aboard their ships.

Koslova hoped they had done the right thing by removing the retrofitted missile launchers from the corvettes' cargo holds in order to make room for the contragravity tanks and APCs. Now each corvette only had its original missile and rifled cannon ammo capacity to feed the two internal missile launchers and the four large-caliber turreted rifles. Each corvette had been given a name when it was re-commissioned, but now each one would answer to a number.

Alpha One was not only Alpha Squadron Leader but also the flagship for the overall operation. It's normally cramped interior was even more cramped as a result of the extra command and communication equipment she had insisted on. Koslova climbed aboard Alpha One and settled down at her command station.

Time to Zero Hour was now twenty-one minutes.

Commodore Koslova knew this was the most important battle of her life and if her plan failed, a lot of good people would pay dearly. She practiced some meditation relaxation techniques while she listened to the background chatter as the other corvettes checked in.

II

Nimitz Captain Fernandez yawned and glanced at the overhead chronometer. Another two hours to go until his duty shift was over and he could go to his cabin for some rack time. He looked around Combat Control. His crew looked equally bored. It was different when the ship was actually going somewhere, because at least you knew when the trip would end. But this endless patrolling, with its random microjumps, was mind-numbing. He was about to engage in some chitchat with his Tactical Officer when the tactical display pinged for attention.

Fernandez looked up and held his breath. Long range radar showed five...no, six ships coming into detection range. Range was still over half a million miles with a velocity of seven miles per second. Fernandez guessed that the ships were likely to be the other six missile cruisers that now had to use their lift-and-drive units to travel through normal space. What puzzled him was the distance between all six ships, which was over twelve thousand miles.

Why would an attacking force spread out that much? There was no way for each ship to offer support to the others. Fernandez turned to his communications tech. "Get me Base Ops quickly!"

"Aye, aye, sir."

When the base was online, Fernandez said, "Base, *Nimitz*. We have long range contacts with six bogeys approaching at one two mps. I recommend we go to Red Alert and get *Zhukov* into the sky."

"*Nimitz*, base. Stand by for instructions."

A few seconds went by and then another voice said, "*Nimitz*, this is Tarkington. We've got your radar data on our tactical screens now. *Zhukov* is getting ready for liftoff, but that won't be for another five minutes or so. In the meantime, I want you to microjump close enough to one of the bogeys to get a good radar look at it. Then jump back to your current position. Got that?"

"Got that, Boss. We'll take a peek and let you know what we find!"

A minute later, the Nimitz microjumped to a point about five thousand miles "above" the line of advance by the six bogeys. Far enough away that his ship would have enough time to jump away again if the bogeys launched missiles. Radar returns showed that each of the six bogies was a ship of at least three hundred feet in diameter. Fernandez knew that Poictesme's missile cruisers were five hundred feet in diameter. Radar return signals were sufficiently ambiguous that those six bogeys could be the missile cruisers.

When the nearest bogey fired three missiles at *Nimitz*, Fernandez was convinced that these must be the missile cruisers. *Nimitz* microjumped back to its original position and passed the radar data back to Koshchei's ground base.

Tarkington agreed and ordered *Zhukov* to accelerate at top speed to clear the no-jump zone.

Fernandez was ordered to microjump to within point-blank missile range of each bogey and fire a missile barrage at each target. *Zhukov* would act as backup. Because *Nimitz* and *Zhukov* would jump in and out in a matter of seconds, the enemy's cruisers wouldn't be able to fire back fast enough and, since they couldn't jump away, they would have to fend off Tarkington's missile barrages as best they could, so the theory went.

He hoped it would work.

Tarkington couldn't understand why Koslova's cruisers were coming in so slowly. At seven mps, it would take her ships almost twenty-four hours to cross the distance to Koshchei. With his ship's ability to microjump, it would be like shooting fish in a barrel. When radar confirmed that *Nimitz* had again microjumped away, Tarkington allowed himself a satisfied smile. He was looking forward to hearing Fernandez's after-action report.

Fernandez gave the order to microjump to the first target. As soon as *Nimitz* emerged from hyperspace, her radar locked onto the first bogey and fired twenty missiles in a single barrage. The time to target was barely three seconds. Not enough time for counter-missiles, if the target had any, to fire.

Nimitz stayed there just long enough to verify that her missiles had made it all the way, but they seemed to miss because all of them went right past the target.

After another two seconds the target fired three missiles back but due to the target's velocity and position relative to *Nimitz*, they would take longer than three seconds to reach *Nimitz*. Fernandez ordered the prearranged microjump away before they arrived.

After reviewing the radar record with his tactical officer, Fernandez ordered another microjump into close missile range and this time fired thirty missiles at point-blank range. When the results were exactly the same as the previous attempt, Fernandez ordered the ship to microjump into orbit over Koshchei and reported to Tarkington, who was furious at the results.

"Fernandez, you incompetent bungler," Tarkington yelled on-screen. "You're fired! Get your Exec on the screen."

When the XO Nagura replaced Fernandez in front of the viewscreen, Tarkington said, "Captain Nagura? You're in command! If you want to stay in command, get back out there and destroy those ships! Understand?"

Nagura replied, "Yes, sir!"

The connection was broken and after a few minutes to set up both the outgoing and return microjumps, Nagura ordered the ship into action. This attack fired fifty missiles and all fifty missed again. Captain Nagura figured he might as well go for broke and ordered another attack with the remaining fifty missiles, with exactly the same results. When *Nimitz* microjumped into Koshchei orbit and Nagura reported to Tarkington, the expected verbal assault didn't materialize.

Tarkington was surprisingly calm. He said, "You fired fifty missiles each time and not one single missile hit?"

Nagura nodded. Tarkington leaned back in his chair. "Hmm. That is *very* peculiar. So you're out of missiles now, correct?"

Another nod.

"Okay. *Zhukov* is still in the no-jump zone and will be for another thirty-five minutes. I'm going to order her to fire all one-hundred and fifty missiles at one time when she's in position. We'll see what happens then. In the meantime, you get that ship back down here for a reload. Tarkington out."

Fernandez, who was still in the room but out of viewscreen pickup range, breathed a sigh of relief. So it was obvious now that his competence wasn't the issue. Maybe when *Zhukov* failed he might get his command back. However, if they couldn't stop Koslova's cruisers, maybe he wouldn't want his command back.

I think it might be best, he decided, *to leave the ship altogether when it touches down at the base for missile reloading*. He turned and walked to his cabin to pack up his things. *Nimitz* now accelerated to Koshchei even as *Zhukov* was accelerating away from the planet.

III

It was about twelve minutes later when Koslova showed her true brilliance. Tarkington was chatting with one of his aides when his tactical display at ground base Combat Center pinged for attention. He looked up and gasped. Radar was detecting three ships emerging from hyperspace, each at a distance of quarter of a million miles but they weren't together.

One was coming in from above Koshchei's north pole, the second came from the side opposite to the direction that the six bogeys were coming from and the third camc from the side along Koshchei's orbital path. All three ships were moving at twelve hundred mps and as Tarkington watched, they launched six smaller ships each and as soon as they were clear, the three larger ships microjumped much closer. This time, barely beyond the no-jump zone, where they each proceeded to launch thirty-four very small objects, too small to be ships.

Before Tarkington could say anything, the three large ships hyperjumped away altogether. Tarkington was shocked by the sudden change in the situation. Both of his cruisers were unable to jump because they were deep in the no-jump zone and one of them had no missiles.

Zhukov did have missiles, but she now had one hundred and two targets instead of six and those new targets were coming in *fast*. They would be crossing the *Zhukov's* and *Nimitz's* path in less than a minute and a half. While Tarkington was still wondering what orders to give, *Zhukov's* CO called Tarkington and asked for instructions.

He was just about to say something when the display showed that each of the one hundred and two objects had just launched three missiles and with their acceleration of 55 Gs, they would reach their targets, *Nimitz* and *Zhukov* in less than sixty seconds. Neither ship could dodge out-of-the-way fast enough.

Tarkington turned to the viewscreen and said, "I suggest you prepare to abandon ship." *Zhukov's* CO didn't bother to reply as he turned and left his command station.

With three hundred and six missiles divided between two targets, there wasn't much left of the two ships by the time the kinetic-energy warheads struck. Both ships were now coasting and were venting atmosphere from multiple hull breaches. Tarkington knew it was all over except for the mopping up.

Those eighteen ships that were further away were now decelerating and he suspected that they were Poictesme's converted ammo freighters slowing down to arrive at Koshchei with zero velocity. They were probably loaded with contra-gravity tanks or personnel carriers who would land ground troops and take control of Koshchei away from him.

Commodore Koslova had beaten him after all in spite of all the precautions and months of careful planning!

Tarkington had no way to get off Koshchei, and he was sure Koslova's troops would find him if he tried to hide. He decided to make the most of the time he had left and departed for his quarters, where he poured himself a stiff drink and sat down in a comfortable chair to wait for the enemy to show up.

THIRTY-TWO

I

Commodore Koslova was pleased with herself. Her idea to develop missile launching drones, all those months ago, had turned out to be the key to overcoming the microjump capability of Tarkington's two cruisers. And when combined with Tor Handler's idea to use decoys surrounded by missile drones to simulate the PPDF's missile cruisers, the plan worked perfectly.

Tarkington's missile barrages proved useless because they were attempting to hit targets that weren't really there. The decoy at the center of each formation of missile drones, as well as the radar-reflective coating of the missile drones themselves, generated a radar echo that looked much larger than it really was. So instead of a five-hundred foot diameter missile cruiser, the incoming missiles were intersecting with a loose formation of much smaller objects, with lots of empty space in between, and therefore passed right through the formation. The odds of actually hitting one of the drones or the decoy were sufficiently small that it hadn't happened.

The mopping-up operation had gone smoothly, too. Tarkington didn't have a lot of men loyal to him on Koshchei; the rest of the population were pleased to see Koslova's troops arrive. Tarkington's local operatives, whom he had bribed, admitted their crimes and the colony's Planetary Assembly had voted in emergency session to rescind all agreements with Tarkington and to restore the previous agreements with Koshchei Exploration and Development.

With Tarkington himself in custody awaiting trial on Poictesme for crimes within the Gartner Tri-System, to be followed by additional charges under Federation law back on Terra, the danger appeared to be over. Naturally the Government of Poictesme and M-12 were pleased with her performance and the shiny new medal on her chest proved it.

"I hate goodbyes," Sylvie said. They were waiting inside the Litchfield spaceport terminal almost eight months after the Koshchei takeover. "I really like Valentina. We've become good friends."

Conn nodded. "I convinced President Fawzi to offer her a permanent position, as planetary admiral. He thought it was a good idea, after our recent experience, but Koslova wanted to move on. The Navy offered her a position as tactical combat instructor at the Naval Academy. She'll be a damn good one, too."

"Of course," Sylvie said. "That woman can do anything she puts her mind to. She sure saved our bacon."

When Koslova had made her way down the line of well-wishers to Conn, she gave him a hug instead of a handshake and told him to call on her if they ever needed a tactician and naval commander again. Conn told her they would. Little Foxx jumped into her arms and gave her a big hug. After she sat him down, Koslova and Sylvie embraced like friends who probably wouldn't see each other for a long time, if ever.

With all of the goodbyes said and passengers embarked, the *Ouroboros II* lifted off and was soon out of sight. As the crowd dispersed, a small group gathered around Conn and his father: Kurt Fawzi, Klem Zareff, Tom Brangwyn, Wade Lucas, his wife Flora, Conn's wife Sylvie and Lester Dawes.

Conn said, "I'm glad that the Navy recognized Koslova's talents and offered her that teaching position at the Academy."

Everyone agreed.

Rodney Maxwell nodded. "Yes. She deserved to have her Navy career back on track. I understand that the Navy has hinted that after at least a year at the Academy, they might even give her command of a cruiser when the next open position comes up. Let's hope they're able to find Valentina a good ship."

Lester Dawes said, "Conn, your wife tells me you had Merlin do another projection yesterday. What was the result?"

Conn replied, "Almost the same as last month's projection. Without any further pirate activity for almost a year now, the Civilization Index is continuing its very shallow decline. As we continue to sell the new super-freighters with the improved Dillingham hyperspace drives to interstellar shipping companies—including T-B-MS in exchange for dropping the tariff—Merlin projects an actual modest increase in the index over the next fifty years as interstellar trade picks up and faith in the Federation is given a boost. This to be followed by another shallow decline that, with a little luck, might give us another century before people start shooting at each other again.

"We won't live to see that, and our children probably won't live to see it, either. Their children will, though, but there's nothing really that we can do about it except warn them so maybe they'll be able to stay out of the fray."

The group remained silent as each person pondered their own thoughts about the future.

President Fawzi said, "I wonder when the System States Alliance refugees from Abigor will return to the Federation?"

"Harrumph," was Klem Zareff's reply. "Let's hope those scallywags never come back. If they're smart, they'll let the Federation go to hell in a handbasket."

Conn noted a wistful look on the old Colonel's face, as though he wished he'd gone with them.

Perhaps, Conn thought, *I should give some more thought to Merlin's idea of setting up a colony outside of the Federation.* He was, after all, a rich man due to his stock holdings in the various companies. Maybe he could talk some of the others into investing in the venture, too. *Hmm. I'm definitely going to have to give that some more thought....*

The End

www.ingramcontent.com/pod-product-compliance
Lightning Source LLC
Chambersburg PA
CBHW030825310726
48980CB00006B/638/J

* 9 7 8 0 9 3 7 9 1 2 2 3 2 *